THE GIRL IN THE WOODS

LORNA DOUNAEVA

For Lizzy

Thank you for those long summer days down in the woods.

ACKNOWLEDGMENTS

I'd like to thank Virginia Malcolm.

Editor
Hayley Sherman

Cover
Melody Simmons

THE GIRL IN THE WOODS

PROLOGUE

I bolt through the woods, grasping wildly at the trees that block me at every turn. I glance back over my shoulder but my vision is indistinct, a blur of green and gold. I stumble madly, trying to get my bearings. A creak in the undergrowth tells me all I need to know.

She's coming.

I propel my legs onward, forcing my way through twigs and sodden leaves. A thick branch twangs in my face and a cry escapes my bloodied lips. My hand goes up automatically, rubbing the nothingness where my right eye should be. My heart ticks like an unexploded bomb and I gasp, desperate to catch my breath. And still I run, pushing myself desperately onwards. I keep on running right up until the moment I fall through the undergrowth. Then all is still.

1

R ain splatters the windshield. I hadn't expected it to rain, not today. I'm dressed in a light, summery dress. White, with a hem of yellow daisies. I agonised over the choice, wanting to appear fun and playful, yet at the same time, dependable and safe.

Noel shifts in the seat beside me, his gangly legs find it impossible to keep still. His cool, grey eyes are fixed straight ahead as the wipers zip across the windscreen. I don't know why I put them on, when we are just sitting here, have been sitting here for a while.

My phone rings, and I almost drop it in my eagerness to answer. My palms are moist with sweat and anticipation drips from my fingers.

"Suzannah? Suzannah, can you hear me?" Effie's voice trills in my ear.

"Yes?"

"How are you both doing?"

"We're fine." I try not to grind my teeth. "So?"

"Listen, I have good news. You can go and collect her."

Tears slide down my cheeks and soak the front of my dress.

Noel looks at me and I nod. His shoulders sag with relief and the clouds lift from his eyes. He reaches for the door handle.

"All right. Let's do this!"

I have let the phone drop down into my lap. I retrieve it and hold it to my ear.

"Hello? Effie?"

She has gone and I'm glad. We have waited long enough.

"Better lock it," Noel mutters with a brief look up and down the street.

Most of the other cars look old and battered; ours, with its year old number plate, stands out.

We reach the house in a dozen strides. Noel slows his pace to match mine and we walk up the garden path together. He squeezes my hand briefly as I ring the bell. We shiver in the archway, rain tickling my neck. Somewhere inside, a dog barks and there is a great clanging of pots and pans, accompanied by the discordant notes of a recorder.

The barking grows more insistent, until there is thunder on the stairs and then the door opens. It is Orchid herself, her frizzy black hair pulled into two pigtails. She grins broadly, revealing more gaps than teeth.

"Hello Mummy. Hello Daddy."

I can't look at Noel. I will him not to cry. I'm very aware of Emily plodding down the stairs, her face pinched and composed. She comes to a stop behind Orchid.

"Why don't you come in for a moment? We're just saying our goodbyes."

"Of course." I force myself to be courteous, despite my impatience.

The house is no tidier than it was the first time we visited. There are children and toys in every corner, along with baskets of washing and plastic beakers with little plastic straws hanging out of them. I press my lips together. We will not be using plastic straws. We have too much regard for the environment.

IT WAS ONLY LAST TUESDAY, our first meeting with Orchid. Noel and I sat side by side on the grimy sofa, sipping milky tea, while she paraded in and out, bringing various possessions to show us. I tried not to be annoyed as her foster siblings clamoured for our attention. Such a crowd of them, so many small, sticky hands, all too young to understand that it was only Orchid we were interested in.

We don't sit down this time and I shake my head at Emily's offer of tea. We will not be staying. The phone vibrates inside my pocket and my heart jumps.

It's Effie, calling to say that there has been a terrible mistake and we can't take Orchid after all.

The vibrations cease and I pull the phone out, handling it like a hot potato. I let out a breath as I see it was only Noel's mum, Colleen ringing to wish us well. I tuck it away again, giddy with relief and focus on the spectacle of Orchid saying goodbye to all her foster brothers and sisters.

They cluster around her, like baby birds, all chirping and tweeting at once. Tim and Emily have had Orchid for too long, in my opinion. I know it's too much to expect her to forget them all entirely. She will carry a residue of this life with her, even as she leaves them all behind.

Emily trembles as she hugs and kisses Orchid, and Noel motions to me to retreat a little, to give them a moment.

"Why didn't they adopt her?" I murmur, as Emily speaks her last, incessant words to Orchid, imparting some vital wisdom.

"They've got their hands full enough, haven't they?"

"All the same, how could they have had her for so long and not want to keep her?"

Tim looks on silently. His long face betrays little sign of

emotion. Then Emily picks up the neon pink backpack that contains Orchid's belongings.

"You've definitely got Mrs Seal?"

"Yes."

"And your mermaid comb?"

"Yes."

"You're all set then."

She hugs Orchid tightly then releases her, almost pushing her away.

"Are you ready?" I ask.

She looks up at me. Her young face is solemn. "It's okay to be nervous," she says.

I nod, words stuck in my throat.

Tim is moving towards her now and his eyes flicker as if he is passing from a place of lightness into the dark. I watch as he places a gentle arm on Orchid's back and steers her towards the door. I call out a last goodbye to Emily, but I can't meet her eyes. Guilt fills my stomach like a heavy meal.

"Look, a rainbow!" Orchid exclaims from the doorway.

Miraculously, it has stopped raining. The rainbow looks pale and washed out, as if it has stretched itself too thin across the grey sky. The colours bleed into one another like a child's painting. Orchid is entranced. I don't know if it's really the rainbow that holds her interest or a feeling of mixed loyalties. By walking through that door, she'll be leaving one life and entering another. It would be a momentous step for anyone, let alone a child of nine.

Emily coughs behind me. I glance back and see tears streak down her face. I glance at Noel, but I don't think he has noticed. He chews the nails on his left hand as we wait for Orchid to take the step. She lingers even longer and then, without a word, she hops down onto the footpath and we are moving again, leaving all this behind.

"Where did you park?" Tim asks, once we are out on the street.

"Just down here," Noel says. "The Volvo."

"Have you got a booster seat?"

"Of course."

We reach the car and Tim buckles Orchid in for the last time, though I'm sure she is capable of doing it for herself. When he has finished, he shuts the car door but he remains standing in the street. Emily and all the other children are at the window, noses pressed against the glass.

I've put the child locks on in anticipation of Orchid fiddling with the door lock, but she sits properly and waits for me to start the car.

"We can go now," she says.

"I know."

I start the engine.

"I feel like we're stealing their child," Noel murmurs.

I drive carefully down the road, acutely aware of the precious cargo we have onboard. I catch a glimpse of Tim in the rear view mirror. He neither waves nor smiles as we drive away. I hope he knows she's in safe hands.

2

"You wait till you see where we live," Noel says, turning to look at Orchid as I concentrate on the road.

"You're going to love it," I agree.

Orchid does not reply. Instead, she blurts out the names of the things we pass and turns them into a song:

"Cars and buses on the road.

Round and round the roundabout.

Bored scarecrow in the field..."

"Why do you think he's bored?" Noel asks. "I think he looks rather..."

"Birds flying in the sky.

Tractors blocking up the road

Houses. More houses. More houses..."

The nearer we get to home, the less houses there are to sing about. There is nothing but fields for miles. Orchid turns her attention to the tray table in front of her, making it go up and down with fascination. I clutch the wheel tighter. It is too soon to reprimand. Our relationship is still too frail.

I wrack my brains for something to say, but it is hard to think up interesting pearls of wisdom whilst driving. I glance at Noel, willing him to say something.

"What music do you like?" he asks.

"What music do you like?" she returns.

"Me? Goodness, there are so many! I love Blue Cheer, Pentagram, Radiohead. You must have heard of Radiohead?"

"Nope."

"I like Suzanne Vega," I say, "and Sheryl Crow."

"It's okay to like whatever you like," she says. "Everybody has their own taste."

"That's true but are there any particular bands you like?"

"What does particular mean?"

I catch a glimpse of her in the mirror. She has pulled her bottom lip up over the top one and she darts little glances at us and then at the road.

"It means – Oh, we're nearly there!" I exclaim, as we reach the green.

LITTLE MERCY IS a quaint Hampshire village with thatched cottages and bright red pillar boxes. The sort of place you find depicted on biscuit tins. The neighbouring towns are called Upper Mercy and Greater Mercy, purely to confuse tourists. Not that we get many of those.

"Is this where we live?"

"Almost."

The country road meanders on for another quarter of a mile, growing increasingly narrow. Then the tarmac disappears entirely and we bump down a muddy track where the dense hedgerow scratches illegible messages on the sides of the car. I drive cautiously, almost at a crawl.

"Why are we going so slow?"

"I hit a deer once," I tell her.

It had been impossible to avoid, the way it leapt through the air, hefty yet graceful, like Pegasus. I remember holding the creature in the road, my tears mingling with its blood.

"You're not to blame. It's just nature's way," Dad had said

softly, as we buried it in a pit at the side of the road. It was good that it died. I wouldn't have wanted the animal to suffer. I just wished it could have lived.

I drive on through acres of luscious green woodland then I spy the tip of a thatched roof as our cottage comes into view. The car chugs over the gravel driveway, like a dog chewing on biscuits, and I park neatly in line with the house.

This was my childhood home: a small, unassuming house, built all on one level. I have hardly changed a thing since my parents bequeathed it to me. We still eat our meals from their willow pattern china and sleep in their solid oak bed.

"Is that the sea?" Orchid asks, as she swings her legs out of the car.

Noel chuckles. "No, it's just a stream."

We all turn to look at the water that runs alongside the house. It will rise a little in the winter months, but right now, it's scarcely a trickle.

"Are there any fish?" she asks.

"Have a look for yourself."

"It's very shallow," I remember telling Effie, when she came to inspect.

"Not too shallow for a child to get into trouble," Effie had said.

"It's just a few inches of water."

"You do realise it could still be a potential hazard?"

She had made a note of it in that blasted red folder of hers and I had fanaticised about kicking it into the stream.

"Wonky Cottage," Orchid reads on the door. "Why is it called that?"

"Because that's the way it was built," I say, with a smile.

Noel stoops to avoid the low ceiling but Orchid and I have no such problem. A fresh lemon smell greets us. The house will probably never be as clean as it is right now. I have thrown all my energy into dusting and polishing, wanting her to love the place as much as I do.

Orchid squeals as she runs from room to room, bouncing off the walls.

Noel and I exchange resigned smiles.

"We can show her around properly when she's calmed down," he says.

The rooms are irregular in size and shape, filled with little nooks and crannies. There are strong wooden beams and bookshelves carved into the walls. We have converted the spare room into a bedroom for Orchid. I had once imagined we'd have a baby in that room. I had pictured it, a lovely chubby baby, with my light brown hair and Noel's startling grey eyes.

She doesn't have any trouble working out which is her room. I have had a beautiful wooden sign made, spelling out her name in bright colourful letters. I stand in the doorway as she barrels in and jumps up and down on the bed. Beds are there to be jumped on, I suppose. A moment later, she is at the window from which, there is a stunning view of the woods.

"Sometimes, I see badgers and foxes outside," I tell her. "We get hedgehogs and rabbits too, not to mention the occasional deer. Do you like animals, Orchid?"

"Everyone loves animals."

"Yes. Yes, I suppose they do."

Orchid pulls the blinds open and shut, watching the view appear and disappear in turn.

When she tires of that, she opens the wardrobe and examines the clothes inside. Up until recently, it had contained things that had belonged to my mother; all her dresses and blouses and skirts. I couldn't bear to get rid of them, even after all these years. They still smelt of her and held so many memories. In the end, Noel convinced me to have them cut up and made into something. There remains just a small square of each garment, now combined into one beautiful quilt that now lies on Orchid's bed.

"I didn't know your size," I say, as Orchid fingers the clothes in her wardrobe, "but I'm sure some of this will fit."

She shuts the doors abruptly, as if she's been caught doing something wrong.

"It's okay if you want to have a look," I say, but the child turns her attention to the backpack she has brought with her. She pulls out a stuffed seal and sets it on the pillow. It looks like a real child's bed now. The teddy bear I put out for her looks stiff and old fashioned next to the seal, so I place it on the nightstand, next to my old doll, Suzy.

"That doll looks kind of creepy," she says.

"Suzy? No, she's just old. She was my favourite, you know, when I was a little girl."

Orchid looks at me quizzically. "You named your doll Suzy? As in…your name, Suzannah?"

"I know!" I laugh. "Originality was never my strong suit."

"Right," says Noel. "I don't know about you two, but I'm getting peckish. What about a spot of lunch?"

In the kitchen, I sit down on one of the wooden benches, while Noel opens and closes the fridge, assembling ingredients. Lunch is his thing. He is the king of sandwiches. I watch as he butters the bread, the knife skimming the surface with expert precision.

"Noel…"

"What?"

"How many sandwiches are you making?"

"Er…around a hundred?" he says, with a wry smile.

"Cool clock," Orchid says, eyeing the Grandfather clock that stands in pride of place by the fire.

"Thank you," I say. "It's a family heirloom, actually. It

belonged to my mother and her mother before that. Unfortunately, it's not working at the moment."

I gaze at it fondly. It is a beautiful time piece but a little temperamental. I keep meaning to take it in for servicing but I'd need to drive to Winchester for that and I haven't got around to it.

Orchid turns her attention to the french windows.

"There's a man in the woods."

I look up, but I can't see anything except leaves blowing in the breeze.

"This is a public wood," I say. "Some of the locals walk this way."

"He looked like a weirdo," Orchid insists. She hops from one foot to the other.

"What makes you say that?"

"He had a moustache."

Noel lets out a big hearty laugh. That's one of the things I like most about him, how easily he laughs.

It feels like an occasion, sitting down to a meal together for the first time, even if it's just sandwiches. Noel and I sit opposite each other, as we always have. Orchid sits at the head of the table.

I pick up a sandwich and bite into it. Noel has made them without his usual dusting of herbs and spices. Plain and simple, since we don't know what Orchid will like. The resulting flavour is a little bland.

"Please can I have some water?" Orchid asks.

"Yes, yes of course!"

Noel leaps up and fills a jug with water, setting out a glass for each of us. We seldom bothered, when it was just the two of us.

She sips her water slowly, making it last. She hasn't eaten much of her sandwich.

"What's wrong, don't you like it?" Noel asks, his face doing that hang dog thing he does.

"I'm not very hungry for sandwiches."

"What are you hungry for?"

"Sweets and cake. I'm always hungry for them."

"How ABOUT WE go to the park this afternoon?" Noel says, as I clear away the plates. "It's quite sunny now. Might be nice to get out."

He says this as though the thought has only just occurred to him, when in reality, we have carefully planned this day, weighing up the pros and cons of the various options, agonising over whether we should go swimming or to the cinema. Noel had even suggested a trip to Legoland.

"We can't take her to Legoland!" I had exploded. "Not on the first day. Imagine how high her expectations would be after that!"

Noel had muttered something into his collar but he didn't argue. In the end, we had agreed that the park would be the safest choice.

I wipe down the table and hang the damp cloth over the tap. It is only then that I notice the empty plate sitting on the side.

"Where are the leftover sandwiches?"

I look at Noel, who is sitting at the table, checking his emails.

"Dunno. Orchid must have taken them."

We both glance in the direction of the spare room. She has closed the door behind her.

"But why?"

"Maybe she wanted to save something for later. You know, in case there wasn't anything else."

"Should we say something?"

"Nah. Leave it."

I call Orchid and she runs to the door like an eager pup.

We all pull on our boots and coats and step out into the sunshine.

"This way," I say, leading her downhill.

Orchid looks puzzled as we walk past the car.

"How are we going to get there?"

Noel smiles. "You've got legs, haven't you?"

We hop across the stream from one rock to the next and scale the bank opposite, climbing up into dense woodland. From there, we follow a man-made footpath, trodden down through the ages. The path is narrow, so we have to walk single file. Orchid skips along behind Noel and he pulls the pricklier branches out of her way. Eventually, the path widens, and there is room for us to walk together again. The branches extend above our heads, reaching across to one another, as if they are holding hands. It is a lovely first walk and Noel makes a game of it, teaching Orchid to squelch through the puddles and over the stile, into the farmer's field.

"The cows are staring at me!"

"Well, you're looking at them."

"They're being rude!"

"Look, there are the swings!"

"Where?"

"There. Just through the trees."

"WELL DONE," a man says, flatly, as a ginger haired boy swings across the monkey bars. I get the impression that this is not the first time the boy has accomplished this feat. There are other parents milling around. The ones with tiny tots follow closely, while those with older children withdraw to the edges of the park and huddle together and chat.

A couple of mums push their tots on the baby swings. The children remind me of little emperors, sitting high up on their thrones.

"Higher! Higher, Mummy!"

"I want to get off! No, I'm staying on. Why aren't you pushing me, Mummy?"

We freeze, taking it all in then Orchid reaches for Noel's hand.

"Push me on the swings, Daddy."

Noel's eyes widen a little and I grin. Meanwhile, Orchid is already clambering up onto the swing. Noel looks at me and I shrug. She is a little old to be pushed on the swing, but who are we to judge?

"Hold on tight," Noel calls.

I smile encouragingly, phone poised to capture the moment. Noel gives an experimental push, softly at first, then a bit harder. I watch as Orchid rises up into the air and down again, a contented expression on her face. Not once does she use her legs to propel herself along. I wonder if she wants Noel's full attention, or if she genuinely doesn't know how to operate a swing. Maybe no one has ever shown her.

AFTERWARDS, we traipse around the park, following Orchid as she tries each piece of equipment in turn. Then comes the familiar tinkle of the ice cream van.

"Mummy! Daddy! Can I have an ice cream?"

Before I can answer, Noel sets off at a run. The van is some way down the lane and by the time he's halfway there, it's already moving away. Noel charges on like his life depends on it. Perhaps he sees it as his first test as a father.

Orchid scrambles up onto the monkey bars and swings from limb to limb. She is not as slick as the boy we saw earlier. There is a look of intense concentration on her face as she lurches from one rung to the next, her cheeks puffed out with effort. She goes for the third rung but loses momentum. Her arms strain with the effort and then she falls, landing with a smack on the tarmac below.

"Orchid!"

My feet are welded to the spot. I'm certain she's crying into the tarmac. I let out a breath, and my feet come unstuck.

"Orchid, I'm coming!"

A toddler on a tricycle blocks my path and by the time I reach her, another woman is holding her, calming her sobs. My body inflates with rage.

"No! No, get off her, she's mine!"

The woman looks at me in disbelief and I know I must look like a crazy person. I wrench Orchid from her arms.

"I was just trying to help," the woman says, affronted.

She doesn't understand. Noel and I have taken the classes and read the books. We need to be the ones who hug her and tell her she is going to be all right. Not some stranger in the park. Orchid clutches me tightly with both hands. Her head is heavy in my lap and her elbow digs into my ribs. She squirms, twisting and turning her body.

"Let's get you up," I say, aware that everyone is staring.

She clings tightly and it is an effort to pull her to her feet.

"Carry!" she says, her voice weak and pathetic.

She is not a small child, but I scoop her up in my arms and lug her over to the bench. The other mums move aside to make way. I catch the slight shakes of their heads, the sense that I'm making too much fuss.

I settle Orchid on my knee and examine her scrapes, which appear to be superficial: a small red cut on her leg and a graze on her elbow.

"We'll put a plaster on those when we get home," I tell her.

I remember how much I loved plasters, when I was a little girl. A plaster was as good as a scar. A war wound to show your friends.

Am I doing this right? I wonder, as Orchid snuggles in my arms.

The minutes tick by and the sensation of holding her doesn't become any less awkward. Orchid seems incapable of sitting still and I feel uncomfortable as she grinds her knees and elbows into my soft flesh.

THEN NOEL REAPPEARS, clutching three large ice creams. Fluffy white ninety-nines, the chocolate flakes melting in the heat. Orchid leaps off my lap and launches herself at him.

"Sit on the bench here," he says, and only once she is settled does he hand her the ice cream.

The three of us sit in a row, eating our ice creams, as if we do this all the time.

"That was the best ice cream in the world," Orchid tells Noel afterwards, licking her lips. She reminds me a bit of a dog I used to have. A little Jack Russell who was mad for ice cream. He'd be licking it off his nose for hours afterwards if you ever let him have some, reliving the taste over and over.

"Good," Noel says with a broad smile. "And you are the best girl."

Orchid drinks in the compliment. She looks so content, sitting between us with the remains of her ice cream smeared round her face, her accident long forgotten.

"Right," says Noel, handing her his hankie to clean herself up with. "How about we go home and watch a film?"

"Sounds good to me," I say. Once again, this is part of our pre planned day.

"I don't like films," Orchid says, throwing a spoke in the wheel.

"What, none of them?" Noel says. "Not even Back to the Future or ET?"

"Haven't seen ET."

"Right then. You're in for a treat."

AT BEDTIME, we take it in turns to tuck Orchid in and kiss her good night. Then Noel switches on the night light by her bed.

We retreat down the passage, too exhausted to do anything but drink wine and read: me, a historical romance set in ancient Greece, and him something clever and humorous. Every so often, he reads me a particularly amusing paragraph and I laugh, but I am still buzzing with the events of the day.

"We have a little girl!" I whisper to him, as I get up to refill our glasses. Then I set the glasses down, overtaken by the urgent need to check on her.

There hasn't been a peep out of her since we tucked her in but when I peer into the spare room, I see that the blinds are wide open. Moonlight streams in, creating a shaft of light that runs around the walls and although Orchid lies still and silent in the bed, her eyes are wide open.

3

"Orchid? What's the matter?"

"There's someone out there, Mummy. I saw a face at the window."

"Are you sure?"

I rush to the window and shine the light from my phone, but the light reflects back at me and I can't see anything except the wind rustling through the trees.

"There's no one there. Would you like some hot milk?"

"I want Daddy."

For a moment, I think she means her biological father, with whom she's never had any contact. Then Noel is in the room, his face etched with concern.

"What's wrong, poppet? Can't you sleep?"

"Someone's watching me."

"There's no one there," I say quickly. "I checked."

Noel strides over to window and takes a look for himself.

"No one there now," he says, confidently.

He pulls the blinds, shutting out the moon and the stars and any number of woodland creatures that might happen to look in. He tucks Orchid in again, smoothing the blanket with care and precision, then kisses her gently on the cheek. She seems placated.

"Can you stay with me until I fall asleep?"

"Of course."

I back out of the door, still in awe at how easily Orchid has conferred on us the titles of Mummy and Daddy. We told her in that first meeting, that she could choose what she wanted to call us, that we were equally happy to be Noel and Suzannah, if Mummy and Daddy didn't feel right. But there was never any doubt in her mind.

"You're going to be my Mummy and Daddy, aren't you?" she had said. "So that's what I will call you."

NOEL HAS band practice on Sunday mornings, every Sunday morning, without exception. All the same, I thought he might skip it this once.

"This is our first Sunday as a family. I thought we might go to church together?" I protest, as he slips out of the covers and into one of his grungy T-shirts.

Noel pulls a face. "I don't do the church thing. You know that."

He wrestles his tight black jeans up over his narrow hips and rakes a hand through his long hair.

"Still, I thought we might start a tradition."

"The pub lunch after can be the tradition. I'll meet you in the Plough at half twelve."

"Oh, go on, then."

I'm disappointed but I never could get him to come to church. I haven't been in a while myself. Whilst we were struggling to conceive, it seemed like everyone and anyone was popping out babies. The last christening I attended made me feel physically sick. I remember racing out of the church and dry heaving behind a car, while my best friend Lila held my hair out of my eyes. Even then, I made her stop at the chemist for yet another pointless pregnancy test, hoping that the sickness had been brought on by something other than an overwhelming fit of jealousy and frustration. But that is all behind me now. Something about having a child makes me want to return to the fold, if only to give thanks. And much as I shouldn't care what people think of me, there is a small but intensely vain part of me that is eager to show my daughter off.

"What's that smell?" Orchid asks, wrinkling up her nose. It is as if the surrounding fields have been bombed with manure.

"That, poppet, is the smell of the countryside."

"Wow, farmers must fart a lot!"

I allow myself a smile as we walk along the country road.

Down in the valley, a more pleasant smell awaits. The lavender beds are in full bloom. There is an explosion of purple, blue and indigo, and the bees hum gently as they work. We stop to take a selfie, Orchid and me. We grin at the camera, in the midst of the purple haze.

We walk on through the centre of Little Mercy, past the cricketers on the green, down to the Five Sacred Wounds of our Lord Jesus Christ Church. People are already making their way inside. I lead Orchid to the door, but she hesitates, as if waiting for an invitation.

"Shall we go in?" I say.

Still, she stands there, gazing up at the entrance way, as if she thinks the old building will come tumbling down.

"It's all right," I insist. I lower my voice. "It's structurally sound."

Reluctantly, she follows me in. Once we are inside, she runs over to the window and presses her hands against the stained glass.

"Mummy, why are windows made of plates?"

"They're not plates. It's coloured glass."

I gently pull her away, but she slips from my grasp and

runs over to a table where there are candles. She stands so close to the flames, I'm afraid she'll catch her hair alight. But she won't be pulled away, not until she's had a good look.

"What are they for?" she asks.

"We light the candles for people we want to pray for," I tell her. "And for people we've lost."

"Lost?"

"Died," I elaborate. I glance around, eager to change the subject. "Come on, we'd better go and sit down."

I nudge her into the back pew and she settles down, flipping through the hymn book. I nod at a couple of people I recognise. The vicar, or Howard, as he likes to be known, steps up to the podium. A hush falls over the congregation as he begins his sermon.

THE CHURCH SEEMS GLOOMIER than I remember but the service is as familiar as a pair of old slippers. Howard recycles a lot of his material, uttering the same phrases and jokes. His voice has a pleasing rhythm to it, like an old man reading a bedtime story. He could talk about car insurance and I'd probably still enjoy it.

Orchid wriggles in her seat.

"How much longer is it going to go on for?" she asks loudly. "I'm cold."

I glance at her naked arms and wish I'd made her wear a cardigan.

"Just a few more minutes. Then we'll go out for lunch."

She starts to hum, the noise growing louder by the minute. I shush her gently, but it makes no difference. She is imitating the bees we saw in the field. A couple of the villagers turn and stare. I stare back. Yes, Orchid is being annoying, but she has as much right to be here as they do.

The choir sings 'Whispers in a dream' while Howard passes round the collection box. When he gets to us, Orchid goes googly eyed at the sight of the money. Her lips move as if she is totting it all up in her head, all those shiny coins, the coppers and the silvers. I stuff a tenner into the collection box to make up for my prolonged absence and Orchid's fingers stretch towards it. I think she is going to burst with the effort of not snatching it.

"It is nice to see you, Suzannah."

Howard glances curiously at Orchid. "And who is this?"

I clear my throat. "This is my daughter, Orchid."

I glance at Orchid. Do the words sound as alien to her as they do to me?

"It's very nice to meet you, Orchid," Howard says. "Welcome to Little Mercy and might I say, what a lovely name."

Not a Christian name though. My mother's voice fills my head, but I'm not the one who chose it. Her birth mother got to pick her name and it could have been a lot worse. I remember a woman I once met at an adoption fair. She had adopted a beautiful pair of twins, three years old and totally adorable.

"They are called Chardonnay and Acid," she told me in an undertone. "We call them Charlotte and Adam but it's still there on their birth certificates and there's nothing we can do about it."

Childless and desperate, I could only nod at the time but now that I too have a child, I'm grateful that her given name is agreeable. I would have gone with something more traditional, like Rachel or Joanna, but Orchid is pretty and unusual, much like the girl herself. Perhaps a Rachel or a Joanna would have been destined to blend quietly into the crowd, but Orchid is not going to allow herself to be ignored, of that, I'm certain.

"Can we have a look in the graveyard?" Orchid asks afterwards, as we spill out into the sunshine.

I shrug. "Why not?"

We have a few minutes to kill before we meet Noel anyway. It's not in his nature to be early. He'll be late for his own funeral, his mum always says.

So, we go around to the back of the church and bumble about, looking at the graves. The grass around the stones is overgrown and there is moss growing on some of them, to the point where I can barely make out the inscriptions. Orchid grows quiet as she walks up and down. It makes me wonder if she has done this before.

"It's peaceful here," I venture.

"That's because everybody's sleeping," Orchid says, her brown eyes earnest.

I pick out names and dates: Anne Copper, 1904, Edwin Copper, 1908, George Hammersmith, 1938…

"Mummy, is that your grave?"

"What?"

I follow her line of sight. There, just to the right is a lone grave, with a faint inscription on it.

Suzannah Decker, in ever loving memory.

"Holy cow!"

I rub at the dirt on the head stone but it's no use, I can't make out the date. It has to be old though. All of the stones look ancient and crumbly. I haven't seen a single one dated later than the 1970s.

"It's not really my grave," I say.

I don't know if I'm trying to reassure Orchid or myself. "This woman just had the same name as me. It must belong to one of my ancestors. I didn't know any of them were buried down here. Grandma and Grandad Decker are in the crematorium at Raven's Hill."

"Weird."

Orchid looks at it with fascination. I open my mouth to say something more, but a thousand invisible needles prick my skin. I feel light and jittery and I fear that I might be sick.

Orchid continues to walk up and down, but I'm utterly

entranced by my namesake. Noel took my name when we got married, since I refused to become a Higginbottom so I have been Suzannah Decker my entire life. Was I named after her, this other Suzannah?

My parents never told me why they chose my name and I never thought to ask. You only think of these things once your parents are gone and you can no longer reach them on the phone. With a trembling hand, I rub at the stone a little more, cleaning off a cobweb from the back of it and buffing the surface so that it shines.

4

The Plough is packed with the usual Sunday rush. Noel has found us a table round the back. He seems surprised that we are late - I'm never late - but I needed time to pull myself together. I can't shake the feeling that I've just stepped out of my own grave.

We place our order and Orchid doodles on a napkin while we wait. Eventually, the waitress brings our pizzas. They are steaming and hot and freshly prepared, none of that frozen rubbish. She hovers over us with the parmesan, but we wave her away. The pizzas look lovely just as they are.

Noel and I dig in. Orchid merely picks at hers, pulling bits of melted cheese off the top and examining it closely.

"What's wrong?" I ask. "Don't you like it?"

"It has olives on it."

"You might like them if you try."

"You haven't eaten your mushrooms," she points out.

"Mushrooms are not food," I say quickly. I have never, ever liked them. No matter how many times people pile them on my plate. Horrible slimy things, they remind me of cold slugs quivering on the plate.

Orchid pushes her pizza aside and delves into her backpack, producing her cuddly seal.

"Mrs Seal is hungry," she says.

"Well, maybe she can help eat your lunch," Noel suggests. For such a wisp of a man, he certainly knows how to put it away.

Orchid shakes her head, sadly.

"Mrs Seal only eats pudding."

The waitress reappears at the table. "Is everything okay?" she asks, homing in on Orchid's uneaten pizza.

"All very lovely," Noel reassures her. "We'll have that one to take home please, and would you mind bringing us the dessert menu?"

I shoot him a glance.

Expectations! Surely, we shouldn't be rewarding Orchid for eating so little. He gives me his puppy dog look and I relent. Mainly, because I live for pudding. We order apple crumble with custard for Orchid and a passionfruit cheesecake for me. It's what I always have. Noel doesn't even have to ask.

"What about you?" Orchid asks.

"He never eats dessert," I say. "He prefers a plate of mouldy old cheese."

"Yuck!"

"Yum!" Noel says, drumming his fingers on the table. "Don't knock it till you've tried it."

He is always extra fidgety after band practice. His foot moves incessantly and his eyes have that faraway look. I suspect that if you were to tap his ears, musical notes would pour out of them. Music is and always will be his mistress.

"How was band practice?" I ask.

"Not bad. We've got a gig coming up."

"That's great."

Noel has been a member of Toxic Fish since uni. The name derives from a poster about global warming that was once taped to the wall of the Student Union. They only play small gigs in pubs and social clubs but Noel's not looking to hit the big time. He plays for the joy of it and I find that rather endearing.

"We're playing Salisbury University," he tells me, with a gleam in his eye.

"You're kidding!"

"No, really. There's a battle of the bands. We're going to be the warm up act."

I smile to myself. Salisbury University. Our alma mater.

"Hey, you should come! It'll be like old times."

"Maybe." I don't go to many gigs these days. "What are you going to play?"

"Rock covers mainly, along with a few originals."

"Yours or Kurt's?"

"Kurt's."

"I might give it a miss then."

His best friend Kurt writes dark, moody music full of anger and angst. When he starts a guitar solo, that's my cue to head to the bar. He'll still be at it when I return, but a cool glass of cider takes the edge off. I prefer Noel's stuff. His songs have a melody to them. I remember the first one he wrote for me, before we were officially an item. He played it in public, in front of a small but loyal crowd at the Student Union. Then he looked me right in the eye and said in a small voice:

"Could the girl who stole my heart please bring it back?"

That was the exact moment I fell in love.

WE FINISH our meal and the waitress brings the bill.

Noel places his card on the plate.

"How much is it?" Orchid asks.

"Thirty two quid."

I catch the look on her face. Astonishment, bordering on fear.

"How can they charge so much?"

"That's just what it costs."

"But it's so much!"

"Do you need the toilet?" I ask, trying to change the subject as the waitress hovers awkwardly with the card machine.

"No."

She never needs the toilet. Emily warned me as much.

We sit in awkward silence, while Noel bashes his pin code into the machine with thick thumbs. You'd never know those fingers could play such haunting melodies.

The machine churns out a receipt and the waitress hands it to Noel.

"Was everything good?" she asks.

"Yes indeedy," he says and Orchid giggles. I smile too and the tension dissolves.

I DON'T TAKE Orchid back to the church the following Sunday. It sounds daft, but I don't want to pass by my own grave again. Besides, I don't think Orchid got much out of the service. Maybe we'll try again when she's older.

Instead, I take her for her first riding lesson. I watch nervously as the instructor helps her mount the horse. She sits rigid with concentration as she's led around the field. Her eyes look wide and uncertain, like she's lost something. Then I realise that it's me she's looking for. She's scared I'm going to leave. I stand up and wave, making it easier for her to spot me. She looks more relaxed after that, even cracks a smile at something the instructor says but a few minutes later, she's looking for me again. That's when it hits me: Orchid doesn't believe that we are never going to leave her. We still have to earn her trust.

That evening, Orchid soaks in the bath while I tidy the cottage, picking up toys and books from the floor. I lay out her pyjamas on her bed and a big fluffy towel for her to wrap herself in when she's ready to get out. I want everything to be perfect for her so that she feels nurtured and loved. I want to speed up the process of bonding so that we can be a proper family already. I wish I knew how long it will take so I could count down the days, the way I once did for Christmas.

Once Orchid has put on her pyjamas, I have the unenviable task of brushing her hair. She winces when I pull too hard on a tangle.

"Sorry."

I brush more softly.

"Have you been on your holidays?" I say, in an attempt to lighten the mood.

"What?"

"You know, it's one of those things hairdressers say, isn't it? I was pretending to be a hairdresser."

"I've never been to a hairdresser."

"Oh – I didn't know."

I could kick myself for my insensitivity but I've always been like that, hoof in gob. How am I supposed to know what she has and hasn't done? I never thought of going to the hairdresser as a luxury, but I suppose it is.

"Who cut your hair then?" I ask.

"Emily. She only did it after Sally came round, because she was always on about nits."

I roll my eyes. What is it with social workers and their obsession with nits?

"How much longer? I'm bored!"

She draws out the word 'bored' until it feels like the longest word in the universe.

"Almost done."

Right away, I run into another tangle.

"You're hurting me!"

"I'm sorry poppet, I don't mean to."

The problem is that her hair isn't like mine. It breaks more easily and needs a different sort of touch.

A mother's touch.

I set down the brush.

"Can I have a story?"

"Of course."

The bookshelf is filled with my own childhood favourites. My parents were keeping them for the grandchildren they never got to meet. I swallow the lump that always forms in my throat when I think of them. I feel so hard done by sometimes. I lost them both the year I got married. They were gone within months of each other: first Dad had a heart attack and then Mum passed away in hospital. She had only gone in for a simple hip operation. I believe she died of a broken heart.

Orchid flicks through the Famous Fives and Nancy Drews, then settles on Hansel and Gretel. She hops into her bed, clutching Mrs Seal. I sit down beside her and begin to read but as I do, I grow increasingly uncomfortable. What am I thinking, reading this, of all books to Orchid? A story about children who are abandoned in the woods.

It is too much. I break off as Hansel and Gretel approach the witch's house, which is made entirely of sweets and biscuits and other things young children like to eat.

"As you know, you should never take sweets from a stranger," I say, quickly turning the page. "So Hansel and Gretel turned around and there, waiting for them were their Mummy and Daddy, who had come to take them home."

Orchid glares at me, betrayal written all over her face.

"You changed the ending."

"I couldn't help it. It's a terrible book. Those children deserved better."

"Are you ready to be tucked in?" Noel asks, sticking his head round the door.

"No," Orchid says. "Daddy, you read me a story. Mummy did it all wrong."

Noel gives me an amused glance and picks up Cinderella. I watch for a moment. You would never think he was new to all this, from the way he reads, creating different voices for each character. I could listen to him read all day but instead, I haul myself to my feet and go and stack the dishwasher, leaving him to tuck Orchid in. We probably shouldn't both do it every night.

"WHY IS THIS SO EXHAUSTING?" I ask later, as we climb into our own bed.

I don't remember being so tired, before we had Orchid and I often worked twelve hour days. I thought the commute was tiring but it really wasn't. Not compared to this.

Noel smiles as he flicks through a photography book he keeps by the bed.

"I'm amazed at you," I say. "You'd never think..."

"You'd never think what?"

"Nothing." I plump the pillows. "I can't believe you've used up all your paternity leave already."

"I know!"

He's not as bothered as he makes out. He is one of those rare people who actually enjoys their job. He works for a small, obscure charity in a pokey office near Elephant and Castle, where he spends all day fundraising for people with obscure diseases. He is endlessly optimistic and tirelessly enthusiastic about it all, despite the impossibility of saving them all.

"Come a little closer."

I inch myself nearer.

"Closer," he wheedles. "I want to smell your hair."

We sleep as we always do, entwined in each other's arms. Some couples need their space, but not Noel and me. Our bed is a tangled mess of limbs, his arm snaked protectively around my middle. I am naturally a cold person and I enjoy the heat of his warm, slightly sweaty body pressed against mine.

IT IS pitch black when I stir. The window is closed, so it's not the sound of birdsong that has woken me. Then I hear the music. It sounds like an ice cream van but it's coming from inside the house. I close my eyes again. It must be one of Orchid's toys but I can't fathom which one. I know the tune.

NOEL RISES EXTRAORDINARILY early in the morning. The first I know of it is the coolness of the sheets on his side of the bed. I stretch out my hand for him but he is not there. Groggily, I roll over and try to go back to sleep but it's no use. I'm awake.

I get up and walk down the passageway to the kitchen. I make a pot of tea and pour myself a cup which I drink as I always do, watching the wildlife. I'm not one of those people who rush about in a frantic hurry in the mornings. I need to adjust gradually to the shock of being awake. I drain my tea to the very last drop, even the bitter layer at the bottom of the cup. I haven't heard a peep out of Orchid yet, so I go and peer into the spare room where my mother's quilt lies in a messy heap on the floor.

"Orchid?"

I lift up the quilt but there is no one underneath. She's not hiding in the wardrobe or under the bed either. I dart back into the living room, the kitchen, the bathroom and finally, my own bedroom but Orchid is not in the house.

5

"**O**rchid!"

I fly around the cottage, calling her name. I try the front door and find it unlocked. I consider the possibility that she has gone out to play in the woods. Would she really venture out there on her own?

"Orchid!" I call into the darkness. "Orchid!"

The only answer is a rustling in the bushes and the trickle of the stream. I hop into my boots and dive out the door.

"Orchid!"

A murmuration of starlings take off in fright.

"Orchid!"

I run down to the stream. The water glimmers, gentle but never still. I listen intently. That's the sound of a twig snapping but it doesn't mean it's her. The twigs in these woods are like tightly wound coils; they don't need a human being to set them off.

"Orchid?"

I picture her playing somewhere, oblivious to my panic. Or worse, huddled under a tree, lost and frightened. I quicken my step, while my conscience drags me to places that exist only in the darkest recesses of my mind. There are no witches in the woods, no wolves or bears. But what if her birth mother has snatched her back? I still don't know the full story there. Did she give her up or did some well meaning social worker, someone like Effie, wrest her from her mother's arms?

"Orchid!"

I call her name with rage. I am furious that this is happening to me and I feel a deep desperation that so many minutes have passed since I discovered she was gone. My hands tap the familiar bark of each tree. I pass the weeping willows and the island but Orchid is not there. I stumble upon the large hollow the locals refer to as a canyon. Legend has it that the devil dug it deep to drown the non-believers.

"Orchid!"

I stand on the edge and squint into the half light, shining my phone around to see if she's down at the bottom. There are places for a child to hide amidst the junk that has collected down there for generations. I spot the old motorbike, the ancient computer, numerous beer cans and old boots, but no Orchid.

I pelt back to the house and check again that Orchid isn't there. I rip back the curtains in each room and get down on all fours to search under the beds but I can't find her. There is nothing for it. I will have to call the police.

They'll think I'm a bad mother.

My whole body shakes as I dial the first 9. At that very moment, the display lights up. It's Noel. I press the phone to my ear.

"Suzannah? Sorry to wake you but it's Orchid. She's followed me to the station."

"Oh, thank heavens!"

Tears stream down my face. Orchid is okay.

"Where are you?"

"Still at the station. I'll have to bring her back."

"Maybe next time you'll lock the door behind you when you leave," I say, before I can stop myself.

"How was I to know she was going to follow me?"

"What I don't understand is how you got all the way to the station before you noticed!"

"I had my headphones in. I was listening to my music."

Of course, he was.

"I would have noticed. I don't walk about with my eyes half closed."

There is a pause. It only lasts a couple of beats but it feels longer.

"Look, why don't you walk up and meet us? There's another train in twenty minutes, I need to catch it."

"All right."

I hang up, wishing that just once, Noel would argue back.

I STRIDE BACK OUTSIDE. The sun has come up now and I have a clearer view of everything. I hop across the stepping stones, over the stream and through the woods. I step out into the lane just in time to see them coming down the hill. They walk hand in hand, Orchid skipping along by his side. They look like a proper father and daughter. I smile in spite of myself.

Orchid is still wearing her pyjamas. She must be cold without her coat but she doesn't seem to have noticed. She is looking up at Noel like he's the greatest legend that ever lived. She never looks at me that way.

"Say goodbye to Daddy," I say. "He has to go to work now and we should get home for breakfast."

She pulls a face. "Why can't I go to work too?"

"Oh, you will, when you're older," Noel tells her, ruffling her hair. "For now, you should enjoy your freedom. I'll be back by bedtime, okay? We can have a couple of rounds of Uno."

"Do you promise?"

"I promise."

Effie is in my head, warning me we shouldn't make too many promises but this one seems harmless enough. I let it lie.

. . .

Orchid looks downcast as she watches Noel walk back up the hill.

"You must be hungry!" I say, with false cheer. "What would you like for breakfast? Cereal? Toast? Eggs?"

She looks at me out of the corner of her eye. "What do you want?"

"It doesn't matter what I want. I want to know what you want."

Orchid shrugs.

I panic and make everything: eggs, pancakes, cereal and toast. I know I'm loving her with food but it never did me any harm. I had a safe, happy home life. Is it too much to want that for Orchid?

I set all the food out on the table and Orchid picks at this and that. I try not to mind as she cuts all the crusts off her toast. I eat too much to compensate, not wanting the food to go to waste. The conversation is a little strained and unnatural, without Noel and his easy going chat.

"Can I leave the table?" Orchid asks, after a few minutes.

She has hardly eaten a thing, despite dismantling the toast. It annoys me but I know I mustn't push it.

"Can you take your plate to the sink?"

The counter is already full of empty bottles and packets that need to be taken out to the recycling bin. I set the breakfast things down and gather up the rubbish in my arms.

"Can you open the door for me?" I ask.

She does and I'm about to step outside, when I feel something brush against my leg.

"Oh, look!"

It is a fat tabby cat with a big bushy tail. His whiskers are a little dented, like he's got caught in the bushes but his face is fuzzy and sweet. He purrs as he rubs himself against me and almost trips me on my way to the bin.

"He looks like a tiger," Orchid says, stepping towards him. His tail twitches and he rises up on his legs.

"Nice kitty!" I say. "Careful, he might scratch."

"No, he won't."

She leans over to stroke him and he closes his eyes with satisfaction. He has the loudest purr, like a motor boat zipping around a pond.

"See? He likes me. I think I'll call him Tiger."

WE SPEND the morning out in the woods. I enjoy pointing out all my favourite haunts: the weeping willows, with their short, colourful trunks make wonderful climbing trees, then there is the rope swing, that hangs from the tallest oak and the little island where I used to play pirates or Robinson Crusoe.

"Who's Robinson Crusoe?" Orchid asks.

"I'll have to get you the book."

Orchid's favourite place is the stream, where I spent hours of my own childhood building dams. Even though she has a perfectly good pair of wellies, she prefers to go barefoot, carrying her boots and socks across to the other side.

At lunchtime, we picnic on the little island, with our feet dangling in the coolness of the water. Afterwards, I duck into the cottage to chop some fresh fruit for dessert. I watch Orchid from the window as I peel and chop the fruit but she does not stray far from where I left her. She's perfectly content as long as she knows where I am.

I'm carrying the tray of fruit outside when I spot a couple of other children walking through the woods. They look familiar - Robert and Catriona, I think. I don't know their last name, but I suspect it's something like Ploughman or Pitch-fork. Their parents own the farmhouse on the corner, if I'm not mistaken.

The children sit down on the bank to pull off their socks and shoes, before joining her in the water. Catriona glances at

Orchid carefully, sizing her up. They look about the same age, I suppose. Robert is a couple of years younger. His face still has that cute, chubby quality and his hair is a mass of ginger curls. Catriona, on the other hand, is tall and slim, her hair pulled back in a sensible hairband. She wears cut-off denim shorts. Fashionable, yet practical. Ideal for paddling in the water.

Should I say something? Maybe introduce them? Offer them some melon? Even in my own mind, it sounds a bit naff. Reluctantly, I stand back and watch. The girls conscientiously ignore each other, each focusing on their bit of the stream. Catriona appears to be digging for rocks while Orchid fishes for sticklebacks with her socks.

After a while, Robert wades across to the shore and sits on the grassy bank to put his shoes back on. He frowns in concentration as he ties his laces but while he is working on one shoe, the other slips off his foot and hits the water with a plop. It drifts quickly downstream, floating close to Orchid, who is standing in the middle.

"Orchid!" I yell. "Orchid!"

I expect her to look up but she is too intent on what she's doing. The shoe drifts away, carried along by the force of the water, heading towards the bridge at the end. Catriona heaves a loud sigh, as if this sort of thing happens all the time and wades after it, while Robert hops into the water on one leg. The shoe eventually gets stuck in a muddy crevice in the bank and Catriona fishes it out with a long stick.

Orchid still does not look up but I catch a sparkle in her eye. She wriggles about in the water, then triumphantly holds up a fish. Not just a stickleback but a small trout. I rush towards her. I can't believe she's actually caught it.

Robert and Catriona drop all pretence at coolness and crowd round to see.

"It's a big 'un," Robert says. His voice is full of admiration.

"Huge," Orchid agrees, holding it up. It flaps about in her hands, struggling to get away.

"You have to let it go now," Catriona tells her.

Orchid continues to hold on to it, as if she hasn't heard.

"You can't take it out of the river," Catriona persists. "Fish can't breathe out of the river."

"This one can," Orchid says.

I grab a bucket and give it to Orchid to put the fish in. Robert fills his shoe with water and pours it in. The shoe is already soaked, so I suppose it doesn't matter.

"Do you have a fishing licence?" Catriona asks me, hands on her hips.

I stare back at the small girl, amazed at her audacity.

"Yes, I have as a matter of fact."

I watch her mouth open and close. She knows I'm lying but she can't prove it.

Orchid and I take the fish back to the house and leave it on the kitchen counter until Noel gets home. He'll know what to do with it.

Of course, Noel chooses today to be late.

"The trains are screwed," he says over the phone. "You should probably go ahead and put Orchid to bed without me."

"I can't. She's got her heart set on seeing you. You made a promise."

I don't mean to sound so judgemental but I am angry nonetheless. I knew he shouldn't have said anything.

EVENTUALLY, Orchid falls asleep on the sofa. I think about carrying her to bed but I'm not sure I can manage it without waking her and in the morning, she'll remember that Noel let her down. I cover her with her quilt and tiptoe around her until Noel finally gets in.

"Sorry," he says, as he unplugs his earphones. "Signal failure at Waterloo."

He drops his rucksack onto the table.

"Is Orchid…"

"There," I say, indicating the sofa.

She looks so angelic when she's asleep, her cheeks rosy and pink.

Noel picks her up, his movements smooth and gentle so as not to wake her. She stirs as he lifts her up. Her eyelids flutter.

"I caught a fish for you Daddy. A really big one."

"Excellent. I'll have it for supper."

He carries her into her room and sets her down on her bed. I put the nightlight on and draw the curtains.

"Are you really going to eat the fish?" I ask, when we come back out.

"No. We'll release it back into the stream, shall we?"

I nod. "Yes, indeedy."

"Haven't you got a home to go to?" I ask the tiger cat when he comes back the next morning.

I'm careful not to let him in but he is there every time I go to the door. Later, as I'm mopping the kitchen floor, I notice him sitting on the table. He keeps absolutely still as if he's merely an ornament someone has placed there.

"Cheeky!"

I pick him up and post him out the door but it is as though he is on a spring. I take a basket of laundry into the spare room and find him curled up on the bed with Orchid.

"Oh, for pity's sake!"

Orchid looks up and smiles. "He's a stray like me," she says.

"I'm not so sure. He looks well fed to me. I think he's just trying his luck."

I don't bother to shift him. It's pouring with rain outside and it seems cruel to chuck him out in such weather. Orchid cuddles up to him and strokes his fur. He purrs so loudly, I can hear him across the other side of the room as I fold her clothes and tuck them into the drawers. I swear there is a smile plastered across the cat's face.

At lunch time, I catch Orchid slipping lumps of cheese to the cat.

"You know that's not good for him," I say. "Cats are allergic to milk. It will give him an upset stomach."

Orchid won't stop. She feeds him crisps and cereal, anything she can lay her hands on. When the rain stops, we go out and buy some proper cat biscuits and a plastic bowl to put them in. We place them in the corner of the kitchen near the back door. Orchid adds a water bowl, so he'll have something to drink. Noel raises an eyebrow when he comes home and sees it all but in his inimitable way, he says nothing.

THE DOORBELL RINGS EARLY in the morning, jerking me from my bed. Groggily, I pad down the hall and see Robert and Catriona on the doorstep. Smiling, I open the door.

Robert stands to one side, exploring his nose with his finger while Catriona steps forward, ready to press the bell a third time.

"Orchid's just getting dressed," I tell them. "Perhaps you'd like to come in and wait?"

"We came to get our cat back," Catriona says, her young face unexpectedly hard. "We know it's her who's got him."

"Your cat?" My heart plummets. "We thought he was a stray."

But I knew. I knew he looked too well fed.

"Well, he's not," says Catriona, boldly. "She must have taken his collar off."

"It must have fallen off," I say firmly. "Orchid wouldn't do a thing like that."

Orchid's bedroom door opens and she bounds out, dressed in jeans and a T-shirt.

"Orchid," I say. "It seems there's been a bit of a misunderstanding. Tiger already has a family. I'm sorry, poppet."

"Tiger?" Catriona grunts. "His name is Arnold."

"Well he's mine now," Orchid says. "You can't just take him."

"Yes, we can. Our dad paid money for him. He's our cat, not yours."

Catriona darts a warning look at me, telling me that it's my job to uphold the law.

I catch my breath. "Catriona's right, I'm afraid, Orchid. He is their cat."

I turn to Catriona, wishing I could think of a way to wipe that obnoxious smile off her face. "Give us a few minutes to say goodbye to him, please. I'll drop him back at your place in a bit."

Robert and Catriona look at each other, unsure if I'll keep my word.

"I promise," I say firmly.

Catriona looks ready to argue but Robert whispers something in her ear and she reluctantly withdraws.

"Thank you," says Orchid, when they are gone.

I rub her shoulder. "I meant what I said, I'm afraid. We do have to give him back."

"Why?"

Her eyes flash with betrayal and I wish with all my heart that there was a way we could keep him.

"You heard them. Tiger already has a home. It wouldn't be right for us to keep him."

"What does it matter – what's right? You can't take him away from me!"

Tears stream down her face.

"Oh, Orchid!"

I reach for her but she shoves me away. She crouches on the floor with Tiger and holds him, her tears dampening his fur.

"Orchid…"

She sobs and sobs and I dither, unsure what to do. Eventually, I pluck the cat from her arms and place him in Mum's old pet carrier.

"I will never forgive you for this," Orchid's voice shakes as she says this. "I hate you! I hate you! I hate you!"

6

Orchid shuts herself in her room and pushes her bed up behind the door. I try the handle, but it's no good. I can't get in.

"Open the door, poppet. Let's talk about it."

"I'm never talking to you again!"

"Tiger is sad, sitting in the pet carrier. We've got to take him home. It isn't fair."

Tiger lets out a pathetic mew and his eyes glow.

Can I leave Orchid here for a few minutes, while I take him home? No. What if something happens? She might freak out.

"Orchid?"

I stand outside her door and knock.

How ridiculous is this, knocking on the door? In my own house, in my own spare room.

I picture how my own parents would have handled this.

"Come out here right now, young lady! We've got to take Tiger home."

Orchid opens the door. She has her head down so I can't see her eyes. I open my arms ready for a hug. Instead, she showers me with Lego bricks.

"Stop that!"

Little cow!

I retreat into the living room and wait for her to calm down. Wait for *me* to calm down.

She's just a child. An angry, frightened child. I'm the adult here.

Tiger mews plaintively. I walk over to the pet carrier and he sticks out a paw.

"I'm doing my best, okay?"

I'm in half a mind to set him free but he'll only come bouncing back if I do and then I'll have Robert and Catriona knocking at my door again.

Orchid is quiet so I creep back to her room to see what she's doing. I inch open the door and she turns her music on full blast. The walls of the cottage shudder and shake and I'm tempted to storm in and steal her speakers. Instead, I switch on the Hoover to drown out the noise. Poor Tiger cowers in his pet carrier and I wonder once again if I should let him go. I leave the Hoover on and peer into the spare room again. Orchid is sitting cross legged on her bed, clutching Mrs Seal. Pages torn from a book lie scattered about on the floor.

All behaviour is communication, I remind myself as I step over the damaged pages. I switch off the music.

"Do you want to go out for ice cream?" I ask.

"Do you?" she returns.

"Get your shoes on."

I RETURN to the living room and turn off the Hoover. Then I pick up Tiger's pet carrier and lug it outside to the car. I place it on the front seat.

"Not long now," I tell the cat.

His little paw comes out of the carrier and I feel bad to have imprisoned him. I go back inside to find Orchid looking for her shoes.

"Your wellies are by the front door."

"No, I want my trainers."

I help her to hunt them down. I find one under the sofa and the other in the toy box. She wriggles her feet into them, without once touching them with her hands, then she follows me outside.

We sit in the car in silence. I glance back to check that she's buckled up, but I'm careful not to touch her. Her face is twisted into a pout and she hugs herself with her arms. Normally she hums or sings while I drive but today, she glowers at her own reflection in the window, her face tight and solemn as if the world is about to end.

I drive slowly down the dirt track and onto the country road that leads to Catriona and Robert's house.

"Wait here."

Robert and Catriona's dad actually has hay in his hair when he opens the door. He is blond and gormless and not at all grateful. Perhaps, like Catriona, he believes we stole their cat.

"Better keep him indoors till we've gone," I say. "Otherwise he might try to follow us."

He turns his head sideways. "Do you think so?"

"Yes, I do."

I wait on the doorstep while he takes the pet carrier inside and then returns it without a word of thanks. Little Robert gives me a wave from the window.

Orchid sits in noisy silence. She doesn't speak a word but she is otherwise as loud as can be. She winds the window up and down, sniffs and sighs mournfully and fidgets in her seat.

"What about that ice cream?" I say.

She sticks out her lower lip. I take that as a yes.

. . .

I INTRODUCE ORCHID TO CONES, an ice cream parlour I've loved since I was a kid. She stops sniffling long enough to tell the server exactly what she wants on her ice cream.

"Any toppings?"

"I want chocolate sprinkles and some of those bats and ghosts and the mini marshmallows, not the big ones."

"Please," I hiss under my breath.

"Please," she repeats and she treats the lady to a dazzling smile.

"Anything else?"

"I'd like a scoop of vanilla," I say, handing over a ten pound note.

We take our ice creams and turn to find a seat. I recognise the woman who has just come in. She's an old school friend of mine, well, not a friend exactly but someone I know well enough to acknowledge. The girls I went to school with are all married now, mostly to local farmers. They bore me senseless with their talk about lambing and crop rotation and they're all terrible gossips. Such teeny, tiny minds. She smiles in my direction but I keep my head down. I'm sure she's curious to see me with Orchid but I don't feel like introducing her right now.

We eat our ice creams in silence, Orchid's spoon chinking the sundae glass. I wish she would say something. Talk about the weather, the ice cream. Anything. When I can't bear it any longer, I reach across the table and take her hand.

"Shall we start again?"

Orchid looks at me from under her long lashes.

"Yes please."

It works. Orchid points out some birds she has seen in the tree outside and we speculate as to what their names are.

"That one looks like a Kevin," she says, pointing to the smallest of the three.

"I think the big one is a Sid," I say.

"No, the big one is a girl. Look, she's wearing a skirt."

I giggle. The bird's long feathers do look a bit like a skirt.

"Her name is Emily," she decides.

The smile freezes on my lips. "And the other one?"

"His name is Tim."

She has chosen the names of her foster parents.

ON THE WAY HOME, Orchid points out a freaky looking scarecrow in the field.

"It's watching us!" she says. "Suzannah, I think it's following us home!"

"Ahh!"

I pretend to be scared but really I'm wondering if she has called me Suzannah on purpose.

I point out the 'Pick your own strawberry' farm as we drive past.

"Maybe we could go there one afternoon?"

"Yummy. Is there a pick your own chocolate farm too?"

"Don't I wish!"

Orchid grows quiet as I drive up the mud track to our cottage. I glance in the rear view mirror and see her scowling at her reflection and grinding her teeth.

"You okay?" I ask gently.

"Are you okay?" she returns.

When we arrive back at the cottage, she hops out of the car without a word. Once inside, she goes straight to her room and stays there.

"Do you want some lunch?" I ask but she shakes her head.

I'm tired so I sit and watch TV. After a while, I go and look in on her.

"Are you sure you wouldn't like a sandwich?"

"No."

She glares at me, her pretty face turning sullen. She has not forgiven me for taking Tiger away.

I wander back to the living room and flop down on the

sofa again. I suppose Orchid will come out when she's hungry but I can't relax. Her bad mood spreads through the house like a foul vapour. It's raining outside, so there's no chance of going out into the woods. I'm trapped inside with a child who hates me. A dark cloud passes overhead and I curl myself into a ball. Three more hours till Noel comes home. It's going to be a long day.

Aside from putting supper in the oven, I get little done. I don't enjoy the time off. I feel guilty and annoyed. I keep checking the clock, my ears alert for the sound of keys in the door. Even the sight of a deer in the woods does not bring me any cheer.

"Orchid!" I hiss. "Orchid! Come out here!"

The deer stops still, startled by the noise, its ears flicker slightly and then it skips off into the trees. I glance resentfully at the spare room. It should have been a beautiful moment but now it's gone.

Later, the oven timer bleeps and I get up to check on the chicken. While I'm bending over the oven, I hear Noel pulling his boots off in the porch. He whistles to himself as he shakes and folds his umbrella.

"Daddy!" Orchid comes charging out of her room and throws herself into his arms.

"Well, this is a nice welcome!" Noel says, picking her up and whirling her around.

I set the chicken down on the table and watch them both in stony silence.

"Hi Suzannah," Noel leans over and kisses me. "Supper smells good."

"Do you want me to help set the table?" Orchid asks.

"Yes please," Noel says. "What a good girl!"

Orchid glows with his approval.

We busy ourselves carrying everything to the table. I dish up the food and Orchid bolts it down, earning more praise from Noel. Of course she's hungry, she missed lunch. She chatters away as if nothing has happened and I feel petty even as I plan on telling Noel about it. How can this sweet, cheerful girl be the same one who threw Lego at me and ignored me all afternoon?

As for Noel, I watch the way he fusses around her and I can't help wondering if it's his fault somehow. Maybe he shouldn't be quite so attentive, seeing to her every whim.

She's still smiling as we tuck her into bed. I force myself to smile back.

"Sleep tight," I say, but there is no real warmth in my words. My heart feels strangely empty.

"DARLING!"

My best friend, Lila hugs me and air kisses each cheek. Then, never one for understatements, she hugs me again.

"So? Where is she?"

"Off out in the woods."

"Don't you worry about her being all alone out there?"

I shake my head. "I check on her every so often, but she's fine."

"What on earth does she do out there?"

I laugh. Lila is such a townie.

"Same things I did when I was nine – climbing, paddling, building dams. Cup of tea?"

"Go on then."

She tucks a loose strand of her ash blonde hair behind her ear. The tip of her ponytail looks as if it has been dipped in blue ink.

"It's been too long," she says, as she follows me into the kitchen. "I haven't seen hide nor hair of you since you became a mum."

She's right. It's been almost eight weeks and in all that time, I haven't seen any of my friends.

"We'll, we're supposed to be love bombing," I say. "You know how it is."

"I know, I know, but I can't tell you how much I've missed you!"

I'm sure she has. We always used to meet up in London for shopping and a show, but that was before I had a child to think about. There won't be so many frivolous days out now. Or nights for that matter. I'm too exhausted by the time Noel gets home. Of course, it doesn't help that I live so far out. Lila has never understood why we choose to live out in the sticks. She's too enamoured with the glamorous London nightlife, the endless shops and shows. She has never understood my desire for a quieter pace of life.

I CARRY the teapot through to the living room, checking on Orchid through the window before we settle on the sofa.

"How did you wangle a day off?" I ask as I pour the tea. "Aren't you supposed to be working?"

Lila laughs. "There's a teacher strike on. I'm supposed to be standing on the picket line, harassing any student who dares to cross, but sod that for a game of soldiers."

"I admire your lack of political conviction."

"Oh, before I forget, I have something for you."

I wait expectantly as she fumbles in her huge Mary Poppins style handbag. She pulls out a bundle, wrapped in pale yellow tissue paper and presents it to me eagerly.

"Oh, you shouldn't have!"

I unwrap the paper to reveal a beautiful green duffle coat that will be perfect for the winter.

"There's a hat too," Lila says, prompting me to check underneath.

I find a knitted lilac bobble hat and picture it all on Orchid, her dark hair streaming out behind her. It is a lovely gift, kind and thoughtful. But a conflicting image flashes through my mind: one of a new born baby.

Lila would have brought clothes for the baby if I'd been able to have one. I'd be unwrapping tiny vests with ducks on, or perhaps a hand crocheted blanket with the baby's initials embroidered across the front. The vision is so real, I think I hear a baby cry. Then I realise it's just Tiger, mewing to be let in.

I set the coat and hat to one side, feeling unaccountably guilty. I'm happy to have Orchid in my life. It's not her fault I missed the baby years. I look down at the beautiful clothes Lila has brought and realise that I should have let Orchid open the present, since it was really for her.

"So, how's it going?" Lila asks, sipping her tea.

"Fine."

Her eyes widen with concern.

"That's not what I'm supposed to say, is it?"

Things are wonderful, amazing. Every day is a gift.

I lower my eyes. "It can be a bit of a…challenge."

Lila's used to this stuff. Her background was in social work, before she became a teacher.

"You know, you don't become a family overnight," I say.

Lila is nodding. Of course she is, I stole that line from Effie. All that guff about not expecting it to happen straight away. That I have to allow Orchid time to get to know me.

"You have to give her time," Lila says, right on cue.

"I know. I didn't say it was going badly. We're still on the getting to know each other stage, that's all."

I wait to see if she has any more pearls of wisdom but she just sits there, a sympathetic look on her face. I've always wondered how people cultivate that expression.

"How about Noel? How is he finding it?"

"Same as me."

How is Noel finding it?

"Orchid has taken to him."

She cocks an eyebrow. "And not to you?"

"He's the fun one," I explain. "He comes home and reads her a story or plays cards with her. I'm the one trying to keep to a routine. You know, bed at a reasonable hour, making her eat her peas. That sort of thing."

"That doesn't seem very fair."

"Yeah, well I'm the one who gets to stay home with her."

"You've been lucky with her name," she comments. "Orchid – such a beautiful flower."

"Yes, I like it. You have to wonder how someone could have chosen such a pretty name, only to put her up for adoption."

Lila sips her tea. "Often it's not the parent's choice. Do you know much about them, her biological parents?"

"No. Effie didn't even tell me why she was given up. Only that the parents weren't suitable."

Lila frowns. "I'm surprised you haven't had the whole story. They usually provide a pretty comprehensive file."

"Not in this case," I say, sadly. "All we got was her birth certificate and a few other details. Not enough to fill in the gaps."

"How strange. I wonder…"

At that moment, there is an ear-piercing shriek and I almost drop my tea.

"Orchid!"

I'm instantly on my feet.

"Orchid, what is it?"

I dash outside and my soft, plaid slippers slide in the mud as I race down the path towards the stream. There is no sign of Orchid.

"Where are you?" I call.

I scan the trees.

"Over there!" Lila says.

I catch a blur of movement. I push through the branches, batting them out of the way. We burst into a clearing and there in the middle, stands the tallest oak tree. It has two thick branches that stick out like limbs on either side. There should be a tyre hanging from the left branch. It has always been there; the local children use it as a swing. But now, the tyre has vanished and in its place hangs a limp, bloodied rabbit, the rope secured tightly around its scrawny neck.

7

The rabbit's eyes bulge like two plastic marbles, fixed in a horrified stare. Its head looks the wrong size for its body. Bloody red tears drip down its neck, which is pink under the weight of its body. Flies buzz like tiny black vultures around its neck. And the smell…

Where is Orchid?

I swallow the saliva that threatens to spew from my mouth and reach out with shaking fingers to check for a pulse.

"Don't touch it!" Lila cries in alarm.

My fingers brush the soft, mottled fur. The animal is still warm but there's nothing I can do to revive it. Its legs sway slightly and I watch them intently, slightly afraid, as if they might spring back to life. Which makes no sense because there are no two ways about it, the rabbit is dead.

"What the hell?" says Lila. "Who would kill it and just leave it there?"

"Teenagers," I seethe. "Sick little bastards."

A SMALL HAND tugs at my sleeve. Orchid's brown eyes are large and confused. She reaches up as if to take my hand but instead she delves inside the pocket of my jeans and brings out my phone.

"Take a picture!"

"I don't want a picture! It's horrible."

I can't stand looking at it, at the way its broken body sways in the breeze.

"Don't," Lila begs, as I attempt to extract the rope from its neck. The more I tug, the more the rope tightens. I can't work out how to pull it loose.

"Leave it," Lila hisses. "Deal with Orchid."

She's right. Of course, she's right.

I take Orchid by the hand and march her back down the path. Away from that thing, that atrocity.

"That rabbit was dead. Do people eat rabbits?" she asks.

"Yes," I say as lightly as I can, "but I'd rather have a nice leg of lamb, wouldn't you?"

I'd planned to take her back to the house, to talk about what we'd seen, but when we reach the stream, she jumps straight in.

I glance at Lila. "She seems fine. I can talk to her later."

"She's your daughter," Lila says, sounding doubtful. "If you really think that's best…"

"I do."

I'm not sure Orchid even understood what she saw up there in the branches. She might not know what we know, that somebody caught that rabbit quite deliberately and left it hanging there until it couldn't take another breath. Perhaps she'll realise later, when her brain has processed it. If she does, I'll talk to her then. Maybe at bedtime, before we settle down with a story. Or maybe Noel can talk to her, when he gets home.

"WATCH OUT!" I yell as a horse splashes through the stream, dropping bombs the size of tennis balls from its rear end.

Orchid has the sense to hop up onto the little island as the horse's movements cloud the shallow water. The rider does not meet my eyes. I couldn't recall her name, but I know her face, just as I know everybody in this village. We all watch as she trots away.

"I thought horses didn't like water?" Lila says, as Orchid hops back into the stream to resume her play.

I shrug. "Noel's a man and he doesn't like cars. Or sex for that matter."

She raises an eyebrow. "Trouble in paradise?"

No. Not any more.

"We're just so exhausted at the moment. I never knew having children would be so tiring. I mean, I knew that about babies, what with all the night feeds. But Orchid's nine…"

"And still very new to you both. Of course, there will be a period of readjustment."

There she goes again, sounding like Effie. I bite my tongue.

WE HEAD BACK to the house. The tea is cold, so I make a fresh pot.

"You've gone quiet," I say, as we sit back down on the sofa.

"I'm sorry," Lila says, covering her face with her hands. "I can't stop thinking about that poor bunny. Its face was so wretched." She glances out the window. "Are you sure Orchid is all right?"

"I think so. Death is part and parcel of living in the country. People hunt animals and slaughter them for food. It isn't such a big deal here."

Lila bites her lip. "But that rabbit was something else. Someone… murdered it. They must have done it for the kick. That is not the kind of behaviour you want to expose a young child to. Especially one as vulnerable as Orchid."

She breaks off abruptly, as Orchid appears in the doorway.

My stomach twists as I catch sight of her. She has a strange expression on her face. Is she…yes, she's smiling. Not quite a smile, her mouth looks a bit lopsided.

Lila's words stick in my head.

Someone… murdered it. They must have done it for the kick.

"Can you leave your boots outside?" I call, my voice shaking slightly.

"Listen, I'd better head off," Lila says, gathering up her phone and glasses case and zipping them into the front pocket of her enormous handbag.

"Aren't you staying for lunch? I've got a roast vegetable quiche in the oven."

I don't want her to go, I'm still creeped out.

"I'm sorry, I can't. I've got a Botox appointment this afternoon but let's do lunch soon, okay?"

"Okay."

I rise to my feet so she can hug me but I don't hug her back. She never mentioned anything about a Botox appointment before. It's that bloody rabbit that's done it.

Orchid watches as she zips up her boots. She looks confused too. I told her how excited Lila was to come and visit and she now can't wait to leave.

"It was lovely meeting you," Lila tells her, with a smile. Orchid doesn't smile back.

Lila's eyes flick down to our wellies, all lined up against the wall. Noel's tall brown ones, my green flowery ones and Orchid's pink sparkly ones, all girly and cute.

"You should totally put that on Instagram," she says.

"I don't even know what Instagram is."

"You're such a country bumpkin, Suzannah!"

As she opens the door, Tiger darts inside. He jumps straight up onto the window sill and hides between the flower pots.

"I didn't know you had a cat?" Lila says.

"We don't."

ORCHID WANTS A BRUSCHETTA FOR SUPPER. I don't know where she gets her fancy ideas from, but I reckon I can rise to tomatoes on toast, which is all it really is. She is quite taken by the idea, and insists on chopping all the tomatoes and onions herself.

"They'll make you cry," I warn.

"Not as much as they'll be crying," she returns, with a wicked smile.

Her eyes water as she slices into a large purple onion but she soldiers on, regardless.

"Do you want garlic?" I ask.

"Garlic? Yuk!"

"What, are you a vampire or something?"

A smile tugs on her lips. "I wouldn't tell you if I was."

At that, I pull the garlic out of the pot and hold it up to her. She pretends to writhe about on the floor, as if the garlic is melting her. Abruptly, she stops.

"Was that the doorbell?"

"What?"

"Didn't you hear it? Listen."

The sound is so faint, I can hardly make it out. The batteries must be low. I brush my hands on my jeans and go to the door. Catriona stands sullenly on the doorstep, her arms folded in a belligerent fashion.

Robert stands in her shade. His lip quivers slightly.

"You've got our cat again."

"Yes, sorry about that but he just keeps coming back. Cats are like that."

I lift Tiger from his perch on the window sill and plonk him into Robert's arms. There is no way he'll allow himself to be carried all the way home but I'll let them worry about that.

"Okay, happy?" I say, when they don't move.

"Someone stole our rabbit," Catriona says.

8

"Your rabbit?"

I hope my face isn't as flushed as I think it is. I had assumed the strangled animal was a wild one but come to think of it, it was rather large. Still, I'm not about to tell the children what has happened to their poor bunny. Better to keep them in the dark.

"Did it get out of its hutch?" I ask.

"You know it did," Catriona says.

"No, I'm afraid I don't."

I'm appalled at her cheek but even though I've had nothing to do with the fate of her rabbit, I feel guilty as sin. I should have cut the poor thing down right away. As it is, they're in danger of stumbling upon it.

"His name is Cinnamon," Robert says. "You know, like Cinnamon Bun."

"Yes, very good," I say, even though I loathe puns. "Did you try the Hancock farm? Their dog has a good nose. He might be able to help you, if you give him the scent."

What am I saying? The last thing I want is for these children to find their strangled bunny, but in my bid to look innocent, my tongue has run away with me.

Robert's eyes are like saucers. "Hey, that's a cool idea!"

He looks at Catriona, who shrugs.

"Well, if there's nothing more I can help you with, I must be getting on," I say, all but slamming the door in their faces.

I fetch the shovel from the shed. Of course, Orchid wants to follow me outside. I convince her to play in the stream while I return to the death site. Even though I know what awaits me, it still turns my stomach to see the rabbit hanging there, swinging in the breeze like a toy hung out on the washing line. I always wanted a rabbit when I was a kid, but Dad said it wasn't a good idea. We had three dogs and he was afraid that one of them might eat it. He was probably right.

I breathe through my mouth as I cut Cinnamon down, but it's impossible to avoid the putrid smell. I wish I had thought to bring my marigolds. Still, I was brought up in the country, I ought to be able to handle it. I carry the poor animal by the ears for a few paces, then set it down. I try to dig a hole, but the ground is harder than I expected and the roots are so tightly bound together that it's impossible to make any progress. I curse the rhododendron bush for its beautiful pink blooms but welcome the fragrance which tickles my nose. I get a good whiff to offset the stench of the rabbit. I will have to find somewhere else.

I pick up the shovel and reluctantly, the rabbit and plod towards the swampy banks of the stream. The earth is muddy here, the ground loose and wet beneath the shovel. Better. I hear Orchid singing to herself as she splashes about in the stream. The words drift over to me, more of a chant than a song:

The fishermen have gone to sea,
The sea is calm and mild,
All alone, I watch them go,
For I'm an only child.

The fishermen are out at sea
The sea is rough and wild,
Who will live and who will die?
Sings the fisherman's child:
One
Two
Three
Four...

I DIG HARDER, determined to get this done. The wooden handle presses into my hand, blistering my skin and my back aches with the effort. I shovel the earth for a good ten minutes until I have cleared enough space to create a shallow grave for Cinnamon, then I lay him in the ground. I close my eyes for a moment and try to picture him hopping about in a meadow, except he wasn't that type of rabbit, was he? I picture him instead pressing his nose against the wire bars of his hutch.

"Dearest God," I whisper. "I pray that you will take this creature from the earth and release him from his sorrow."

I open my eyes again and commence covering the rabbit with soil. Once it is sufficiently covered, I mark the spot with a couple of pebbles.

"What are you doing?" asks Orchid, casting a shadow over the ground.

"Oh, you made me jump!" I say, with a nervous laugh. "I've buried that poor rabbit. Don't tell Robert and Catriona. I think it must be theirs."

"Who are Robert and Catriona?"

My eyes narrow. "You know, that boy and girl, Tiger's owners."

"Oh, I didn't know they had names."

I open my mouth to say something more but don't bother.

Orchid needs time to learn to play with other children, we've been told that much.

"NICE DAY?" Noel asks, when he gets home.

"I've had better," I say, stacking the last of the dishes in the dishwasher. The cleaning seems to be endless. Orchid has left a muddy trail that leads all the way from the kitchen door to her bedroom and no sooner had I mopped it up than Tiger reappeared. My newly cleaned kitchen floor is now covered in muddy pawprints. I thought cats were supposed to be clean creatures.

"Had company?" he asks.

"How did you know?"

"You always drink gin with Lila."

I glance down at my gin and tonic.

"Do I?"

"Always."

"That's funny. She was only here for an hour or so. I didn't start on the gin till later. Hey, I meant to tell her about your gig. When is it again?"

"A week Saturday, but don't feel you have to come."

He takes off his rucksack and sets it down on the table, unpacking the bread and milk he bought on the way home.

"I want to."

"I know, I was just thinking that it might be a bit soon to leave Orchid. You know, we've never had a babysitter before."

"I hadn't even thought about that. Who would I even ask?"

I rack my brains, but I can't think of anyone local I could call upon. My real friends are all in London.

"Maybe it's about time you mingled with the other mums in the village?"

I pull a face. "Do you think so?"

"Don't you? I mean, just look at the pair of us. Still hanging around with the same friends we've had since uni. Don't you think we should have moved on by now?"

My mouth hangs open. "Noel, you and I met at uni. What are you saying?"

"I'm not saying anything, I just think it might be nice for you to make some new friends now that we have Orchid. You can't keep looking down your nose at the whole village."

I almost drop my drink.

"Is that what you think of me?"

"I just meant… maybe you could go to a few coffee mornings or something? Try to meet a few people."

I hug my drink to my chest. "I'm fine as I am, thanks."

"Daddy!"

We both turn as Orchid catapults herself into the room and makes straight for Noel. She clutches him tightly, hugging him as if she hasn't seen him in years. He laughs and hugs her back. I move quietly away and set the table for supper.

"WE NEED to go into Greater Mercy," I tell Orchid in the morning. "We have to get you measured for school shoes. You'll be starting in a couple of weeks."

I try to gage her reaction as I relay this information, but she looks about as interested as if I had said we were off to buy carrots.

"I want to play in the stream."

"Well you can later but first we have to buy shoes."

"Will they be red and shiny?"

"No, sorry. They have to be brown to go with your uniform."

She pulls a face. "Can Tiger come?"

"No. We can't take a cat shopping."

I wait patiently, while she wriggles into her boots and coat then we walk out to the car. Orchid insists that she can't do her seatbelt so I have to buckle it up for her, even though I know she can do it. When I get into my own seat, Tiger leaps up onto the bonnet and sits there, licking his front paw.

Orchid laughs hysterically while I try to shoo him away. Tiger does not get the message, so I have to get out of the car and set him down on the ground. He is right on my heels as I go to get back in.

"You'll have to shut him in the house," Orchid says, "Or he'll get run over."

It seems ridiculous, but when I start the car, he darts out in front of me again. There is a very real chance I could hit him.

"Dippy cat!"

I get out of the car again and pick him up. I don't want to shut him in the house, but it is better than running him over. At least that way, I know he's safe.

9

When the big day arrives, Orchid is up and dressed in her school uniform by the time I come out of my bedroom. There are splashes of milk on the kitchen counter and cereal crumbs on the floor.

"What time did you get up?" I ask.

"I don't know, but the birds were already up."

I clear away the debris. It narks me how much mess she makes, but I try not to grumble. It's good that Orchid has made herself breakfast. She's learning to be more independent. And her uniform still looks immaculate, which is a blessing. She must have eaten first, before she got changed.

I take about a million pictures of her in her school uniform, first in front of the mantlepiece then standing by the front door. I don't normally care about Facebook, but this morning I feel a pang. I know Colleen would love a copy of these pictures and I'm dying to show her off to Lila and Jennie. But I know the rules. We had it hammered into us at the parenting classes: we cannot put her face on social media, so I don't.

"I'm not sure I'm ready for her to go to school," Noel confides in an undertone. "What if she gets bullied?"

"All kids get bullied," I say, working an extra layer of polish into my already shiny shoes.

"I wasn't," he says.

"Lucky you."

I think back to my own school days. There was so much to deal with at school, quite aside from the academic work. How was I supposed to know who it was and wasn't acceptable to sit next to in the lunch hall? Why did Elsie Bowman invite everyone in the class to her birthday party, except me? And why did Tina Pearson cry when Mr Slater put us together for the history project?

"I'm excellent at history," I remember telling her. "Far better than you, in fact."

For some reason, this had made Tina cry all the more. She had sobbed so much that Mr Slater had relented and let her work with someone else. I got stuck with sniffly Jimmy Snodgrass, who kept wiping his nose on his jumper, whilst Elsie and Tina laughed at us from across the room.

"You take the higher ground," Dad had told me. "Turn the other cheek."

Mum had sat there, nodding sagely until he went out into the garden to mow the grass, then she gripped me by the shoulders.

"You've got to show those little cows what's what!"

There was a fierceness to her voice I'd rarely heard before.

"You think I should punch them?"

"No, you have to make it subtle. Hide Elsie's pencil case in Tina's bag and they'll soon show their true colours. They'll be falling out in no time."

"Do you think so?"

"I know so."

WE DRIVE to the school together, Noel, Orchid and I. It's walkable, but it's a bit of a hike and the roads get so muddy.

The old building looks much the same as it did in my day. I remember queueing at the water fountain in the playground. It's not even there any more. These days, they all have their own plastic bottles, which Orchid will no doubt spill inside her bag.

Orchid seems unfazed as we pull up. I suppose she has been to a number of new schools, as she moved from one home to another. Perhaps that's why she seems so calm, while my heart chirps inside my chest like a hummingbird. Noel has fallen silent and I realise he is nervous too. I can't believe how much he has changed since Orchid came to live with us.

"Mummy! Is that my school?"

"Yes, it is poppet. Do you like it?"

"Do you?"

The children form a disorderly queue outside Luna class and when the door opens, you'd think they were giving out Jaffa cakes, the way they scrabble to get inside. I spot the teacher, Miss Gibb writing on the whiteboard, in precise round letters. Whatever happened to blackboards, I wonder. I picture them, burning in heaps on Guy Fawkes night.

"Miss Gibb?"

I feel ridiculous greeting her so formally but I don't know her first name. She looks young to me, scarcely old enough to vote. And here we are, about to entrust her with our daughter.

She turns and looks at us, taking in Orchid and her big bushy pigtails that have expanded on the walk from the car.

"Good morning Orchid," she says, looking directly at her.

"Hi," Orchid says, looking around the busy classroom. "How's it hanging?"

"Orchid!" I exclaim.

Miss Gibb seems unphased.

"You can go now," she says, in a low voice. "Don't worry, she'll be fine."

Noel takes my hand and we walk silently back to the car.

"She'll be okay," he says, as I start the engine.

"I know."

I drop him off at the station and drive back home.

The silence hits me as I walk in the door. No music blaring from the spare room. No TV left on, no incessant demands about what's for lunch and when it will be. I'm stunned to find actual tears in my eyes as I potter about, making the beds and fluffing the cushions. I switch on the Hoover then switch it off again. I can't do it. I'm not cut out to be a housewife. If I stay in all day, I'll lose my nut. Instead, I grab my brolly and walk outside. I could go down to the village and browse round the shops, maybe visit the library. Anything to keep me occupied.

LITTLE MERCY IS NOT BUSY, but there are people milling around the dozen or so shops. I walk into the library and check out the new releases but nothing takes my fancy so I cross the street to the baker's. I'm always startled by the contrast between this place and London. No one is in a rush here. They all stop and have a chinwag, not caring if it takes half an hour to purchase a loaf of bread. If a London shop-keeper took this long to serve people, a fight would break out, but here it is completely unremarkable.

Coming out of the bakers, I almost collide with an old man on a bicycle.

"Smile love, it might never happen!"

I glare at him until he moves out of my way. If I were Lila, I would have stamped on his foot. No one ever tells her to smile.

"Suzannah!"

I turn to see Howard, the vicar hopping off his motorbike. He walks towards me, a warm smile on his face.

"Well hello, my dear. I can't tell you how lovely it was to see you in church and with young Orchid too. Do you think we might see that husband of yours one Sunday?"

"Probably not," I admit. "He has band practice on a Sunday and nothing gets in the way of that."

Howard smiles, "I too used to play in a band, back in my youth. Good for the soul, so they say."

I could see Howard in a band. He doesn't even dress like a vicar. I mean he wears the dog collar, but he usually pairs it with something casual, like chinos or a pair of jeans.

"It's not becoming of a clergyman," Mum used to say.

"It's not becoming of any man over forty," Dad used to say.

I think Dad was secretly jealous. He'd had his tractors in his heyday, but nothing made his eyes light up more than the sound of a noisy motor. Something shiny and unnecessarily showy. If only Mum had let him.

"Howard, I was meaning to ask you something. It's about a headstone I found outside the church. Did you know there was another Suzannah Decker buried there?"

His eyes widen.

"I…"

His mouth contorts slightly and he looks uncomfortable.

"Howard? You know something, don't you? Come on, I have a right to know."

He sucks in his breath through his teeth and shifts his weight.

"Yes, yes. I think perhaps I should tell you but it won't be an easy conversation, Suzannah. You're going to want to sit down."

10

I follow Howard into Jane's Café and wait impatiently for a table.

The waitress is chatting to another customer and seems in no hurry to get us seated, despite the pointed stares I send her way.

When she finally comes over, Howard enquires after her health and that of her family, including her grandmother who is recovering from gout. Only then does she show us to a table.

"Don't you want to see the menu?" she asks.

"Just a pot of tea, thanks," I say.

She stands there for a moment, a disapproving look on her face, but Howard nods and says, "That'll suit me, thank you."

"If you're sure I can't tempt you with the lemon pie?"

"Does that come with cream?" he asks.

I sit on my fists as this exchange continues. I think Howard's getting pie whether he wants it or not.

"Well then," he says, when she finally leaves us alone. He takes his napkin and tucks it into his shirt. "Such weather we've been having. Three days of rain last week and then that perfect day of sunshine. I've never seen such green grass."

I don't recall the sunshine. I don't give a fig about the

grass. I'm dying for him to get to the point but that is not how things are done in Little Mercy. First tea, then talk.

As I wait for Howard to collect his thoughts, a gaggle of mothers and babies walk in and take up residence at the big table in the corner. They are noisy and self-centred and I try not to glare. Mother and baby groups are like an exclusive club to which I'll never be invited. How I have envied those mothers with their big, cumbersome buggies, as they shared their birth stories over endless cups of tea. How dare they complain about a single minute of it? They are so lucky and most of them don't even appreciate it. They chat away, ignoring their offspring as they toddle back and forth, desperate for their parents' attention. All the old, familiar feelings stir in my stomach and I push them back down with an effort.

It doesn't matter because I have Orchid now.

A different waitress materialises with our order and Howard conveys his blessings for her injured dog. I wait impatiently for her to leave.

"I'll be mother, shall I?" he says, as he pours the tea into each of our cups and adds a dash of milk.

He stirs sugar into his tea, then drops the spoon onto the saucer with a clink. I wait with bated breath as he begins.

"I knew the other Suzannah."

My body goes ridged. "You did?"

"It was back in the seventies, before you were born."

"Who was she?"

He draws a breath. "This may come as a bit of a shock, but your parents had another daughter, before you were born."

"You're kidding me!"

I almost spit out my tea.

Howard looks at me, waiting for me to say something, but I can't even form a sentence.

"Are you sure?" I finally ask. "Could she have been a cousin or something?"

Even that doesn't ring true. Dad was an only child and Mum's sister is practically a nun.

Howard rests a gentle hand on mine. "I'm sure," he says, carefully. "I knew her well."

"She…she lived here, in this village?"

Howard nods. "She was a beautiful little girl, with pale blonde hair and the most brilliant blue eyes. A lovely child by all accounts, but also a bit of a terror. She never listened to your mother, refused to hold her hand when they went out walking together and she threw the almightiest tantrums."

He drops his gaze.

"She had just turned four when it happened. Your dad was washing the car in the driveway, and your mum was pulling up weeds. Suzannah was right under their noses, playing in the garden in her Wendy house. It only took a moment for her to wander off and then she was gone. They searched for her for over an hour. The neighbours searched too. They had half the village out looking for her, but it was the police who eventually found her. She had been knocked down by a farm vehicle as it came around the corner. The driver hadn't seen her until it was too late. It was no one's fault, just a terrible tragedy."

"How awful!"

I imagine my parents, my poor dear parents, coming to terms with such a loss.

"But why did they never tell me?"

I think with guilt, of all the times I begged my mother for a brother or sister and she had silently shaken her head.

"You were born a few years later and you looked just like her. It was like their lost child had come back to them. Your mother insisted on calling you Suzannah too. I tried to talk her out of it, but she wouldn't listen. Your father chose your middle name."

"Hope," I say.

"Whereas your sister had been Suzannah Mary."

"I still can't believe they called us both Suzannah!"

"When they came to get you baptised, I told them that you were a different child, for all the likeness. I explained that you would have a character of your own and that you could never replace the first Suzannah, but your mother, she was adamant. So Suzannah it was.

At first, she used to tell you about the other Suzannah, but then I suppose she became ashamed that she hadn't given you a name of your own, your own identity, because of course you were a different child. By the age of four, the age she died, you didn't even resemble her any more. Your hair was darker, as were your eyes. You were so different, happy to sit and play quietly in the corner, whereas the first Suzannah had always demanded everyone's attention. In a way, you were more like your parents than she was. They were quiet, bookish people, as you know. They wanted to tell you about her, I'm sure they did. They just never got around to it, I suppose."

The waitress comes over with Howard's lemon pie and sees that I've pushed my tea to one side.

"Something wrong with the tea?"

"No – I."

I can't even begin to give her a reason. I lean back in my chair. The whole room is spinning. In the space of a few minutes I have gained and lost a sister. It is an awful lot to take in.

I'm the first one at the school gates, a ridiculous twenty minutes early to pick Orchid up. As I sit in the car waiting, my conversation with Howard rattles around in my head. I can't get over what he has told me. Why weren't there any pictures amongst my mum and dad's things? I have looked through all their photo albums and I don't notice any photographs of my sister but perhaps If I had seen them, I would have assumed the little girl in the photo was me. I will have to go through all the old albums again. It would be nice to have a picture of her, much nicer than a grave.

I realise with a jolt that people are getting out of their cars and walking up the lane to the school. We huddle like cattle, waiting for the gates to open. I feel curious eyes upon me, but nobody says anything, even though I know who most of them are. Eventually, one of the other mums sidles over to me.

"Hi, it's Suzannah, isn't it?"

Tina Pearson. I manage a tight smile, but I can't bring myself to say anything in reply. I wish she hadn't bothered. I feel stupid and awkward, with her standing beside me. She's dying to hear about Orchid, but I don't want to talk just now. Certainly not to the likes of her.

THE CARETAKER WALKS down the path in his high vis jacket, swinging the keys like a jailor. The gate opens with a loud creak and he herds us toward the classrooms. I don't remember which one Luna class is, until I see Catriona coming out. Yes, there's Miss Gibb. She calls out each child's name in turn, as she recognises the parents. I wait and wait, but her eyes never settle on me. Finally, when every other child has been excused, she looks at me, and I realise that she has known I was there all along.

"Can I have a word?"

I run over the possibilities in my mind. Has Orchid wet herself or had a tantrum and upset the tables? Miss Gibb clicks her tongue. I wish she would bloody well spit it out.

"Orchid is settling in quite nicely, but she needs to work on her listening skills. Three times, I had to ask her to come and sit on the mat this afternoon."

Is that all?

"She has been in care," I say, defensively. It doesn't seem fair to expect her to behave to the same standards as all the other children.

"And…there has been a bit of language."

"Really? I've never heard her swear."

Her face is pinched and I'm not sure she believes me.

"Seriously, I've never heard her swear. What has she been saying exactly?"

"I'm not about to repeat it. I'm just letting you know."

"Hmm," I say with suspicion. It dawns on me that her threshold for swearing could be a lot lower than mine. Does 'bloody hell' count as swearing in her book? Or words like 'crap' or 'damn'?

At that moment, Orchid comes to the door. She has her drinking bottle in one hand, her bag in the other and her coat tucked under her arm.

"Mummy, can we go now?"

"Yes," I say, taking her bag. "I think that would be best."

The crowds have thinned out as we make our way to the gate. Orchid skips along, humming to herself in her usual manner. Her hair has come loose from her pigtails and formed a cloud of frizz around her face. There are ink stains on her uniform and her new shoes are already scuffed.

"Looks like you've had a busy day?"

She nods.

"What did you do?"

Silence.

"Come on, you must have done something?"

"Register."

"What did you have for lunch?"

"Jacket potato with cheese."

"Did you make any friends?"

"Stop asking me questions. You're making my brain ache."

She is of course ravenous and I have failed to bring her anything to eat, so we race home and I allow her a packet of crisps. The ultimate treat. I pour myself a gin and tonic while I'm at it. It has been quite a day for both of us.

I'm on my third G&T by the time Noel arrives home. I had planned to wait until Orchid went to bed, but the whole story comes tumbling out over supper.

"I can't believe your parents never said anything," Noel marvels.

"They probably thought they had all the time in the world, didn't they?"

My head is filled with visions. I picture the other Suzannah as a more lively, vivacious version of me. The fun sister. The daring sister. What would my life be like now, if she was still alive?

"They might not have had you at all," Noel points out, then he looks at me in horror. "Sorry, I shouldn't have said that."

"No, no you're right. If she hadn't died, then I might not even be here. I was a replacement child."

"Just like me," Orchid says.

I stare at her. It never occurred to me that she knew that. That if Noel had been able to give me a child of my own, then we wouldn't have gone looking for her. A lump forms in my throat and I stretch out my arm to hold her hand.

"I'm so glad we found each other."

"Me too, Mummy."

"So, what did you do today?" I ask, when I collect Orchid from school the next day.

"Register."

We walk through the playground, dodging kids on scooters and mums with pushchairs, little ones weaving their way in and out.

"What about lunch? What did you have?"

"Jacket potato."

"What again? Did you make any friends?"

"Mummy, I wish you would stop asking me that. It's so embarrassing."

"Sorry, I'm just interested, that's all."

"Did you bring crisps?"

"No, sorry."

"I told you to bring crisps!"

For a moment, I think she's joking. Her eyes grow small and hard and she kicks out at me. I step out of her way and she has a royal meltdown, throwing herself on the floor and thumping her fists on the ground. I stand there flabbergasted, not knowing what to do. Am I supposed to say something? Hold her? I feel the eyes of the playground upon us. Tina sends me a sympathetic look but I don't meet her eyes. I do not need anything from her. I just need Orchid to get up off the floor.

Gradually, without any interference from me, she calms herself down, or perhaps she simply grows tired. She stops screaming and thumping the ground.

"Let's go home," I say, casting an eye around the empty playground. We are the last ones there, though I spot Miss Gibb watching from the window.

I pull Orchid to her feet and we walk to the car. She leans heavily against me and I wrap my arm around her as we walk. The occasional sob ripples through her body like an after-shock and I make soothing noises.

I let her have the crisps when we get home. She takes them wordlessly and walks off to her room. I drag out the Hoover to clear up the permanent trail of crumbs.

A little later, I open the oven to check on supper.

"What's that weird smell?" Orchid wants to know.

"I made fish stew."

She wrinkles up her nose. "It smells rancid."

"Fish has a strong smell," I say but now that she mentions it, there is a bit of a whiff.

I sniff the pan, but the stew smells normal. Perhaps it's coming from outside. I open the door and step outside. I can't smell anything. Maybe the wind has changed.

My phone beeps. It's Noel.

Running late.

How late?

Home by 8. Love you.

I purse my lips. He'll miss supper.

ORCHID FIDGETS in her seat as I put her bowl in front of her.

"I'm not eating that. It's minging."

"You ate it last week."

"It was more tomatoey."

"This is tomatoey." I give it a stir to show her.

"Mummy, I'm sorry, but it's making me feel sick."

"That's not very…"

All of a sudden, I too feel a wave of nausea. I set my spoon down and rest my hand on the table. It's no good. I can't eat this. I pick up the bowls and carry them to the sink. I don't know why I didn't notice it before. The smell is overwhelming.

"Do you want anything else?"

"No. I can't eat now."

"Me neither."

I tip the stew into the bushes outside and stack the dishes in the dishwasher. The moment I turn my back, Tiger climbs into the dishwasher, his big fluffy tail in the air.

"You don't want to get in there, you daft apeth. Cats don't like getting wet."

I pick him up and dump him in the spare room. Orchid is busy making paper chains and hardly looks up. Tiger settles among the scatter cushions on her bed and I leave them to it.

The smell is still there when I return to the living room.

"Ugh, what is that?"

I've got rid of all the stew now, but the stink lingers. Maybe there's something in the drains. It reminds me of the time we found a dead mouse down in the cellar: like a combination of methane and rotten eggs.

I swat a fly away from my face and walk around the living room, picking up toys and other items that Orchid has left strewn about. I throw it all into a basket, too tired to sort it out. More flies appear as I walk past the curtain, and I bat them away in disgust. The smell hits me again. It's so bad, it makes me gag. Then I see the patch of earth on the ground.

"What the…"

The curtain flutters in the wind, revealing a dark shadow that shouldn't be there. Slowly, I reach out with my hand. Even the soft velvet of the curtain feels creepy against my skin.

"One, two, three…"

I rip back the curtain and force myself to look.

The stench of decay goes right up my nostrils as I stare at the dead rabbit sprawled out on the floor. Clumps of mud cling to its bloody body and its neck has turned black. A piercing sound escapes my lips and I jump back as if I've touched a live wire. It's like something out of a horror film. I stare at the liquid leaking from the body and the flies feasting on the carcass. The smell. The smell is like nothing else. I cough and splutter and my heart thuds like an old man falling down the stairs.

It's the same rabbit, it has to be. Its neck is all…I can't even look at it. I have a gamey flavour in my mouth, repulsive and at once familiar, like chicken that's gone bad. I shudder and squeeze my eyes tight, hoping the wretched thing will disappear. I will never, ever, ever eat rabbit again for as long as I live.

My ears pick up a sound: *clicking, knocking, clanking.*

I listen intently. It's coming from outside the house. I move to the window and peek through the net curtains. There is someone out there.

"Orchid?" I hiss. "Orchid, is that you?"

Light footsteps disturb the gravel. Then a muted cough. My throat contracts. There is a figure on the doorstep, tall and shadowy, features hidden beneath the hood of a navy blue raincoat. The doorbell rings, a single, brisk note. The figure pulls down the hood and I see that it's Effie, our social worker. I had completely forgotten she was coming.

11

My first thought is that this is some warped kind of test. What will Suzannah do if we hang a dead rabbit in the woods? Perhaps I failed by burying it. Is that why they've dug it up again and dumped it in my living room?

I forage for a simpler explanation. The cat. Perhaps Tiger brought it in. Cats bring you mice, don't they? And small birds. Perhaps he dug up the rabbit for me. I laugh at the ludicrousness of it. Tiger is trying to teach me to hunt.

But now Effie's waiting on the doorstop, expecting me to invite her in. I feel a surge of adrenaline, as I jump to my feet. I grab the oven gloves from the stove and hover over the grisly body. It really reeks now: worse than the flesh that comes from the butcher's van. Of course, the butcher's meat is fresh and decently refrigerated, whereas what we have here is basically an unsanitary corpse. It smells worse that the stench of the portable toilets at the festival Noel dragged me to last summer.

My stomach flutters as I reach down and grab the thing by its neck. Its ears flop in my arms. Ugh, it feels like it's moving, twitching and gasping for breath. I cart the thing across the room but it's hard to keep hold, using only the oven gloves. It's slimy and the gloves have no grip to them. I watch in horror as it flies through the air in slow motion. I put out a desperate hand to grab it but only succeed in knocking it further out of reach. The wretched creature spins like an astronaut in space and crashes down hard, splatting on the floor in the centre of the living room. Blood seeps into the cream carpet, leaving a permanent reminder and its head rolls under the sofa.

I stare at the mess: claggy mud mingled with blood and decay. Clumsily, I pick up the corpse and deposit it in the kitchen bin. Then I dive under the sofa to retrieve the head. It is a horrible thing to hold in my hands, but I have no choice. I have to get rid of it. It's not the time to be squeamish.

I wrench open the cleaning cupboard, securely fastened with a magnetic lock to keep Orchid out. I grab a bottle of fabric spray and dart back to the living room, where I spray liberally to soak the stain. I rub furiously with a wet cloth. The stain does not come out and nor does the smell, although it is now mingled with a chemical smell that makes me want to sneeze and vomit simultaneously. The doorbell buzzes again, more insistently this time and I can't put it off any longer. I'll have to let her in.

Effie has her phone out by the time I reach the door.

"Suzannah!" she simpers. "You do realise I've been ringing your doorbell for the past ten minutes? I thought you must have forgotten!"

"No, no!" I say, as lightly as I can. "Sorry, I was busy. I was having a... problem with the boiler."

I laugh too loudly and she shoots me a puzzled look.

"Do come in!"

I lead her into the living room, wishing desperately there was somewhere else we could go. Unfortunately, our house is too small for any alternative. I can hardly take her into my bedroom or the bathroom and it's standing room only in the kitchen.

. . .

EFFIE'S VISITS are meant to be somewhat informal at this stage, but even a simple cup of tea feels like an interrogation to me. I can't wait until the day when she stops visiting us. We don't need her 'support' and we never have.

Effie takes a seat on the sofa and I go around opening as many windows as I can.

"A cup of tea?" I ask.

"Not for me, thanks."

"You don't mind if I make one for myself, do you? I'm parched."

I go into the kitchen and boil the kettle. While it's boiling, I take out a can of air freshener and spray it in the direction of the living room. Then I brew a pot of peppermint tea, hoping the aroma will offset the stench of dead rabbit.

"So," says Effie, when I finally join her. "Where is Orchid?"

"Er…"

I've been so caught up in the dead rabbit drama, that Orchid has temporarily slipped my mind. Is she still in her room? Or has she gone outside?

"Orchid!" I call.

To my relief, Orchid materialises and plonks herself down on the opposite sofa. She automatically reaches for the remote and turns on some terrible trashy TV.

Effie's forehead creases and I know that she's judging me for letting her watch such crap, but if I put my foot down, it might spiral into another full on tantrum. I can't let her see that.

"Now, Orchid. You've been here for what, two months now?"

"Three," I correct her.

"Three," she says, flicking through her papers. "And how has it been?"

Orchid shrugs.

"It's been great," I say, forcing my mouth to smile.

My hands are still trembling from the gristly discovery and the living room is filled with the bad smell.

Orchid scratches the back of her neck and Effie picks up on the gesture.

"Have you been checking her hair regularly for headlice?"

"Yes," I say through clenched teeth. Do I have to answer these stupid questions? Effie spends her days monitoring unfit mothers, so she doesn't know how to approach normal, civilised people. How I wish Noel was here now to help bat back the answers. It's such a strain, always worrying about saying the wrong thing.

"And how has Orchid settled into school? Are you still accompanying her there and back?"

"Of course."

Effie looks at Orchid, who has drawn her knees up to her chin.

"How do you feel about school, Orchid?"

Silence.

It's clear to me that Orchid doesn't want to talk to her either but Effie doesn't take the hint.

"Perhaps we could pause the TV for a minute?"

Why, oh why?

Orchid turns and looks at her like she's out of her mind, then she returns to her TV watching. Effie is flummoxed. She's probably not used to people saying no to her.

"What do you like best about school?" I ask, desperately trying to draw her in to the conversation.

Now it's my turn to be ignored. It's humiliating but the smell of decaying rabbit is still strong and I'm fighting the urge to vomit.

"Have you made any friends?" Effie chimes in.

Oh boy.

There is an awkward silence which Orchid breaks by laughing hysterically at her TV programme.

"Did you see that?" she says, clutching my sleeve.

"Yes," I reply dully. We've watched this same episode over and over.

"Perhaps we should get some fresh air," says Effie. The stench of the decaying rabbit must be getting to her too.

"Good idea," I say. "Sorry about the smell. I was just... defrosting the freezer."

"I thought it was a bit ripe in here."

"Do you want to see my vegetable patch?" Orchid asks, out of the blue.

Earlier in the summer, Noel took her outside and they planted a variety of different vegetables. I had forgotten all about it but apparently Orchid hasn't.

We go outside and Effie looks impressed as Orchid points out the different plants. We all admire the green shoots which are beginning to appear.

WHEN IT IS time for Effie to leave, Orchid and I follow her round to the front, where her silver Fiesta is parked beneath the shade of the large birch tree. I glance with satisfaction at the squirrel poo on the windscreen. I wouldn't dream of parking my car under that particular tree. Effie's mouth forms a straight line, but she doesn't say anything. Then I spot Tiger, prowling round the car's tyres and I pick him up to ensure that he doesn't get run over.

I'm standing there, holding him as two children come in to view. It's Robert and Catriona. They are heading directly for us.

"Hello," I call out to them, with as much cheer as I can muster.

Orchid says nothing but Robert offers a watery smile.

"Oh, are these your friends?" Effie asks, in delight.

Of course, Catriona has to go and spoil it. "She's not our friend. She's a pet thief."

Effie laughs lightly and I stand there, wishing the earth would swallow us up.

"Orchid is not a pet thief," I state clearly but Catriona won't have it. Her eyes are as round and beady as her rabbit's as she peers at me, her hands planted on her hips.

"I know it was her. First she took our cat and then she took our rabbit."

"What's all this?" Effie asks. She looks uncertain, as if she's not sure if we're playing a game.

"I'm just holding the cat so he doesn't get run over," I say. "He keeps trying to jump under the car."

"He never jumps under our car," says Catriona. "Cats are cleverer than that."

"Well, this one isn't."

I rattle my brains, trying to think of something final to say. I need to get rid of Robert and Catriona whilst still playing nice in front of Effie.

"Do you want to see my vegetable patch?" Orchid asks.

Robert looks interested but Catriona won't hear of it.

"I'll take my cat, please," she says to me. I hand Tiger over and hope that he bites her.

"Well, got to get back to defrosting my freezer," I say, with false merriment.

"I suppose I had better leave you to it," Effie says, finally taking the hint.

ONCE EFFIE HAS GONE, I open the kitchen bin and pull out the bag. I tie it up tight and lug it out to the grey wheelie bin outside, cringing as the plastic bag brushes my thighs. It's bin day tomorrow. I can't wait for the wretched thing to be gone.

I return to the house and pull on my marigolds. I attack the stain with a vengeance, banishing Orchid to her room while I spray it with more chemicals and flood it with boiling hot water. I scrub until I feel high and still I can't shift that infernal smell, so I open the doors and pray that the scent of the nearby pine trees will freshen up the room.

Afterwards, I peer in at Orchid, but she is still busy with her paper chains. I try not to mind the mess, all those little snippets of paper and the sticky tape stuck to her bed. I try not think about how many trees we are squandering with all this artwork and tell myself that at least she's doing something besides watching TV.

Noel arrives home, all laughter and smiles. He has brought chips from the van. The strong chip smell is just the thing to drive the rabbit smell away. He makes a big production of it, setting the chips out on the table, fetching the ketchup and vinegar. He presents Orchid with a can of Coke.

"Thank you Daddy! Thank you!"

She hugs him tight and smiles up at him, like this is the nicest thing anyone has ever done for her. I don't begrudge them these father-daughter moments, at least, I try my best not to. I just wish there was space inside their circle for me.

Once Orchid is in bed, I take a long hot bath and wash the icky feeling from my body. I use a huge handful of bath salts and watch them fizz and foam. There is nothing quite like the smell of vanilla and eucalyptus to make you feel human again and I emerge feeling lighter and revived.

"You're in a good mood," Noel says, when I enter the bedroom. He sets his book aside and pats the space next to him on the bed.

I move towards him, admiring the way he looks in his tight vest. His body smells fresh and musky and his eyes are sexy and inviting, but I can't quite kick the image of that dead rabbit. I picture its eyes boring into me as my lips brush against Noel's and it's all I can do not to jump back from the bed.

"Mummy!

I rub my eyes groggily. "What time is it?"

It's light outside. Noel must have left for work, but my alarm has not yet gone off.

"Mummy, you have to get up!"

I peer out of the covers. Orchid's face is obscured by her huge cloud of hair as she pulls on my arm.

"Give me five minutes, poppet."

"But Mummy…"

She grabs my arm again and tugs on it until I climb out of bed.

"Really, Orchid. I wish you wouldn't…"

I stop. I can hear the sound of running water. Lots of it. Where's it coming from?

I follow her out the door and into the passageway.

The bathroom. It's coming from the bathroom. I throw open the door and water sloshes out. The bath and sink are both overflowing, all the taps running at once. The bathroom floor is several inches deep and the water keeps coming.

12

"What on earth?"

I rush into the bathroom, but the water is hot.

"Stay back!" I snarl at Orchid.

I leap back and run to the front door to pull on my wellies, then back to the bathroom, to turn off the taps. I can't believe how much water there is, can't even begin to think how I'm going to get rid of it all. I turn and look at Orchid, who is standing close behind me, pressing against me to see into the bathroom.

"Did you do this?"

"No, Mummy. It was like this when I got up."

Of course, it was.

I send Orchid to her room to get ready for school, then I fetch the mop and the bucket and clean as best as I can. The water takes ages to drain out of the bath and no matter how many buckets I fill, the mess on the floor doesn't seem to be going down. Eventually, I leave it and go and change so that I can take Orchid to school. She has made her own breakfast, creating a fresh mess of jam and crumbs on the table and there are sticky finger marks on the wall.

Rage boils inside me as I rush around, getting ready.

"Come on, Orchid, get your shoes on. We're going to be late."

Orchid stands by the door.

"Mummy, I want to bring Tiger to school. He could come on a lead."

"No, Orchid, he wouldn't like it. Besides, he's not even our cat."

"He is too."

I take a breath. "Maybe we could get you a cat of your own?"

I should not have suggested this without talking to Noel first, but I'm desperate.

"I don't want another cat," she says, stamping her foot. "I want Tiger."

"Let's talk about it later," I say, passing her her shoes.

I stand over her as she puts them on and finally, we walk out to the car.

WHEN WE ARRIVE at the school, she starts up again.

"Mummy, can you bring Tiger when you pick me up?"

"No, Orchid. I don't think so."

"But why not? I want to show him the school. He's curious."

I roll my eyes. "Really, Orchid, I think Tiger is perfectly happy at home."

"Mummy, you're not listening to me," she whines, her voice growing loud. "Why don't you care about me?"

I sigh with frustration. "I do care about you, Orchid but right now, I'm worried that you're going to be late and I have a lot to do back at home clearing up that mess you made."

"I didn't make any mess!"

Her voice is getting louder and louder and I realise that

these are delay tactics. She doesn't want to go in. I remember what that felt like.

"Promise me you'll bring Tiger!"

"Orchid, stop shouting. Everyone is staring. You'll make a fool out of yourself in front of all your friends."

"I don't have any friends!"

She stamps down hard on my foot and stomps off to the classroom like a sulky teenager.

I stare at her for a moment, not knowing what to do. I don't want to part on such bad terms. Should I go in after her? I stand in the classroom doorway.

"Orchid!" I call, but she has already gone through to the cloakroom.

I feel Miss Gibb's disapproving glare.

"The parents are not supposed to come inside the classroom. It's for the children's safety."

"That's all very well, but Orchid is upset."

"We'll take good care of her don't you worry."

I stand there dissatisfied. I could block the doorway just to be difficult but other children are still coming in and I don't want to get in their way.

I think for a moment about pulling Orchid out and telling Miss Gibb to "eff" off, but then I'd have her at home all day and I'm not sure I could stand it. Instead, I take a deep breath and withdraw. My heart is thumping hard inside my chest and there is a primal, animalistic part of me that wants to climb to the top of a mountain and scream. Instead, I skulk back to my car and drive back home to my messy house.

It takes me a good hour to get the place looking anywhere near normal again, and the hems of my jeans are soaked. Afterwards, I flop down on the sofa with a cup of tea. It is only then that I spot Orchid's PE kit sitting by the door. She'll need that this afternoon.

For goodness sake!

I finish my tea and drive back to the school. Since I'm not

allowed to enter the classroom, I hand it over to the stony faced receptionist. The children are outside in the playground when I walk back to my car. I see them through the fence, running and laughing and playing games. I spot Orchid sitting alone on a bench. She looks entirely separate from the rest of the school. They're all wearing the same uniform but it looks different on her, somehow. She is tall and gangly and her hair is thick and woolly, whereas all the other little girls have neat little ponytails and bunches. She is not one of them and I think they sense it. I felt the same way when I was at school. I might have looked the part, but there is something inside me that makes it hard to gel with people.

What you looking at, Frosty?

I remember it well, that feeling of isolation. I did not mind sitting there all by myself, but I dreaded the others noticing. I didn't need girls like Tina pointing out how inept I was. I just wanted to be left alone with my thoughts.

As I watch, two dinner ladies approach Orchid and speak to her. From the wide smiles on their faces, I guess this is an attempt to jolly her along. After a bit of an exchange the ladies walk off again patrolling the grass at the periphery of the playground where the children are playing a muddy game of football.

Orchid is not the only child on her own. There is a boy who seems entirely absorbed with emptying the contents of his pockets into his hands and examining them in great detail and there is a girl who stands near a group taking part in a skipping game. The other girls sneak little glances at her but pretend not to see her. She pushes her glasses up her nose and stares intently. She would be left standing there all break time if it weren't for the football that comes totally out of left field and smacks her in the face. There is instant drama as blood spurts from her nose. Suddenly, everyone in the vicinity is paying attention to her. The girls stop their skipping game. It is now their turn to stare. I look at Orchid hoping she will help but she is laughing, howling hysterically, like it's the funniest thing ever to happen. I feel unsettled as I walk away. Every time I feel a bit closer to my daughter, I feel her moving further away.

———

I SPEND the afternoon at the big library in Upper Mercy researching my sister, the other Suzannah. I have looked online but failed to come up with anything. It was all too long ago. The librarian sets up the micro fiche for me in a quiet room at the back.

"There's a coffee machine downstairs if you need it," she says.

"Thank you."

I wait while she closes the door behind me. I am impatient for her to leave.

I spend the next few hours searching through local news-papers from around the time the other Suzannah must have died. I feel excited. I want to find my sister, but I'm also a little nervous about what I might find. This girl, this Suzannah must have been someone incredible for my parents to name me after her. I feel something akin to jealously that I was not their one and only, mingled with sadness that they kept this from me for all these years.

My eyes grow tired as I churn through the pages. There are so many of them preserved here and so much of it is of absolutely no use. Articles about garden parties and royal weddings, debates about joining the European Union and stories about giant marrow crops and homemade jams. Then finally, finally, I find what I'm looking for:

Tragic Suzannah, 4, killed in road accident.

I stare at the headline and shiver. The words wriggle in

front of me. I struggle to make sense of it all, until I see the picture. I trace the outline of her face with my fingers. I have seen pictures of myself as a young child. This girl has the same blonde hair and angelic expression. I see that our noses are different. She had a little button nose, whereas mine is straighter and longer but all the same, the resemblance is uncanny…

Tears prick my eyes. I wish I could reach in and pull her out. My sister. My flesh and blood. If only she was still here, then perhaps I wouldn't feel quite so alone. It is such an enormous burden, to be the last of the line. I have felt it keenly, with each failed attempt to get pregnant. The Deckers die with me. Or they would have, if it weren't for Orchid.

I read and reread the article, desperate for details. It all seems to have happened pretty much as Howard said. It was a warm day and my parents were working outside, while Suzannah played in the garden. She was in and out of her Wendy house - a little plastic tent with a cat painted on the door - so my parents didn't realise at first that she was gone. According to the report, Suzannah's pet rabbit, Toby had gone missing from his run. It seemed he had burrowed his way out and it was thought the little girl may have wandered off looking for him.

My throat runs dry. The image of the dead rabbit looms large in my mind. I picture it, brown and fluffy, its dark eyes lifeless and still. It's one creepy coincidence. I glance behind me and all at once, I don't feel like being on my own any more. I stand up and grab my handbag. I can't get out of that room quick enough. I take the stairs down to the break room and put a pound into the drinks machine. My own reflection peers back at me as I wait in for it to dispense my coffee. I press my fingers against the glass and imagine that I am touching her, the other Suzannah. Would she still look like me if she were here today? Would we be friends or would we avoid each other, meeting only for special occasions like Christmas?

"Excuse me, miss?"

"Yes?"

"You have to press the button."

"Oh."

Feeling like an idiot, I press the button and the coffee churns out. The paper cup is hot to the touch and I carry it by the rim over to the window. I watch the car park as I sip the hot liquid. I watch as a tall woman climbs into her silver Fiesta and I imagine that it's her. She has a noisy exhaust. She ought to get that looked at. I will nag her about it next time she comes round for tea. She will protest at first, but then she'll agree to go to garage and I'll relax, happy that I have done my sisterly duty. I shake my head. I wonder if this is what it feels like to go mad.

ORCHID is in a better mood when I pick her up from school. She chatters on about her music lesson and the arguments of the morning are forgotten. I give her a bag of salty pretzels just to make a change from crisps and she goes off to her room while I make lasagne for supper. Immediately, I hear her music go on, the loud bass booming through the house.

"Can you turn it down?" I call through the door.

To my surprise she does. I leave her to it and get on with the cooking, stirring the sauce and chopping carrots and courgettes like a pro. Goodness knows if she's actually going to eat any of it, but I have a popular children's cookbook in front of me and the book says, 'it's your job to serve and her job to eat.'

I feel quite pleased with myself as I place the lasagne in the oven and wipe my hands on a cloth.

"You okay, Orchid?"

I push open the door to her room. She is sitting on her bed, cutting out some pictures for her scrap book.

"Oh, Orchid!"

On the floor beside her lies her quilt, the beautiful quilt I made out of all my mother's clothes. It has been snipped into hundreds of tiny pieces. I feel like someone is sitting on my chest.

"What?" she says, all innocence.

"That was my mother's! How could you? You selfish little brat!"

I fall to the floor and pick up the biggest bits of the quilt but it's no use, it cannot possibly be mended. I snatch the scissors from her hand and walk out of the room, tears streaming down my face.

"Mummy!" Orchid comes after me and I know that I should take the opportunity to talk to her and explain what she's done wrong. But I can't be reasonable right now. I'm far too upset.

She puts her arms around me but I push her away, a little harder than I meant to.

"Get away from me."

Now it is Orchid's turn to be upset. She runs back to her room and slams the door with deafening force. I feel the whole house shake and for a moment, I think the ceiling is going to come down on top of us.

I return to the kitchen and pour myself a gin and tonic. I swear I never drank this much before I had her. I never needed to. Orchid does not emerge from her room, not even when it's time for her favourite programme. I put it on and turn it up to make sure she can hear it. I don't know if I'm trying to lure her out or if I'm doing it just to spite her. I don't feel like myself any more. I'm hot with rage and my body shakes so badly that I drop a plate and I feel irrationally angry when it doesn't break.

The door opens and Noel comes in, his backpack slung

casually over one shoulder, exactly the way he wore it when we were at uni. He's wearing a black cap with the logo of one his favourite bands emblazoned across the front. It annoys me that he wears that to work, when it doesn't go at all with his work clothes. I wait impatiently as he removes the earphones from his ears. First one, then the other. I hear the tinny drumbeat as he reaches down and switches off the sound. He has gone too long without a shave and he has a face full of stubble. He never shaves unless he has to. He would rather look homeless, and it makes me unreasonably angry.

"How was your day?" he asks, as he steps into his slippers. He doesn't actually look at me and I can see that he's still thinking about whatever he did at work or perhaps about some song he's in the middle of composing.

"It was awful! Bloody awful."

"Suzannah, what's wrong?"

I take a deep breath and spill the beans. I tell him about the flooded bathroom and what Orchid did to my precious quilt. How it will be impossible to fix.

"It can't be that bad," he says calmly. Oh, so calmly.

"It *is* that bad. You go in there and see for yourself."

I don't tell him that I screamed at Orchid. I already feel guilty about that, but Noel is home now and I know that he will make it right.

"Will you talk to her?"

"Of course, I will."

He goes into the spare room, knocking first to show her that he respects her privacy. I hear them talking in low, muted voices. I picture him seeing the quilt, seeing how bad it is and I feel my anger welling up all over again.

I wait for Noel to emerge, but he doesn't seem to be in any hurry. My anger drains away as the time passes and guilt sets in its place. All that anger. What was it all for? I sit down and pick up a book, but I keep rereading the same sentence over and over and I can't take it in. I shouldn't have yelled at her.

Has Orchid told him how badly I behaved? Has she told him what a horrible mother I am?

My chest aches as I remember the shock and hurt on Orchid's face. I remember being nine, and going through my father's bookcase and taking down his copy of Robinson Crusoe. It was the most beautiful illustrated story book, and I cut out every picture and pasted them on to a big piece of scrap paper. I had thought I was creating a wonderful piece of art for him. I had thought that he would be chuffed. How was I to know that once I cut up the book it would be ruined? I hadn't thought about that at all, only about the wonderful collage I was making.

I pull myself out of my chair and walk with the lightest of footsteps into the spare room. Noel has left it ajar and I watch the two of them doing Orchid's princess puzzle together. They work in perfect synchronicity, Noel slotting in all the edge pieces and Orchid building the picture in the middle. The atmosphere is calm and relaxed, in sharp contrast to the adrenaline buzzing inside me. They look so natural, as if they belong together. I feel like an intruder, stepping on their turf.

I clear my throat. "I wanted to say sorry," I mumble. "I was angry and upset but I shouldn't have shouted. I didn't mean the things I said. I love you very much."

Orchid looks up and there is a hint of triumph in her eyes.

"Do you have anything to say to Mummy?" Noel prompts her.

"That's okay," she says, her smile growing into a wide, cheeky grin.

I swallow my anger, before it can rise up and bite me again. "I would like to know why you did it," I say. "What made you cut up the quilt?"

"It wasn't me," she says, slotting a piece of puzzle into place. "It was the other Suzannah."

13

My heart pounds and all the muscles in my body grow tense. I look to Noel for support, but he is looking at Orchid.

"What do you mean?" he asks.

"She did it," Orchid insists. "She was lonely. She said she wanted to play with me."

"You actually heard her say that?"

"Yes."

She looks right at me, challenging me with her eyes. I glare back at her, heat flooding my face. I wait for her to blink but she holds my gaze until I can't take it any longer. I turn on my heel and run from the room. Noel does not follow.

My hands shake as I occupy myself with the laundry. There is no urgent need to do it right now, except that I have to do something or I'll explode. I sort the darks from the whites and check the pockets of Noel's jeans before I put them in the wash. Once I've got it running, I pick up the basket of clean clothes and take it into my bedroom to sift through. I make three piles on the bed, mine, Noel's and Orchid's. I ball up the socks and fold the T-shirts and then I pick up one of Orchid's dresses. It is one of the first ones I chose for her, covered in bright yellow flowers with big beaming smiles. There is something charming and childlike about this dress. I hold it in my hands and try to remember how it felt before Orchid came to us, when my heart ached so badly for a child. I had felt so alone then and now I have Orchid and I still can't be happy.

Noel interrupts my thoughts by walking in at that moment and I wipe a stray tear on my sleeve.

"I think she's lonely," he says, perching on the end of the bed. "She's making up an imaginary friend to keep herself company."

"But does it have to be my dead sister?"

"Sorry, but we should never have discussed her in front of Orchid. Children have vivid imaginations."

"All the same, I don't like it. She needs to take responsibility for her actions."

I know I sound all hoity toity, but I can't help it. Orchid has hurt me deeply.

"She's nine," he reminds me, gently.

"She's nearly ten. Nearing the age of criminal responsibility. We need to keep her on the right track."

He laughs. "You're not suggesting Orchid is about to become a criminal, are you?"

"No, but it matters. Actions matter and so do words."

"Of course."

He tugs at his shirt, pulling at the material as if he's not used to it. "Is there time for a quick shower before supper? It was so hot and sweaty on the train."

I sniff his neck.

"You smell fine to me."

"Still."

I watch as he walks towards the bathroom and listen for the sound of running water.

ORCHID's tenth birthday is fast approaching and I latch onto it, like a lighthouse in a vast ocean of uncertainty. All tenth birthdays are a big deal, but this one more than most. It is her first birthday as part of our family and as such, I want it to be special. This is a day I want us all to remember. I want it to be the kind of birthday that normal families have, one that will help us push past the weirdness and tension of the past few weeks.

I long to throw her a big birthday party with jelly and cake and party games like 'pin the tail on the donkey'. The trouble is, Orchid doesn't have any friends. She's been at school for over a month now and she doesn't seem to have come any closer to making any. So I take the bull by the horns and organise something anyway, just a small birthday tea. I collar Miss Gibb and ask for a list of names of Orchid's classmates, but she is less than helpful.

"I'm sorry, but I can't give you that information; it's confidential."

For goodness sake!

I'm reduced to nobbling other parents outside the classroom door and asking if their children would like to come. I emphasise that Orchid is new and recently adopted and that it would mean a lot to us both if they would come, but there are no bleeding hearts in Little Mercy. Of the ten I invite, only three accept.

ORCHID's BIRTHDAY falls on a Thursday. I buy her a deluxe art kit that includes a sketch pad, paints, brushes, pens, pencils and pastels. I also buy her a nifty easel that I set up in her room while she's asleep so it's the first thing she sees when she wakes up in the morning.

"Wow," Orchid says and her eyes brim with tears, as she examines the easel. She tries out various pens and pencils and Noel brings in a pot of water so she can try out the paints. We watch as she makes a big sweep of green with a wide brush. The picture quickly transforms into trees and I recognise the weeping willows from the woods.

"She has talent," Noel says.

I nod. She is completely engrossed.

She catches us watching and stops, the smile sliding off her face.

"What is it?" I ask.

"Will I be able to take this with me when I go?"

"When you go where?"

Noel looks at me.

"Oh," I say, as I realise her meaning. She still does not consider this her forever home.

"But you are home," I tell her, wishing I had more than those measly words to give her.

I HAVE all day to prepare for the birthday tea. I blow up balloons and bake a cake and organise party bags. Then, at three o'clock, I pick Orchid up from school and she goes to her room to change. At four o'clock, the cars arrive. I'm relieved that the other parents are so punctual. I don't think I could take the anxiety if they were late. I have read posts on Facebook about children whose parents invited the entire class but nobody showed up. Horrendous.

Priscilla and Primrose are the first to arrive. Twins with thick glasses, sticking out ears and prominent teeth. Despite what you might glean from this description, they are both unconventionally gorgeous. Then comes Dilly, the dreamer, with glazed eyes and a lazy smile. I'm not sure she listens to a word I say, but she seems nice enough. Last but not least is Catriona, dressed in her best pink party frock. I hadn't even realised I'd invited her. I'd simply asked a group of mothers outside the classroom if their children wanted to come. It hadn't occurred to me that one of them was Catriona's mum.

Still, she's here now, so perhaps she's willing to give Orchid another chance. If not, I'll be watching her. Catriona seems to be friends with the twins, whereas Dilly is one on her own, so maybe she and Orchid will play together.

Catriona asks for a glass of water and then the others all want one too. Dilly manages to spill hers on Primrose's feet and I have to go and get her some spare socks of Orchid's. Primrose refuses to wear them, because they don't go with her outfit.

I bite my cheek. How to get things back on track?

"Who wants to decorate the biscuits?" I say, and they all congregate at the table.

Both the twins want to sit next to Catriona, which nearly causes a fight because Dilly is already sitting next to her. I ask her to move next to Orchid and she does as she's told. They all look excited when I bring out five large unicorn shaped cookies and little pots of edible glitter.

Orchid is meticulous in her decorating, but the rest seem to be in competition to make as much mess as possible. Since they are already at the table, I bring out the food as soon as they've finished. That way, they don't have to clean their hands twice. Nobody touches the tuna sandwiches. They munch through the crisps like a plague of locusts, barely pausing for breath as they inhale the biscuits and cupcakes. The melon balls sit in a sorry heap and the carrot sticks are shoved to one side in order to make room for the jelly.

After the food, Orchid begs me to get out the piñata. It is a pony shaped one we found in the pound shop, though it cost more than a pound. The colours are bright and gaudy and the girls cheer as I hoist it up into position.

"Orchid can go first," Catriona says. "Since it's her birthday."

I'm not sure who put her in charge but Orchid looks pleased so I go along with it. I give her the stick and she whacks the piñata violently. It shatters, showering the girls with sugary sweets. The girls squeal and throw themselves under the chairs and tables to retrieve them. I realise too late that I should have given out the party bags so they'd have something to put them in. Orchid has the most and Orchid is not good at sharing.

We attempt a game of musical statues after that, but the girls are pumped with sugar and nobody can stand still.

"Can we watch the 'My Little Pony' movie?" Orchid asks.

It's not what I had in mind but the others seem to like the idea so I let them. Dilly and Catriona settle beside her, clutching their sweets, while the twins continue to play musical statues on their own. All of a sudden, the TV switches itself off.

"Spooky," Dilly says.

I get up and switch it back on. It's odd. There doesn't seem to be anything wrong with it and it's such a mild day outside, no storms on the horizon. They continue watching but a few minutes later the TV turns itself off again and this time, the lights go out as well. It is not quite dark yet but the girls are alarmed, nonetheless.

There are screams as the twins come bounding into the room, freaked out by the power cut.

"It's all right," I say. "Probably just the trip switch. I'll go and sort it out."

THE TRIP SWITCH is down in the cellar which will be full of spider webs, I realise with a shudder but hopefully not mice. We had an infestation of them last summer and had to get the place fumigated. It should be all right now though. Especially with Tiger around.

"Mummy, can you hurry?"

"Okay, but you girls stay together till I get back, right?"

"I'm scared," says Dilly.

"Of what?" Catriona says. "It's not even dark yet."

I suppress a smile. "You'll be fine for a few minutes. Just stay put until I come back."

I don't relish the thought of going down into the cellar but I'm not about to become one of those women who waits for their husbands to do everything.

I leave the girls huddled together and walk down the passageway to the end of the house. I open the cellar door and flick the switch. Nothing.

Oh come on!

I whizz back to the kitchen and take the torch down from the fridge. Then I hurry back, eager to get it over and done with. I promise myself a nice glass of wine once all this is over and a large slice of birthday cake to go with it.

I shine the light down into the dark, musky room. There are concrete steps that lead down into the depths. I prop the door open with a wedge and move onto the first step. There are boxes upon boxes down there. We keep our camping equipment down there, along with the ski gear we only used a couple of times. There is also a large wine rack and any number of things that belonged to Mum and Dad. I make my way down the stairs, shuddering slightly at the size of the cobwebs. At the bottom, I side step a pile of suitcases and find the switch box. I flip the power back on and a shaft of light comes down from upstairs.

"There."

On my way back up, I pick up a box of my parents' photographs and lug it back up the steps. The door creaks as I approach and begins to close. Perhaps one of the children has inadvertently nudged the wedge that was holding it open. I start to run up the steps, but the rusty old rail comes away in my hand and I lose my balance. The box of photographs tumbles out of my hands, landing with a thud on the floor below. I just manage to save myself from toppling down after it when I hear the door slam.

14

The TV has come back on, louder than before, blaring pop music. I picture the girls dancing about, having fun.

"Help!" I yell. "I'm trapped in the cellar."

The darkness closes in on me in. Damp fills my nostrils and I cough up the dust I hadn't noticed before.

I fumble back down the stairs and step into the depths of the dark, dank cellar.

When I reach the bottom, there a scuttering movement that sends a jolt of fear to my heart.

That had better not be mice.

I stand stock still. It sounds like something is rolling across the floor.

Where is that torch?

I follow the beam of light, fragments of dust and dirt dancing in its path. The wind rattles at the door and I urge my legs onward. I bend down. The torch is within my grasp, but as I reach for it, I touch something cold and slimy. I pull back sharply.

Ugh, what is that?

I wipe my hand on my trousers and dive for the torch. I clutch it tightly and shine it from one side of the room to the other, but all looks still.

I edge back towards the stairs. It seems further than I thought. I scramble up on my hands and knees, still clutching the torch tightly. My heart is racing as I reach the cellar door.

"Orchid? Girls? I'm stuck in the cellar! Let me out!"

I try to keep the panic from my voice, but I can't help it. I feel the lightest touch on my shoulder and I pound on the door, convinced that there's a spider crawling down my neck.

"Orchid!"

Where is she?

Are they all out there, giggling as they ignore my cries? No, she doesn't know them well enough for that. One of them would rebel.

"Help!" I yell again. My own voice echoes back to me.

"Please!" My voice is weaker now. "I'm scared."

I slump down on the step and hold myself in a tight embrace. I can't bear it any longer.

"Let me out!"

I wait and wait. Every so often I call out again, but nobody answers and I feel more and more wretched. They've got to notice when somebody wants something, but the food and drink is still out on the table. They can probably help themselves. I suck in air through my teeth. If I had known I would be stuck down here, I would have brought my phone and a nice warm jumper. I fantasise about the thick angora cardigan I have hanging in my wardrobe. I hate brushing against the cobwebs with my bare arms and I can't stand the thought that there may be other creatures down here. And I dread to think about what the girls are getting up to in my absence.

After a long while, I hear a knock at the front door and I

realise the parents have arrived to pick up their children. I expect the girls to answer the door, but no one does. Then I hear my phone ringing in the kitchen. Surely they can hear that? The girls must still be in the living room. I told them to stay there, didn't I? There is more banging on the door as the parents grow increasingly irate. I hear the door rattling but it's no use. I locked it myself. They won't be able to get in.

I look around, desperate now. There are no windows in the cellar, no other way out. I pull at the door but it locks from the other side. There is no way to get it open. The voices grow louder. The parents are getting frantic.

"Let me out!"

I bang on the cellar door until my fists feel like they are on fire.

I stop and listen. The voices are getting nearer. Are they…

Yes, there are voices in the passageway. The girls must have finally let them in.

"In here!" I yell. "I'm locked in! Help!"

I thud on the door so hard that when it finally swings open, I fall through it, colliding with my stone faced rescuers. Multiple hands help to steady me, and I scramble to my feet. For a moment I stand there, blinking at the light. When my vision swims back into focus, I find myself looking at Catriona's mum and the twins' dad. Neither of them is smiling.

"The power went out." I struggle to catch my breath. "Then I got locked in the cellar."

I glance about to see if anyone is hiding, sniggering in the shadows. Then I spy Dilly's mum, standing quietly in the background. Her face is pale and unsmiling.

"Where are the girls?" she asks.

I blink. "Didn't they let you in?"

"No, I had to climb in through the window," Catriona's mum says. "Then I let Samuel and Emma in."

I feel a flash of panic.

Where are the girls?

The house is silent. Surely they haven't gone out into the woods? Not at this time of the evening? My throat closes up like I've swallowed a wasp. It has begun to rain, fat droplets racing one another down the window. If the girls are out there...

With one last dash of hope, I stride towards the living room. The door is closed and when I pull the door handle, I find the room in darkness. It is only then that I hear it. A voice so deep and eerie that I can't quite believe it's Orchid's.

THE GIRLS SIT in a circle on the floor, clutching an assortment of cushions and teddies while Orchid holds their attention, speaking in a slow, deliberate monotone. Her voice rises and falls at just the right moments and my hackles rise as I listen.

"The other Suzannah chased them down to the stream and made them swim and swim until no one could swim any more. All five girls drowned, one by one. Starting with..."

Abruptly, she shines her torch on Catriona. "You!"

The girls scream and I flip on the lights. It's hard to tell who is actually scared and who's just having fun. The other parents push past me and grab their children and hug them as if they are rescuing them from some great disaster. I want to hug Orchid too, but something stops me. That voice...

She smiles at me but the guilt shows in her face. Is it because she told the other girls a scary story or because she locked me in the cellar? I wish I could tell.

"I was scared," I say, making the first move. "I got locked in the cellar. I thought I was never going to get out."

"Poor Mummy."

She reaches out and hugs me and I try not to freeze as I feel the warmth of her arms around me. It feels nice, the hug, if only I could make myself relax. But she is hugging me too hard and I have to pull away.

"Mummy!" She sounds annoyed. Her voice is whiny and shrill, but I can't help it. I need to breathe.

"You shouldn't have told that story," I tell her.

Her bottom lip wobbles. "Why? Didn't you like it?"

"You know I didn't. You shouldn't be talking about my sister like that. It isn't nice."

Orchid tilts her chin towards me. "She wanted me to tell it."

The twins' dad is looking at me.

"Come on girls, let's get out of here. Your mum will be wondering where we've got to."

Catriona's mum mutters something and they all gather up their things.

"Don't forget your party bags!" I call, and Orchid springs into action, handing them out as the girls are hurried out the door.

From the faces of the other parents, I can tell there won't be any more play dates any time soon.

"Sorry I got locked in the cellar," I say again but no one is listening.

I follow them all to the door. The whole house seems to have been turned upside down in the hour or so that I was down in the cellar. Tiger is up on the table, nibbling on the leftover tuna sandwiches. There is a satisfied look on his face as if he has masterminded the whole thing. Catriona picks him up on the way out and lugs him to the car. He gives me a look over her shoulder to tell me he'll be back. I can see why they called him Arnold now.

I close the window and lock it, then pour myself a large glass of wine. I look around at all the mess, but I can't face it. Not after the evening I've had. I'm still wondering who knocked the wedge that was holding open the cellar door. Was it one of the girls or simply an accident? If not Orchid then could it have been Catriona? We got off to a rocky start with her. Maybe she was out for revenge.

"Orchid?" I call. "Where are you?"

There are cushions and teddies strewn about the living room, but Orchid is not there. I peer into her room. She lies diagonally across her bed, still in her party dress. She is drawing on her new sketch pad. I move closer and take a look. She has drawn a small blonde haired girl, playing in the woods. The details are impressive, from the long, light eyelashes to the freckles scattered about her cheeks.

"Is that one of the twins?" I ask.

"No, it's…"

"Who?"

"You don't want me to talk about her."

I bite my cheek. "Go on."

"The other Suzannah."

THE THING IS, I saw a ghost once. It's not something I talk about much because I know that no one will believe me. But when I was about thirteen, I was on holiday in Skegness with my parents. We were staying at a hotel that used to be a ball room. One day, I left my cardigan in the dining room. When I went in to get it, I saw a pale young woman in a crinoline dress. I watched as she danced through the room. Her movements were incredible; I remember vividly how she soared through the air and then disappeared behind the curtains. I waited for her to come out but when she didn't, I decided to investigate. I pulled back the curtains. There was nothing but a solid wall.

I told my father but he just muttered something about hidden bookcases. I think he believed I'd made it all up. Mum, on the other hand, had more of an open mind.

"Children are more susceptible to seeing ghosts and spirits," she had explained. "Especially teenagers, because of your hormones."

I remember being embarrassed at the mention of

hormones. I was going through an incredibly awkward stage and the last thing I needed was to be reminded of my raging acne. I wondered at the time if she had ever seen a ghost but stupidly I didn't ask. Now I wish I had.

15

Following the birthday tea fiasco, the reception at the school gates is even less welcoming than before. Apparently, Orchid's ghost story gave some of the other girls nightmares and Catriona told it to Robert, who told it to his friends. Now everyone is staring at Orchid like she's some kind of witch, instead of just a girl with an overactive imagination. It's pretty pathetic really. It's not like I let them watch an 18 rated film or anything.

"You were supposed to be supervising our children," Catriona's mother complains. "Those of us who've lived round here all our lives, we have a certain way of doing things…"

"I'm local," I butt in. "Little Mercy, born and bred."

"Yes, but you went off for a few years, didn't you?"

"I was at uni."

"Well then."

I have no idea what my having gone away is supposed to prove, but you just can't argue with some people. No wonder Catriona is so full of herself.

SATURDAY IS our long awaited trip to Legoland. Ostensibly, we are going to celebrate Orchid's birthday, but Noel loves Lego. I think he is almost as excited as she is. I wish I could share their enthusiasm, but I take one look at the queue to get in and feel a headache coming on.

"Jam sandwich?" Noel says, opening the picnic bag.

"No thanks," I say, but Orchid thinks this is a cracking idea. Within minutes she has crumbs all down her T-shirt and there are wasps buzzing around us. I take a wet wipe from my bag and mop her face with it. I swore I was never going to be one of those mothers, burning through the environment with their wet wipes, but they come in so blooming handy. They have become my guilty pleasure.

"Cup of tea?" Noel offers, holding up the flask. I shake my head. The only way I like my tea is fresh and from the pot. I take a couple of steps forward and sigh. We are hardly moving.

HALF AN HOUR LATER, we are finally inside. All I can think about is finding a toilet.

"Come on, Orchid," I say to her, but she refuses to come.

"I'll take her on the first ride," Noel says, pointing it out on the map. "Take your time, Suz, get yourself a cup of tea. We'll see you when we get off."

His kindness rubs me up the wrong way. I don't need to be pandered to like a child. I just don't enjoy this sort of thing. Why couldn't we have gone for a nice day out at Longleat? It would have been so much more civilised.

Noel and Orchid emerge, laughing and exuberant from their ride. They both have flushed cheeks and Orchid's hair and clothes are all damp.

"What happened?"

"The water ride was a bit wetter than we expected but never mind, she'll soon dry off in this heat."

"She'll catch a cold."

"She'll be fine."

Noel peels off his shirt and pulls it over Orchid's head. It comes all the way down to her knees and she laughs and twirls around as if she's wearing a new dress. Noel is now down to his vest, but he doesn't seem to mind at all.

"Come on, Suzannah. This is supposed to be fun."

We go on a roller coaster ride together. I grip the bar tightly as the roller coaster edges up and up. I know it's coming but I still struggle to catch my breath as it rolls over the crest of the hill and plummets. The blood rushes to my head and my hair stands on end. I glance at Orchid but she is giggling like a hyena, not caring at all as we dip further and further down and then whoosh, we are climbing again. Noel is grinning his head off. He's like a big kid, really. He shows off, waves his hands in the air while I grip the bar for all I'm worth. The coaster is climbing again, up and up and up. The contents of my stomach rattle around like cups and saucers in the sink. When the ride finally ends, it takes a few minutes for the message to reach my brain. Noel takes my hand as I climb down and stagger towards the exit.

"How about something a little calmer?" I say, pointing to the land train.

Noel nods in agreement and we join the queue. While we are waiting, the man in charge notices the big birthday badge Orchid is wearing and has everybody sing happy birthday. Orchid beams and I feel happy for her. I'm not so old that I don't remember what it's like, that wonderful feeling of a special birthday.

"I'm hungry," Orchid says, when we get on the train.

"We'll have our picnic next," I say.

"I'm hungry now!"

"Here, have an apple," I say, passing her one from the bag.

"I'm not hungry for apples."

I roll my eyes and Noel distracts her by pointing out all the different sights. It is a pleasant way to explore, way better than the roller coaster.

"I want to go on another ride!" Orchid says, when the train comes to a stop.

"I thought you were hungry?" I say. "Come on, let's go and have our picnic near the miniature Lego world."

I march off in that direction before Orchid can object. I am pretty hungry myself now, probably due to the all the fast food smells wafting about the place.

We find ourselves a nice spot and settle on the grass. Noel pulls out the sandwiches and crisps and we all dive in.

"When we get home, I'm going to make our house in Lego," Orchid announces. "The woods and everything."

"You'll need a lot of green bricks," I say, with a smile.

"And blue for the stream," she says. "The stream's my favourite bit."

Once the sandwiches are all gone, Noel produces a birthday cake. It's a lovely, gooey chocolate one and Orchid squeals in delight when she sees it. The cake is so delicious that a toddler runs up to me and tries to wrestle my slice away. His mum and dad are embarrassed and apologetic.

"It's okay, we've all been there," I say.

Except of course, we haven't. I wonder if anyone looking at us would know we're not Orchid's biological parents. I mean, she doesn't look anything like us, with her black hair and dark eyes. But children don't always look like their parents, do they?

"You've got cake all down your neck," Noel tells me afterwards. "It's even in your hair."

"Oh dear, I'd better go and clean myself up. Do you need the loo, Orchid?"

Orchid shakes her head. I just hope she doesn't wet herself.

. . .

THERE IS a toilet block close to where we're sitting, so I go and wash my face and neck at the sinks. Then I open my bag and fish about for a comb. I feel something hard and close my hand around it but it's not my comb. It feels slimy and horrible. What is that? Did I leave a banana in there to go rotten? I reach for it but it slips through my fingers and all I pull out is a bit of fluff. No, not fluff, fur. A vile smell hits me and I peer inside. There is something disgusting in my handbag. It is too dark in there to see what it is, so I tip the contents out into the sink, not caring that my library book is getting wet. Out it all comes, the comb I had been looking for, an empty tube of smarties that I had meant to throw in the bin and a spare pair of Orchid's socks. And there, in the middle of the sink is the most disgusting thing imaginable. It smells as ripe as a wedge of stilton and it's gone mushy around the edges but the shape is still there, long and distinctive. It is the rabbit's foot. I swallow the urge to scream.

What on earth?

There's a sour taste in my mouth as I run into a cubicle and hurl my guts up. The vile smell of the rabbit's foot is mingled with the sickly smell of toilet cleaner and it smells all the more unpleasant. My throat contracts and I can't stop vomiting. It comes up fast and violent, exploding out of me and spraying the surrounding walls. Finally, it stops and I pause to catch my breath. I am aware that I have left my things in the sink and that anyone could walk in and steal my wallet, and yet I am such a mess I'm not sure how I'm going to stand.

I rise, shaking from head to toe and wipe my face with some toilet tissue. I look through the open cubicle door and see to my relief that the room is still empty. I haul myself along, using the walls to support me. My bag is still positioned by the taps. I peer into the sink, hoping that the rabbit's foot will have mysteriously vanished, but it is still there lying amongst my possessions. Gingerly, I pick out my wallet and keys and remove the comb and library book and place them all back in my bag. Then I stare at the rabbit's foot, wishing it away.

I could just leave it here.

I discount the idea quickly. If I leave it there, then it might find a way back to me. I have to get rid of it, in some way that it can't possibly come back. I grab a wad of paper towels and pick it up, shuddering and carry it back to the cubicle I've just soiled. I drop it into the loo. It makes a splash as it hits the water. Quickly, I pull the chain. The water whirls round and round, before getting sucked under. I turn to walk out but something draws me back. It's still there, floating on top of the water, bobbing about like a boat in the ocean. I force myself to breathe. I wait a moment, then pull the chain again. Once again, it's sucked under and once again it rises to the top. Maybe I should break it up? If I hack it into pieces, it would have to go, wouldn't it? I roll up my sleeve and reach down into the loo, but I can't bring myself to touch it. Instead I pull off a wad of toilet roll and throw it on top of the rabbit's foot. Even then, I can still see it poking out. I pull off another big wad and throw that on too, but it will never be enough.

I walk back to the sinks, my head pounding as I scrub my hands with soap. I am shaking badly, my brain pedalling furiously to catch up.

How the hell did it get there?

I disposed of that bloody rabbit, it should be gone. Did Tiger somehow dig it out of the bin and deposit it in my bag? A fresh wave of nausea hits me, but a group of people have come in now and none of the cubicles are free. I lean over the sink, ignoring the stares of the women in the queue.

"Pregnant?" Someone asks with sympathy. "I felt like that the whole nine months. Face as green as cabbage."

I can't speak. I splash more water on my face and stumble out into the sunshine. I don't want to ruin Orchid's birthday, but I'm not feeling well at all now. That bloody rabbit. Will I ever be rid of it? A rabbit's foot is meant to be lucky, but not when it's decayed and rotting in your Louis Vuitton handbag.

It must have been Tiger. There's no other explanation. How else would it keep coming back to me? But a nagging feeling claws at my insides as I look around for my family. What if it wasn't the cat? What if it was Orchid?

I HEAR a peal of laughter and spot them, mucking about in front of a Lego sculpture. They both look like they are having so much fun, taking it in turns to pose in silly ways. Neither one of them seems to care if anyone's watching. They are uninhibited in a way I can never hope to be.

I walk towards them, wishing I could be anywhere else in the world. Orchid looks up as I approach and I think, but I'm not sure, that I detect a note of triumphalism in her face. Is she just a girl enjoying her birthday, or is she playing a sick mind game with me?

"Did you fall in?" Noel asks.

"What?"

"You were in there for ages. We were about to form a search party."

Normally, I would smile. Actually, no I wouldn't. Normally, I would roll my eyes, but Noel would act as if I had smiled.

"Shall we go and queue for the new ride?" he asks.

"Might as well," I say, still watching Orchid. I watch as she slips her hand though Noel's and holds it tightly as she skips along.

I let the pair of them lead the conversation and join in only when a response is required. It is so exhausting, trying to keep up with them both, when I feel like I've been hit by a train.

"You go ahead," I say, when it's finally our turn to board

the ride. There's no way I can get on. Even looking at it makes me want to vomit.

"Where shall we meet you?" Noel asks. He doesn't seem surprised that I'm not coming.

"I'll be over there, getting a coffee," I say, pointing at the stall opposite.

"Okay, see you soon."

I watch as they board the ride and Noel leans over to check Orchid is buckled in. They both look so excited, their faces shining with anticipation. At last, Noel has a partner in crime, someone to share his passion for all things fun. The ride starts and I watch their faces as they whizz by, but not once do they look down at me.

Once they get off the roller coaster, Orchid wants to go to the playground, so we follow her around as she climbs and jumps to her heart's content. The walk back to the car is a long one, with my stomach rumbling loudly and Orchid growing slower and slower until eventually, Noel puts her up on his shoulders and strides along, pretending to be a giant. I don't know where he finds the energy.

"She'll never sleep tonight," I say, as we sit in a long tail back. Orchid is out like a light before we even make it out of the car park.

"We made some good memories today though, didn't we?" Noel says with a smile.

His rests his hand on my knee. It feels so intimate that I don't want to tell him about the rabbit's foot. I can't bear to spoil his day.

When we finally get home, Noel carries Orchid, still sleeping into the house. We put her straight to bed, in the clothes she's wearing.

"She hasn't brushed her teeth or anything," he says.

"It doesn't matter just this once, does it?"

"God, don't tell Effie," he says with a grin.

Maybe I should tell Effie, I think to myself. Not about the

tooth brushing, but about all the trouble I've had since Orchid came to stay. Maybe she could help me get to the bottom of it. I feel horribly disloyal even as I have this thought, because I am sure that getting Effie involved would not end well for Orchid. If she is behind all this then it would raise grave questions for us as a family. And it would break Noel's heart.

A NOISE in the night disturbs me. I twitch. It's that music again, a kind of soft, lilting music that is both gentle and eerie at the same time. Where is it coming from? I throw back the covers and climb out of bed, padding down the hall, past Orchid's bedroom. I stand there for a moment, wondering if it could be something of hers. Her musical box perhaps, or the CD player we bought her. But no, the music doesn't appear to be coming from that direction at all. I follow my ears down the passageway and out into the living room. It's definitely getting louder now, the music less soft and more rousing the closer I get. I enter the living room, but as soon as I do, it stops.

I switch on the light and sit down on the sofa, listening intently. All is silent. I check under the sofa and behind the TV but I can't find any toys trapped under there or anything at all that would make that kind of music. It's all rather puzzling.

There is a low murmur as I walk back past the spare room. I peer in. Orchid is sitting up in bed and facing the wardrobe. The beam from her night light spills across the room and I see her gesticulating with her hands.

"Who are you talking to?"

Orchid turns to look at me. Her eyes shine in the darkness.

"The other Suzannah."

I take a breath. "Orchid, you know she's not real, don't you?"

A determined look passes across her face. She opens her mouth to say something but clams up as Noel appears in the doorway.

"Why are you both awake?" he asks.

"Orchid has been talking to the other Suzannah again."

He comes into the room and helps Orchid lie down again, kissing her gently on the cheek. I watch as he fusses over her, tucking her blanket in and passing her Mrs Seal, who had fallen onto the floor.

"Goodnight," I say from the doorway and Orchid smiles at me.

I still don't know what to make of that smile.

Noel and I head back to our own bedroom and I lie awake in the darkness. The pillow feels cool against my cheek and I watch with envy as he turns onto his side. He always falls asleep so easily whilst I could toss and turn all night. I wish I could find a way to put my troubles to the back of my mind for a few hours, but I find it impossible to switch off.

"What's up?" Noel murmurs, as I let out a sigh.

I turn and look at him. "She's turned my dead sister into some kind of imaginary friend. It's not normal."

"I had an imaginary friend when I was a kid. Didn't you?"

"No, though I do have a vague recollection of riding an imaginary horse."

"Mine was a headless knight. He was very swarth. A big hit with the princesses."

He takes my hand and kisses it politely.

"Charmed, I'm sure."

I smile at his display of affection. It must be fun to be Noel, laughing and joking your way through life, but I cannot relax, no matter how hard I try. I can't shake the feeling that we're all in terrible danger.

16

I step off the tube at Piccadilly Circus and follow the directions to Broadway College where Lila works. The campus is streaming with students, many with brightly coloured hair. I pass a group rehearsing lines together and another lot practising their harmonies. One young man sits by the wall, strumming softly on his guitar. He reminds me of Noel.

I have to chuckle when I see the name plate on Lila's office door: 'Dr Delilah Swann.' Lila is not a doctor of anything and 'Delilah' is a joke because she got sick of kids asking what Lila was short for. Still, this is the drama department, so I expect they're all full of it.

Lila's class is practising for a performance in the college's open air amphitheatre, build down in the depths of the earth. The seats are made entirely out of stone boulders, arranged in circles around the stage, rising higher and higher. The sharp climb gives me vertigo. Lila stands in the middle of all this, directing the students:

"Speak up, Rosie! No one can hear you if you don't project your voice."

A skittish young redhead speaks into the sleeve of her polo neck.

"But no one's here to hear us!"

"It doesn't matter!" Lila cries with passion. "It doesn't matter if the auditorium is half empty. It doesn't matter if no one comes to see you except your mum. You still have to get up and give your mum the best show of her life. You have to play it up as if the audience is packed and it's being beamed live around the world to 80 million viewers. You have to play it like you've already arrived because if you can do that, then one day, you might just get there."

Her speech is so rousing, I want to clap. It reminds me of the one woman show she put on when we were at uni.

She booked the local theatre for a whole week and performed her show every night. She wasn't rich, but her family was 'comfortable' so she could afford to take the gamble. She roped us all in, Noel and I were on ticket duty, bringing people in to see her show. Each night of the show, we would go out into the streets, giving away spare tickets so that the theatre would be packed.

Opening night was impressive. We'd bribed everyone we could think of: classmates from my business studies course, Noel's band mates, friends from the film club. We'd papered the town with posters. Our friend Jennie had done the artwork and she had pulled out all the stops. The title 'In my bed' was deliberately provocative and I worried that people would think they were a hooker's business cards but Lila didn't care as long as people came to see the show. She thought that once word got out, her career would be made.

But it was harder to fill the theatre the next night and harder still as the week dragged on. By the final night, Noel and I had run out of favours.

"What do you think of the play?" Noel asked me, as we handed out flyers outside the City Hall.

"It's good," I'd said loyally. *"Really good, but it's a bit long, you know?"*

"Really long."

"I mean, two hours! That is an awful lot of Lila."

"An awful lot."

That final night, we were supposed to stay and watch again to add to the numbers, but we were too busy falling in love. So instead, we walked back to his place and one thing led to another.

"She won't even know," Noel had pointed out. *We both knew the play off by heart by then anyway.*

I smile at the memory then turn my attention to Lila as she continues to instruct her class. Her voice seems deeper than normal. Huskier. Sexier. When you act, you can be whoever you want to be. She's obviously having fun.

SHE SPOTS me and gives me a wave then speaks to a couple more students, telling them how they could improve their performance. She has everybody's eyes and ears, I notice. She has found her calling.

"Sorry, darling. Didn't mean to overrun," she says, once class is dismissed.

I submit to her hugs and kisses, then run a self-conscious hand through my hair. I bet I've got her lipstick on me.

"Do you fancy a drink before the show?" she asks.

"Does a one legged duck swim in a circle?"

She laughs. I don't tell her I stole that line from Orchid. It's nice to be the one to make people laugh once in a while. Too often, I feel like a stiff.

Once again, I remind myself how lucky I am to have a friend like Lila. She sends cards for every occasion you can think of, birthdays, Christmases, Easter. I don't know anyone else who even sends Easter cards. She's constantly forwarding me funny jokes or sending me thoughtful little texts or emails.

She's the one who always insists we meet up with Jennie too. A lot of people would have let their university friendships peter out after twenty years, but Lila has been the glue that has kept our little gang together.

We take the tube to Leicester Square. It's only one stop, but Lila doesn't want to scuff her shoes. A big, burly bouncer opens the door for us as we walk into the bar next door to the theatre. There is a long queue for drinks but Lila somehow nudges her way to the front and orders extravagant cocktails for the both of us.

We carry our drinks to a tall table with no chairs and lean against the wall.

"Shouldn't we get going?" I say, glancing at my watch. "The show's supposed to start in a few minutes."

"It's fine," Lila says. "These things never run on time."

I wait impatiently as she finishes her drink and then checks her make up in the loos.

We arrive at the theatre ten minutes after the show is supposed to start and get glared at by all the people who have to stand up to give us access to our seats. Lila is right though, the performance doesn't start until we're in our seats.

LILA ALTERNATES between clapping excitedly and nudging my foot with her spikey heels.

"Did you see that? Did you see?"

I don't have the heart to tell her that it's not my thing. Too modern and experimental. I spend most of the show thinking about the rabbit's foot. I got rid of my handbag in the end. I had loved it once but after finding the rabbit's foot in it, I couldn't bear the sight of it. I gave it to a charity shop in Little Mercy. It will be a lovely bargain for someone.

I'm ready to go home to bed after the show, but Lila won't hear of it.

"The night is young, Suzannah. Can't you stay for a nightcap?"

She leads me into a secluded wine bar, where she orders us more cocktails. Then she spots a couple of her students and talks with them for so long I get bored. I take out my phone and google train times. When Lila notices, she laughs.

"Don't go yet, we haven't even got to the good part."

"What good part? We've already seen the show."

"There's a pub down the road that does late night karaoke."

I picture myself singing in front of a pub packed with strangers.

"No way."

"Oh, come on, it'll be fun."

"Of course, it will for you. You can sing." I glance at my watch again. "Look, I should get cracking. I have to be up with Orchid in the morning."

She lets out a little hiccup and I wonder if I look as drunk as she does.

"Maybe we could stop for a coffee," I relent. "There's a little Italian place by the station. We could get some dessert too."

She hiccups again and takes my hand as we leave the club. The men by the bar look disappointed to see her go.

WE CLONK DOWN THE STREET, arm in arm. I trip over a paving stone and we both stagger to right ourselves, which sets Lila off giggling. By the time we reach the station, the Italian place is closed but we find a McDonalds open. I order us two coffees and a couple of ice creams and we find ourselves a table.

"Was Orchid okay after that business with the dead rabbit?" Lila asks.

"You won't believe what happened after that!"

I confide about all the weird stuff that has happened since Orchid came to live with us. Lila listens gravely and doesn't interrupt until I have finished.

"What about Orchid's past?" she says. "Did anything like this happen at her foster home?"

"I don't know."

To be honest, the less time we spent at her foster home, the happier I was. I didn't feel comfortable talking to the people we took Orchid from but perhaps we should have asked more questions.

"Well, there must be some clues in her file, surely?"

"Not really, it was kind of scant."

Lila's forehead wrinkles slightly. "That's strange. In the cases I used to deal with, there was usually an abundance of information. There would be minute details, things the adopted family didn't need to know, such as the number of times their kid had been treated for worms."

I get a flash of Effie and her incessant questions about nits.

"It's odd," I agree, "But Orchid's file is so thin. It's as if there are things they don't want me to know."

I dart a glance at Lila, expecting her to laugh but she doesn't.

"It has been known," she says, swallowing the last of her coffee.

She glances up at the board. "I think your train has just been announced. You don't want to miss it."

"But what should I do? Do you think I should talk to Effie?"

"No, leave it with me. I'll see what I can find out."

"You can do that? I mean, how? You've been out of the job a few years now, haven't you?"

"I still have my contacts," she says, straightening her skirt. "One in particular, who owes me a favour. I'll see if I can get a look at the system for you. Now you'd better scram, if you don't want to miss the last train."

"Thank you!"

I hug her tight. I'm sure what we are talking about is not entirely legal but I don't care. I'm Orchid's mother now. If there is something the authorities have hidden from me, I have a right to know.

17

A few days later, I knock on the door to the spare room. Orchid has a book open next to her and there are toys scattered about the floor. In many ways, it looks like a normal little girl's bedroom but it still looks incomplete in some way. I can't quite put my finger on it.

"I think we should redecorate your room," I say, looking around at the plain walls. "What colour would you like?"

"What colour would you like?"

I pull up some colour palettes on my phone.

"Maybe a nice sunny yellow?" I suggest. "Or a rosy pink?"

"I like this one," she says, pointing to the grey.

"Really? You wouldn't like a nice bright colour?"

"Grey," she says firmly.

"It's a strange choice for a child," says Noel as the two of us watch the rugby on TV that night.

"I know but it's her choice. That's important, don't you think?"

He squeezes my hand. "Of course, you're right. You're a great mum, do you know that?"

"And you're a great dad."

I mean it. He makes it look so easy, the way he talks and laughs with Orchid, as if she has always been a member of our family, not just recently slotted in.

"You wouldn't believe this team was nearly relegated last year," Noel says, as the Pythons score another try. He usually supports Salisbury, but it's hard not to admire a team who have clawed their way up from the bottom.

"I think our goalie is asleep," I say, as our team almost concedes another try.

"There are no goalies in rugby."

"Fullback then, you know what I mean. Oh, look he's got the ball!"

I wait to see what will happen but at that moment the TV turns itself off.

"No!" Noel shrieks. He runs over and switches it on again.

The game has already moved on and the Pythons have control again. The ball is fast moving up the field in the wrong direction.

"They're going to score again!"

Noel clenches his jaw.

We watch transfixed as the ball gets closer and closer and then the screen goes black again.

"No!"

Noel is beside himself. He switches it back on and stands to one side, not trusting it to stay on.

"They've scored!" he groans. "They've scored and we missed it."

A moment later the TV goes off yet again.

"Stupid thing!" I thump the set.

"That won't help."

"No, but it makes me feel better."

"It's about time we replaced this ancient TV."

"Maybe."

I'm not keen to fork out for a new one. Noel, like all men, thinks the bigger the better when it comes to TVs. I'd be perfectly happy to have a small, cheap model and save the money for something I care about.

We wait a while but the TV does not spring back to life. I become aware of his hand on mine.

"It's late. Maybe we should get to bed."

"I'm not tired."

He smiles coyly. "Nor am I."

That's when music comes on. It sounds like a xylophone but the notes are a little out of sequence, speeding up and then slowing down.

"Is that...Ave Maria?" Noel says.

I nod, looking around for the source. I feel a chill go down my back as I picture a ghost like presence in the room with us.

"It's the grandfather clock!" Noel cries. We both turn and stare at it. He's right. It's vibrating along with the music.

"I didn't know it played music," he says.

"Nor did I!"

I walk towards the clock but as soon I touch it, it switches to the more familiar chimes. "Perhaps it only comes on at midnight."

I nod, but there is something unnerving about the sudden disturbance. First the TV and then the clock. I feel like someone's playing games with me and I don't like it. I vow to find the settings in the morning. I'm going to silence that clock once and for all.

IN THE MORNING, I drive Orchid to the hardware shop in Little Mercy to get the paint for her room. There are several different shades, some of which are closer to violet or indigo.

But she chooses a dark, stormy grey that the shop calls 'Thundercloud.'

"A fine choice," says the man at the till who reminds me of a walrus.

Orchid beams but what she doesn't know is that I was in there to buy a packet of screws a few weeks back and he called those 'A fine choice' too.

"Is there anything else I can get for you?"

"Yes, I'd like to hire a steam cleaner as well."

The smell of decay lingers on in the living room and I'm desperate to be rid of it.

The walrus nods. "Which one would you like?"

He points out three different models.

"I'll take the big one."

"A fine choice," he says, as he extracts the money from my credit card.

WHEN WE GET HOME, we move as much of the furniture as possible out of the spare room and cover the rest with dust sheets. My mind returns fleetingly to the baby I had hoped to have and the pretty pinks or blues I had pictured myself painting, but if Orchid wants grey, then grey it is.

I begin on the largest wall, while Orchid works on the one opposite. I let her go for it with the paint. I can always put another layer over the top if it looks uneven. We work all morning, until my limbs feel heavy and sore. I wipe the sweat from my brow.

"Right, that's it. I think we've earned a nice cup of tea and a slice of cake."

"What kind of cake?"

I've learned by now, it can't be carrot cake, nothing with fruit or raisins in it. No lemon or marzipan or flaky almonds or indeed, any other kind of nut. And it has to have icing. Any cake without icing doesn't qualify as far as she's concerned, so I've played it safe.

"Chocolate," I respond. "I made a chocolate cake."

Orchid smiles. "What kind of chocolate?"

AFTER TWO CUPS of tea and a large chunk of cake, I'm ready to resume. Orchid sprawls out on the floor with a magazine. I suppose it's a bit much to expect to hold her interest for the entire day. I finish the wall around the window and stand back to examine my handiwork.

"There, what do you think? Do you like it?"

Orchid looks up and gives me a satisfied smile.

"No one else will want my room now."

"What do you mean?"

"Because it's grey."

"Oh, Orchid!" I fold her into my arms and hold her for as long as she will let me. I ask her if she wants to go back to the shop and pick out a colour that she really likes but she refuses, so we leave it Thundercloud Grey.

"I quite like it," Noel says, when he sees it. "It's very alternative."

"But is it Orchid?"

"I really don't know."

Orchid seems quite pleased with herself as we tuck her into bed that night. I get the impression she thinks she's won something. When I look in on her, she's fast asleep, clutching Mrs Seal by the tail. Her face is curved into a little half smile and the room still smells faintly of new paint. I open the window a little wider, to be sure that she can breathe properly, and head for the bedroom where Noel is waiting for me. His head is full of music and he insists on playing me a new tune he's been messing around with.

"Sounds great," I say but my mind is still on Orchid and

her gloomy grey walls. I can't help feeling I've made a big mistake.

A BLAST of cold air nudges me from my sleep and I hear a noise that sounds like waves crashing against rocks. I float up to the surface of wakefulness and then sink back down into the sleepy comfort of the blankets. A terrifying crashing sound echoes through the room, and I jolt awake. My legs hit the floor before my brain has time to catch up. I patrol the passageway, head turning this way and that as I try to locate the source of the noise. I reach the kitchen, but all is well there. The first rays of sunlight shine in through the windows, making the counters gleam. All looks neat and tidy. No sign of broken crockery or vases. No chandeliers lying shattered on the hard stone floor.

I stop and listen. All is quiet now but I definitely heard something. I can't have imagined it. I walk back towards the bedroom and as I do, something sparkly catches my eye. I turn and see that the bathroom mirror has been smashed to pieces and the jagged shards glitter like tiny ice crystals.

I stare at all the pieces and dark thoughts flit through my mind.

She did this.

That mirror has been there for decades. There's no way it suddenly fell down. I walk out, slamming the door behind me and head to the cupboard to fetch the broom. The glass shards clatter together as I brush them into the dustpan. Most of the pieces are minute, but there is one big bit that breaks in two as I reach for it. I hold the two halves in my hands, not caring if the edges nick my skin. I can't believe that this is all that's left.

I glance in at Orchid on my way back to the bedroom but she appears to be fast asleep, her face half hidden under the covers, her black hair billowing out. How is it possible that she looks so peaceful? Even if she didn't break the mirror, surely the noise should have woken her?

When I return to the bedroom, Noel is wide awake and staring at the vanity table.

"Not another one!"

I stare at the broken mirror. This one was newer than the one in the bathroom, but it had a long crack down one side. Noel promised to mend it years ago but never got around to it. I suppose he won't have to now.

"What happened? Did you see?"

Noel shook his head. "I just woke up and saw it."

I feel a throbbing in my veins.

"Unbelievable. First the bathroom mirror and now this one."

I flop back down on the bed. "I can't take it anymore. I really can't."

Noel looks stunned. "I locked the door last night, I swear. How on earth did they get in?"

"I don't think anyone's got in. As far as I can tell, nothing's been taken."

"Then…"

I point towards the door.

"You think Orchid did this?"

"I don't know. I don't know what to think."

"Perhaps she did do it," he says slowly. "She's testing us. She wants to know if we'll stand by her no matter what or if we'll throw her out if she misbehaves. She must be more insecure than she lets on."

I watch as he gets up and sets about cleaning up the mess. So much glass. So much destruction.

"What are we going to do?" I ask as he tips the shattered pieces into the bin.

"We'll talk to her," he says, buttoning his shirt for work.

I wish I had his patience. He reaches out and takes my hand.

"Let's speak to her together."

I nod. I'm less likely to lose my temper with Noel there.

Together, we walk into Orchid's bedroom, where it turns out she isn't asleep at all but reading by torchlight, under the covers. The grey walls make her room appear darker and gloomier. It feels like there are extra shadows on the walls.

Orchid peeks out from the covers.

"Hello Mummy, hello Daddy."

She is all rosy cheeks and smiles.

"Orchid, do you know who smashed the mirrors?" Noel asks, gently.

Her eyes widen, then narrow.

"It wasn't me. It was the other Suzannah."

I nod wearily. I thought as much.

I SUFFER THROUGH THE WEEK, constantly on edge. I can't relax until I deliver Orchid to school each day but as I drive away, I'm overcome with guilt. It weighs me down and once or twice, my foot slips on the pedals.

Concentrate, I chide myself.

I bump the car down the road, paying scant attention to the traffic piling up behind me. I drive at the speed limit and they can do the same. The car behind me sounds its horn. I smile triumphantly and slow down a little more. I will not be told how to drive, not by this bunch of country bumpkins. The other driver makes a rude sign. It gives me a twisted sense of pleasure that I've made him angry.

Help me Mummy!

I have to glance over my shoulder and check that Orchid's not still there. But no, it's just her voice inside my head. Our relationship is as fragile as an elastic band and the more she stretches it, the harder it is to pull her back. I want to love her so much...

The phone rings. Lila's name flashes up on the screen and I pull off the road to answer it.

"Lila? Are you all right?"

Her laugh tinkles down the phone. "I'm fine, you goose! I just needed to talk to you and I thought it would be easier over the phone."

"What did you want to talk about?"

She laughs again but then her voice grows serious. "It wasn't easy, but I got a look at Orchid's file."

"You did?"

I hadn't forgotten our conversation, but people promise a lot of things when they're drunk. "Well? What did it say?"

There is a pause.

"Lila? Are you still there?"

"I'm still here, darling. But listen, the file is definitely longer than the flimsy version you've been given. I found a lot of informal information, hidden alongside the official stuff. Things that case workers have noted but not had the guts to put into the official notes."

"Really? Why?"

"It's not unusual. I often left notes that don't make it into the official records. Thoughts and feelings about the parents we were working with. Hunches we couldn't substantiate, like if I thought the dad might have a gambling problem, that sort of thing. These are clues for other caseworkers to go on, but they don't make it into the official report due to a lack of evidence."

I feel a shift in my stomach, as if someone's moving boulders around down there.

"And what do Orchid's notes say?"

"I thought the best thing would be to make a copy. I can send it to you, if you want. The only thing I ask is that you delete it once you've read it. My friend Meena, the one who helped me to get this, could get into a lot of trouble. You do understand?"

"Of course."

"Are you sure you want to see it, Suzannah? Because once you've read these things, you can't take them back."

18

"Send me the file," I beg. "Of course, I'll delete it when I've read it."

"All right, I'll send it to you, but it's up to you what you do with it. If you decide not to look at it after all, that's fine by me."

"Why wouldn't I want to look at it?"

"Just…just make sure you have a good think about it first. Only you know what's in Orchid's best interest."

The more she says this, the more worried I become. I find it odd that she's gone to all this trouble and now she's practically telling me not to look at it. Why? What doesn't she want me to see?

A few seconds after I hang up, my phone pings, acknowledging the receipt of Lila's email. My finger hovers over the attachment, but I can't bring myself to open it. What am I doing, nosing into Orchid's past? I don't know if I could take it, if I find out she's been abused or something. I suddenly feel fiercely protective of her but at the same time, a little scared. What secrets lie within these pages? What if it turns out my daughter is a monster, as I have feared deep down all along? Maybe it's better I don't know.

I'm horribly torn. Now that I have the file, how can I not look? And yet, the way I came to get this file, through Lila's friend - it doesn't feel right somehow. I'd be committing a crime. I should talk to Noel about it but he's at work. Perhaps I should just take a quick peek and see what it's about. There's no need to bother him till I know. I can't just delete it. I would always be wondering, possibly for the rest of my life. And what if there's something in there that I need to know about? What if she poses a real danger? My blood runs cold and just like that, my mind is made up. My heart beats faster as I open the file.

I act quickly, before I have time to second guess myself. It is a long document, much longer than the one Effie gave me. That one had just the barest facts, the very basics, such as Orchid's date of birth, her childhood illnesses, the name of her birth mother and some basic facts about her life. This report begins in the same way as the other one. It is the same document, word for word. The same basic details I've already received but when it ends, there is another heading: notes.

ORCHID WAS REMOVED *from her mother, aged two and put into foster care but then returned to her aged three. She was then removed again six months later, this time for good. For the next few years, Orchid lived with a few different families but had to move on several times, due to a failure to bond. These placements coincided with some strange and often disturbing happenings.*

A WAFT of cold air blows up my back as I scan the notes. The details are spine chillingly familiar.

AT ORCHID'S *first foster home, she kept talking to a person in the corner, who wasn't really there. The family assumed this was an imaginary* friend that she had invented, except that the name she choose for this imaginary friend was 'Helena', which had been the name of her foster mother's grandmother, who had passed away. Possibly, Orchid had overheard someone talking about Helena. The family could not recall such an occasion as they had all called her Gran. Orchid would constantly whisper to this person, stopping abruptly if anyone else entered the room. The family found it quite unnerving.

At another foster home, the family dog took against Orchid and barked uncontrollably whenever she came near. Since they could not get the normally placid creature to calm down, it was decided that Orchid should be placed in another home.

A new home was found and nothing terrible happened there, but within a week of her arrival, the family cat went missing. Nobody thought Orchid had anything to do with it, but then the family hamster also disappeared and the foster parents suspected that Orchid had let it out of its cage. Once again, Orchid spent much of her time talking to an imaginary person who seemed very real to her and they all heard a strange whistling sound that sounded like a voice howling in the wind. The younger children seemed afraid of her to the point where it was decided that she should move again.

This time, Orchid was sent to live with another, more experienced couple, Emily and Tim. Emily and Tim bonded with Orchid but could not explain some of the weird things that happened around her. Once again, she found herself an imaginary friend and was constantly talking and whispering to this person. She claimed that it was her imaginary friend and not her who pushed one of the younger children off the swing, causing him to break his arm. There was also an incident where all the taps in the house were left on when the family went out to the supermarket and on their return, the bathroom and kitchen were both flooded. Once again Orchid did not accept any responsibility. The family then awoke one morning to find both the front and back doors wide open, when they were sure they had locked both doors for the night. It was only by luck that nothing was stolen. Emily also reported the destruction of a much loved painting, a portrait of her dead aunt. Someone had made holes through the eyes and it was not possible to *restore it. Once again, there was no evidence that this had anything to do with Orchid.*

I CAN'T SWALLOW the grapefruit sized lump in my throat. What does all this mean? Is Orchid just a naughty child or is there something else going on here?

I draw a breath, unable to think straight. It's only half past nine in the morning. Too early for a gin and tonic, even though I feel like I need one. What the hell does it all mean? I have always been open to the idea that there is more to the world than what we can see. Indeed, in all the time my parents have been gone, I have longed for them to get in touch with me. Perhaps that's why I was so adamant that we should live here as opposed to selling the house and using the proceeds to buy a place in London.

I knew there was something different about Orchid. I let out a breath. It's one thing to accept it but quite another to deal with it. If Orchid is somehow channelling spirits, maybe even the spirit of my dead sister then what can I do to help her? I think with a shudder of the dead rabbit and it makes me nervous. I must find a way to help her to use her gifts for good and above all, to turn away from evil. God has brought her to me for a reason but who am I to help her, when I have struggled to take her into my heart? I hold my head in my hands and rock myself back and forth until I start to feel a little calmer. It is only then that I feel ready to make the journey home.

I UNLOCK the door to the cottage and pause in the doorway as if held there by an invisible force. Is she here now, my sister? I am both excited and petrified by the prospect and I fear the not knowing will drive me mad. Abruptly, I push my way into the house and busy myself with menial chores. I pull the dirty clothes from the laundry basket and sort them, checking the pockets of Noel's work trousers and jeans before popping them in the wash. That done, I dust and polish the tables and shelves. It feels good to breathe in the beeswax. The place hasn't smelled right in days.

Afterwards, I take out the steam cleaner and give it a run around the living room. I have to return it on Saturday, so I may as well get some use out of it. I clean like crazy, not stopping until my knees protest. Then I sit down with a cup of tea and a slice of Victoria sponge and watch the Chelsea Flower Show. My parents were keen gardeners and the three of us always watched it together. They had strong opinions about the arrangement of the blooms and would often correct little things that the commentators got wrong. How I wish they were here now, to tell me what to do about Orchid.

I watch as the camera pans over a beautiful garden. The flowers look good enough to eat, an explosion of peonies, dahlias and geraniums. I could just imagine what my father would say:

"It looks more like a sweetshop than a garden."

I set down my teacup and as I do, there is a loud click behind me.

What was that?

I jump to my feet as a loud hissing noise fills the air. It takes me a few seconds to register what it is. The steam cleaner. Somehow it has switched itself back on. I race towards it and turn it off. Then I pull out the plug for good measure. It feels warm to the touch. Perhaps it has overheated. I return to the sofa but every so often, I glance back at it, certain that it has moved. The flower show no longer holds my attention. The neat hedges and perfect lawns belong to another world, one in which it is possible to create perfect order whilst mine descends further and further into chaos.

Howard's words drift back to me: "The other Suzannah. She always wanted attention."

"Are you there?" I call into the nothingness.

I walk into Orchid's room and sit on the bed. I stare at the grey walls, hoping to see what Orchid sees but what do I know about summoning a ghost?

"It's okay. You can show yourself. I want to see you."

I wait expectantly, but nothing else happens. The steam cleaner does not come on again, the TV does not switch itself on or off and I feel foolish. Of course, she's not going to come to me; she only appears for Orchid.

I would have thought if anyone would be able to see my sister's ghost it would be me. I'm the one who most wants to meet her. But as it is, I can't separate Orchid from my sister, the ghost. They have come into my life together, hand in hand.

My phone rings. The third time in an hour. I can't put it off any longer. I will have to take Lila's call.

"Well? What did you make of it?"

I picture her sitting on the edge of the stage, her boots swinging beneath her as she watches her students.

"Just wow," I reply. "This proves that there is something going on with Orchid, something she may not be able to control. I think it's time we got some help."

"What are you going to do?" she asks. "You can't tell anyone, remember? We'd both be in deep shit. I mean it, Suzannah."

"Don't worry, I'm not going to tell anyone."

"And make sure you delete the file."

"I know, I will."

"Okay, I have to go now. My class is coming back from break but let me know if you need to talk."

"I will, thank you. I need to think about how I'm going to handle this."

19

Much later that day, Noel and I curl up together on the sofa and he tells me about his gig at Salisbury University. The one I didn't get to go to because I couldn't find a babysitter.

"The building's a lot posher now, of course," he says. "They sell avocado on toast in the café."

"Very swish," I say with a smile. Then I take his hand in mine and pull him close.

"Is something wrong?" he asks. "Is it Orchid?"

I nod. I know Lila told me not to tell anyone but I have to tell Noel. He has as much right to know as I do.

I take a deep breath and blurt it all out. Then I wait for his reaction. His mouth twists into a shape I've rarely seen before. He opens and closes it a couple of times as if he can't make up his mind what to say.

"Well?"

He shakes his head. "Do you know what you sound like, Suzannah?"

"I know it's a lot to take in."

"No, listen. You are under a lot of stress, adapting to being a mum. I know Orchid can be challenging at times but that doesn't mean she's possessed!"

"I never said she was possessed! You're putting words into my mouth."

"Then what are you saying?"

"I don't know. I think she may have the ability to channel spirits."

He takes a deep breath and looks at me. "Seriously, Suzannah. I love you, you know I do. But you need to stop with this nonsense before you drive us all down the path to insanity. I hate to think what kind of crazy ideas you're putting into Orchid's head."

"I haven't said anything to Orchid."

"Good. Please keep it that way."

"But…"

"I'm going to go and take a shower."

The conversation is over. I feel a tear slide down my cheeks. Then I catch the movements of an animal in the darkness and stare in amazement as a deer comes right up to the french windows. It looks right at me and I don't dare move for several minutes in case I frighten it away.

ORCHID DOES NOT WANT to leave the house the next morning and she has a proper strop when I tell her she has to wear her school shoes instead of her purple trainers.

"I want a packed lunch," she says, as we are about to get in the car.

"I thought we agreed you were going to have school dinners for the first term?"

She tilts her chin forward. "We didn't agree. You did."

"Well, either way, I've already paid for your dinners up until the end of term."

"That's not fair!"

Her foot comes down hard on the ground.

"We have to go," I say. "Let's talk about it on the way."

"I don't want to go to school."

"I'm sorry to hear that, but you have to go. It's the law."

"Don't care!"

She stamps her foot again but I just get into the car. I turn on Radio 4 and listen to the news while I wait. I half expect her to go and play in the stream. She stays where she is, seething, mutinously. Then, after a few minutes, she gets in the car.

"I feel better now," she says, as she does up her seatbelt.

I allow myself a smile.

ONCE I HAVE DROPPED her off at school, I drive to the church. Little Mercy is quiet at this time of the morning and the car park is virtually empty. I go inside and take a deep breath, trying to feel His presence. In all honesty, I have never felt especially close to God in this church, but perhaps that's because I don't visit it enough.

I sit quietly for a few minutes, soaking up the atmosphere then I close my eyes and pray for guidance. The organist arrives and sits quietly at the ancient pipe organ. I hear the rustling of sheet music and then the church fills with the opening notes of Bach's Toccata and Fugue in D minor. I listen in awe as the glorious music fills the air. It is as if the church has burst into life.

I become aware of voices and I notice Howard talking to a young woman. She sounds rather distressed and although I try not to eavesdrop, words and phrases float through the air towards me. Words like 'unfaithful,' and 'unreasonable.' I realise she is asking him if she should get a divorce.

Howard looks at her kindly. "You've tried to make it work. Can't say fairer than that."

"But what about my soul?" Her eyes are frantic. "Will it be all right, do you think? I mean, I know I promised to love him forever, but I didn't know he would be such an arse to live with."

Howard lowers his voice. "Marriage...doesn't have to be forever, you know."

I expect to see shock on the young woman's face, but I only see relief.

I wait until she has left the church, then I slide out of the pew and make my way over to where he is examining the contents of a box of food.

"Plenty of rice pudding for the food bank," he tells me, as I approach.

"That's good."

"It's never enough though. So many hungry mouths to feed. Such a shame."

He tilts his head slightly as if trying to read my expression. "Is there something I can help you with?"

At first, I struggle to find the words. As I start to talk, it all comes tumbling out. I even tell him about the ghost I saw as a child, something I rarely share with anyone. Once I have finished, I look at him, expectantly. His expression tightens.

"Are you sure it was really a ghost you saw?"

"Yes, I'm sure!" I feel slightly irritated that he, a member of the clergy, would question me. This should be right up his alley.

"I mean, couldn't it have just been... you know, a living person, playing a trick on you? There could have been a sliding bookcase or something. You never know."

I'm about to point out that you can't see God either, but I keep my mouth shut.

Howard fiddles with his collar as if it is too tight. He never looks entirely comfortable in his clothes. I get the impression he's one of those people who is straight into their pyjamas the minute he clocks off.

"So, you don't believe it's possible Orchid is being visited by a ghost or spirit?"

Howard scrunches up his forehead. "I have never seen one myself, good or evil, but there are certainly individuals who grapple with spirits of one kind or another. Their own personal demons, if you like."

"You think it's a bad thing?"

"You're probably worrying about nothing."

"But the church…there must be some kind of understanding about this sort of thing?"

His shoulders slump as if the whole conversation is weighing him down.

"In my experience, there is rarely a reason to fear for a child's soul. What a child needs is love and understanding. You can give her those things, can't you?"

"Of course, I can!"

But if I was to be really honest, I have my doubts. Nasty, niggling doubts. Because I'm not like Noel with his endless well of understanding. I'm human and imperfect. Impatient even.

I look at him anxiously, unable to accept his advice. "Are you sure there's nothing you can do?"

"Well, if you've come here looking for an exorcism, you're barking up the wrong tree," he says with a chuckle.

Is he actually laughing at me?

"Seriously, this is the twenty first century. We'd be laughed out of the church!"

"But I thought…surely there must be people…priests who still…"

He closes his eyes for a moment.

"Exorcism is always the last resort. It is far too dangerous to be used lightly and honestly, in all my years, I have never found it necessary."

"What do you suggest then?"

I feel foolish to have brought it up because if the church doesn't take me seriously then who on earth will?

He thinks for a moment.

"You've had Orchid for a few months now, haven't you? Perhaps it's time to celebrate that as a family. Tell me, do you know if the child has been baptised?"

"I don't know, but I'd say it's unlikely. I don't think it's the kind of thing her birth mother would have done if she was unfit and foster parents aren't even allowed to cut their hair without permission."

"Well then maybe you should consider having her baptised. Just a small ceremony, with a few of your closest friends and family."

"Do you think that will help?"

"Baptism is a form of deliverance, Suzannah, where parents agree, on behalf of their child to reject Satan. As Orchid is a little older, she can be included in this. That ought to allay any fears you have concerning her soul, and wouldn't it be a nice way to celebrate the adoption? You could throw a little party afterwards, in that lovely woodland garden of yours."

I think of Noel's parents, champing at the bit to meet Orchid and how we keep putting them off. Maybe it's time.

20

Orchid's baptism falls on a glorious autumn morning. The ground is carpeted in green, amber and gold leaves, and droplets of rain glisten in the weeping willows. The whole of Little Mercy basks in the sun's warmth and the stream sparkles as if it has just been cleaned.

Noel's parents, Royston and Colleen, arrived the previous day, moaning about the state of the B&B I booked them into. It is an absolutely lovely place run by a sweet young couple who would do anything for you, but there was no tea in their room when they arrived, so Colleen will never forgive them.

She loves a good moan, does Colleen. One year, they went on holiday to Majorca and they were put up in a grotty room with a leaking shower and bedbugs. They even had fire ants climbing the walls. I have never heard her sound happier than when she rang home to tell us about it, her description of the ants growing more dramatic as she told me and then Noel. By the time they came home and told us all over again, the ants may as well have been the size of tortoises, carrying off wedges of cheese on their backs.

"What time shall we come over in the morning, pet?"

"You could just meet us at the church, if that's easier."

"Oh no, I think we should come over but what time?"

"Er, all right – eleven o'clock then."

SO OF COURSE, they are round at our house by ten AM, demanding cups of tea and biscuits. We don't even have any biscuits.

I am glad to see they have ditched their anoraks for the occasion, but Colleen is wearing a lime green trouser suit that makes my eyes water and Royston's orange tie isn't much better. I'm beginning to wonder if Noel is also adopted as he is so unlike either of them.

For the baptism, Orchid wears a long white dress that Colleen made by hand. It is extremely frilly and flouncy, but who cares? She's ten years old. She can still get away with a pretty frock. I don't care if all the other little girls are progressing to teenage clothes and trying to look cool. I have missed so much of her life, I want to be allowed to enjoy this at least for a little while.

I brush her hair and put it into bunches, tied with green ribbons to add a splash of colour. I still struggle to cope with her unruly hair, but I'm starting to get the hang of it.

"There, you look beautiful," I tell her, when I've finished.

"So do you," she says, giving me a hug.

I hug her right back and the warmth of her love surges through me. I have been such a fool. She's just a frightened little girl who needs a mother's love. I promise her silently that I will do better.

WE DRIVE to the church to keep our fine clothes from getting muddy. Colleen still manages to get mud on her shoes as she clambers into the car and she fusses about it for the entire journey.

"I've only worn these shoes once and now look at them!"

"Will you put a sock in it?" Royston finally says. "It's hardly the worst thing to ever happen to a person, is it?"

"Here have a wet wipe," I offer, pulling one from my handbag. They are good for everything. I don't know how I managed without them all these years.

We shuffle up the steps to the church and Orchid pauses in the archway, just as she did the last time.

"What is it?" I ask, aware that everyone's waiting.

"It's so cold in there. Why is it so cold?"

"I…I don't know, it's in the shade, I suppose. Go on in, it'll be fine."

"But it's so dark."

"They don't use electric lights, that's all. You'll eyes will soon adjust."

She looks uncertain, so I give her a playful push. It's a bit harder than I intended and she staggers inside.

"Easy now," Howard says, stepping forward to catch her. "Come on in, my child. We are about to begin."

Orchid's eyes go straight to the candles flickering at the back of the church. To my relief, she moves forward. I take her hand and lead her to our seats. We sit right at the front, as Howard instructed. The baptism is going to take place at the end of the Sunday service so we will have to wait a while. I just hope I can keep Orchid in her seat.

"I want to make a stained glass window," she whispers to me, as the first hymn begins. "Do you know how to make them?"

"No, but I'm sure I could Google it."

"What?"

"I said…never mind, we're supposed to be singing now."

"What?"

"Shh!"

Is she doing it on purpose or just totally oblivious to the fact that we're supposed to be singing? Colleen's voice rises from the row behind us, two octaves higher than everybody else and dismally out of tune. Orchid giggles and I nudge her to keep quiet. She glares at me and nudges me back. I hear a loud snore and see that Royston has fallen asleep with his mouth wide open.

No offence to Howard but the sermon is long and boring. There is a lot of talk about sheep and goats - farming analogies go down well with this congregation. I seem to remember sitting through this one before.

"And you have to ask yourself, are you a sheep or a goat?"

This sets Orchid off giggling again. "I'm a sheep, Mummy! I'm a sheep!"

"Sh!" I hiss.

Noel, sitting on the other side of her, distracts her with his iPhone, while I pretend not to notice. Finally, the sermon draws to a close and it's time for Orchid's baptism.

"Thank god for that!" Royston mutters, then he yelps as Colleen digs him in the ribs.

Noel and I stand up and lead Orchid to the back of the church, accompanied by our friends and family. Everyone is dressed in their Sunday best, all except Lila, who is sporting dark glasses and a dress that looks more appropriate for the Oscars, and Noel's friend, Kurt who is wearing the same jeans as always. I think he only has the one pair.

I feel the eyes of the village upon us as we take our places at the font. Out of the corner of my eye, I notice Catriona and Robert sitting good as gold, in between their parents. Dilly is there too, with her mum. She offers me a dreamy smile as we walk by.

"Where are the godparents?" Howard asks, when everyone is quiet.

Kurt and Lila present themselves and he starts talking about what the baptism means and what their job as godparents will be. I can't look at Lila, because if I do, she might start laughing. She has a horrible habit of giggling at the least appropriate moments and the worst part is that it's contagious. Perhaps this is why her acting career never took off.

"Orchid, would you like to step forward?" Howard asks.

Orchid glances at me uncertainly and I nod in encouragement. She moves towards Howard and looks up at him with those big brown eyes of hers. Howard takes a little water from the font and pours it over her head. Orchid makes a strange sound and then screams louder than I've ever heard her scream.

"Orchid…"

"It burns!" she yells, her hands rubbing her head in desperation. I move towards her, but it's too late. She's already running for the exit.

21

I run after Orchid and find her standing in the middle of the road. Luckily there isn't any traffic.

"Does it really hurt?"

"Of course, it does!"

I lead her round to the back of the church and get her to sit on the bench so I can examine her scalp. It feels cool to the touch and I don't see any burn marks.

"Here," I pull the wet wipes from my handbag and scrub her head.

A moment later, Noel comes out and he also examines Orchid's head.

"There must have been something in the water that didn't agree with you," he says. "Perhaps someone cleaned the font and left a trace of chemicals in it."

I finish with the wet wipes. "Does it feel any better?"

She shakes her head. "It still stings."

"Okay, I'd better take you home and we'll wash your head properly. Better safe than sorry."

We leave Noel's parents stranded at the church and race home. I'm sure one of our friends will give them a lift. I can't worry about that right now.

I take Orchid into the bathroom and hose her down under the shower, washing her face and hair to ensure there are no chemicals left.

"Does that feel better?" I ask, as I wrap a towel round her.

"It's still a little bit sore," she says.

I search her eyes but there are no answers there. She does not flinch from my gaze nor does she stare in defiance.

"I'm hungry," she says. "When can we eat?"

I HEAR Colleen's voice outside, commenting loudly on how rude it was to leave them there. *They got here though, didn't they?* I usher Orchid into her room and wait for her to get ready. Her hair is all wet now but I don't dare use the hairdryer, in case that hurts her too.

I step out into the living room and find more people have arrived. Everyone has followed us back here. I don't think anyone knows what to make of it. People talk in uncertain tones, their voices low but not low enough. The house echoes with whispers; they fill the passageway and the living room. If they must speak, I wish they would do it louder. There seem to be twice as many voices as there are people.

Kurt walks over to Noel and raises a sardonic eyebrow.

"What's the deal, man? Is she like allergic to holy water?"

"There was nothing wrong with the water," Lila says. "I dunked my hand in it to check."

She catches my eye and lifts her voice above the whispers. "If you ask me, the kid got stage fright."

HOWARD ARRIVES. He's the only one to ring the bell. I let him in.

"May god be with you," he says as I let him in. He looks a bit rattled.

"There is a perfectly logical explanation for this," he says, scratching his head. "But I can't for the life of me imagine what it is."

"Lila reckons she got stage fright."

Howard considers this but I can see he's not convinced. He thinks for a moment, his left hand resting on his chin.

"A joke, maybe?" he says with inspiration. "Maybe someone put her up to it? You know, how best to freak everybody out at a baptism? Pretend that the holy water burns."

He glances at Kurt, who shakes his head. No one else owns up to it, either.

Colleen eyes the platters of chicken and quiche. "What are we going to do with all this food, pet?"

"I suggest you have the garden party as planned," Howard says.

I feel a slight ache in the pit of my stomach. "I'm not sure it would be appropriate."

"The whole purpose of today was to celebrate Orchid joining your family, wasn't it? We can still do that. We can have her properly baptised another day. In private, if she prefers."

I look around at all our friends and family. I just want them all to leave, but Noel is nodding.

"It would be a shame to let everything go to waste and everyone is here."

I open my mouth but I don't dare say what I'm thinking: *How can we celebrate, after all that's happened?*

I retreat into my bedroom and close the door behind me. It's too much. It's all too much. I climb into bed and pull the covers up over my head. Maybe if I stay here long enough, they will all go away.

THE KNOCKING SOUND STARTLES ME. I don't answer but I hear the door open and someone comes in. I peek out, hoping to see Noel but it's Orchid. She slides into the bed next to me and cuddles up. Her hair is still wet and she leaves a big damp patch on my shoulder, but there is something reassuring about her presence.

"Mummy, are we still going to have a party?"

I turn and see her face, innocent and hopeful.

"Of course we are. Mummy just needs a little rest."

Orchid loosens her hold on me and wriggles about in the bed. It's not comfortable any more, the way she keeps moving about and I force myself to sit up.

"Are you ready now?" she asks, pulling back the covers.

"Ready as I'll ever be," I say, checking my appearance in the mirror.

I comb my hair and smooth my collar but I still don't look right. There is something jaded about my face, a greyness I barely recognise. I reach into the drawer and pull out the expensive bronzer Lila gave me for my birthday.

"Fake it till you make it." Isn't that what she always says?

I let Orchid pull me back towards the living room where people are still milling about. More cars pull up outside and I hear a loud voice in the doorway.

"Babes!"

Jennie is still the quintessential Essex girl, glowing with fake tan, sunglasses perched on the top of her head. I let her embrace me, then turn to look at her thirteen year old daughter, Maisie who has shot up overnight. She has become a full on goth, draped from head to toe in black. Her dangly pink earrings are the only hint at the sweet little girl she used to be.

"All right?" Maisie says, without cracking a smile. Her face is so incredibly pale.

"Glad you could come," I say.

Time was when she would have jumped up and hugged me but she is more self aware now, and we are each wary of spoiling the other's make up. Everybody has headed outside while I've been greeting Jennie and Maisie and the decision to continue with the party seems to have been made. I don't know what they are all thinking. If I was any of them I'd make my excuses and run. But where can I run to? This is my home.

"Right then," Noel says, when we get outside. "What does everyone want to drink? We've got the bar set up on the patio."

That shuts them all up. Everyone congregates around the bar. I watch them all chatting and laughing and I dig my heels into the dirt. This isn't right, the way they are all carrying on. This is no party, it's a catastrophe.

Noel brings me a large Pimms without my even asking and I force myself to smile. I take a gulp, welcoming the heat on my tongue.

I feel Colleen at my elbow.

"That's better, pet. You look so pretty when you smile."

Her words come from a good place, so I swallow my retort.

I take my drink and go back inside to check on Orchid. I find her playing by herself in her room, her damp hair dripping down her back.

"Come on, you can't skulk in here all day. Come and enjoy the party."

"I had a look and it's all grown ups."

"Not entirely. I'll introduce you to Maisie, she's thirteen. Hey, you should show her your bedroom walls. I bet she'll be well impressed."

"Okay."

She follows me outside and I point out Maisie, not that she needs pointing out. She is the only one who looks like she's come dressed for a funeral.

I leave the two of them together and head to the bar where Lila is busy filling her glass.

"Another Pimms?"

"Go on then."

She pours the drinks and leans in close.

"It doesn't matter, darling. About the baptism. Let's just have a good time, shall we?"

"How can I?"

Her arms jangle as she reaches for me. She must have at least fifty bangles on each arm. "Come on, don't let it spoil the day."

"I'll try."

Kurt saunters over and grabs himself a beer. He looks at Lila and she looks back.

"Enjoying yourself?" he asks.

"You?" she returns.

I look from one to the other. They have always had a weird energy. I suspect they might have had a thing once, though Lila insists not.

"What you been up to, Kurt? Still rocking Wembley Stadium?"

"How about you Lila? Starred in any West End Plays lately?"

For a moment, there is total silence then Lila howls with laughter. Kurt smiles politely then backs away, clutching his beer to his chest.

A moment later, Jennie joins us and the three of us prop up the bar.

"Maisie keeps pulling sickies," Jennie complains. "I'm sure there's nothing wrong with her, but she always insists it's her time of the month and it's hard to argue with that."

"If she looks fine, I'd send her in anyway," I say. "They'll send her home if she's genuinely ill."

Jennie gives me this look as if to say, 'who are you to be giving me advice? I've raised four children.'

"You might not find it so easy when it's your own," she says, quietly. "They have a way of getting around you. Even when they are at their naughtiest, they give you this look that melts your heart and you can't be cross with them any more."

She gives my arm a gentle squeeze.

"Right," she says, "I'm popping to the loo. Don't either of you nick my drink, okay?"

Lila pretends to be horrified. "I'm not some kind of common criminal, you know."

"You say that," Jennie smirks "but we know you better, don't we Suzannah?"

"Huh?"

"Don't you remember that time she stole a Christmas tree?"

"Oh my goodness!"

I had completely forgotten. I'd nearly had a fit when a giggling Lila dragged it into our flat. It was taller than she was and already decorated with tinsel and a big gold star.

"Didn't you steal it from a shopping centre?" Jennie says, laughing.

"I really don't remember."

"The funniest part was when Suzannah told you to take it back and you said, 'Don't you like it?' and burst into tears."

I smile at the memory but poor Lila looks perplexed. "I really don't remember that."

"No, you were really wasted."

I watch as Jennie walks off towards the house. That's the great thing about old friends. They help take your mind off the things you really don't want to think about. My stomach churns as I remember Orchid running from the church. Glancing around, you wouldn't think anything had happened. Why aren't people more upset about it? Am I over-reacting?

"Here we go!" Lila says, as the first few chords sound.

I turn and look. It was only a matter of time until Noel and Kurt got their guitars out. A lump forms in my throat as Noel looks in my direction. He is playing our song, "*The Girl Who Stole My Heart*". Then I catch Orchid's eye and I wonder if Noel has written a song for her yet. I bet she would love it.

After a few more songs, Noel bangs his beer bottle with a spoon and everyone looks at him expectantly, especially me because he's not in the habit of making speeches.

"All right, everyone. Who wants to see some fireworks?"

I might have known. Colleen tuts about the money he must have wasted on them and how fireworks will frighten all the birds in the trees. I'm with her on that point but boys and their toys...

Noel places a large rocket in the ground and lights the fuse. We all watch as it soars up, into the field and explodes with a big bang. A dozen little stars appear in the sky and then fizzle out. Another two rise up, soaring in different directions and exploding gracefully above our heads. Everybody claps and cheers and then Howard walks round with a tray of mulled wine that he has kindly brought.

"The Lord would want us to keep warm," he says with a smile, as he hands me a glass.

"Thank you."

I watch Noel as he talks to a couple of locals who have wandered into our midst. He looks incredibly at ease as he chats with the pair, who are both young women in their twenties. One looks a little bored but the other is giggling like a schoolgirl and flipping back her hair, and I can't help but wonder if she fancies him.

"Oh dear!" I say loudly. "I seem to have spilled mulled wine down me."

"You must put your shirt to soak at once, darling," Lila says, taking my glass. "Otherwise it'll stain."

"I think we're already past that point," I say but I excuse myself anyway and go inside to change. I know just the thing to wear too. This morning, as I was getting ready, I spotted my old band T-shirt wadded up at the back of the drawer. It's pretty faded but you can still make out the band's logo on the front. I smile to myself as I pull it over my head.

Noel grins from ear to ear when he sees me.

"I can't believe you still have that T-shirt!"

His companion stops giggling for a moment and turns to stare.

"Of course, I do! This is my favourite shirt." I lower my lashes. "And my favourite band."

I wrap my arms around his neck. I don't generally do public displays of affection so I think he is surprised. He kisses me on the lips and it feels good, an unexpected rush of warmth.

His admirer takes the hint and wanders off with her tail between her legs and I mentally flip her the bird.

Noel's mind has turned back to the music.

"How did we sound earlier?" I hear the anxiety in his voice. "Do you think we've still got it?"

I'm not sure they ever had it, whatever 'it' is. That undefinable quality of a band that forces you to listen and makes you hang on every song. Lila, Jennie and I always enjoyed their gigs, but that was because we knew them. We always had a laugh hanging around together, drinking cider or Archers and lemonade, swaying about to the music.

"Of course," I say, realising a response is required.

Noel frowns. "I messed up on the chorus for the new song. Do you think anyone noticed?"

"You were ace," I say. "A bit of practice and it will all come together nicely."

I don't know why he's so keen to hear my opinion anyway. What would I know?

THE EVENING HAS GROWN COLD. My nose runs and my ears sting a little. Noel wraps his arm around me. I'm not sure if he does this out of affection or because he has drunk too much mulled wine.

"Can I have a glass?" Maisie asks, stomping over in her chunky heeled boots.

"Afraid not," Noel says, "But there is a bottle of Shandy, if you like?"

Maisie rolls her eyes the way only teenagers can.

"Where is Orchid?" I ask.

"How should I know?"

Cracking. I had hoped the two of them were getting along. I guess not.

"She went inside about ten minutes ago," Colleen says. "I bet she's tired, poor mite."

"Thanks."

"She's a lovely child," she says. "Despite everything. We're all very blessed."

I smile and to my annoyance, tears prick my eyes. Those are some of the nicest words anyone has ever said to me. Words that I'm sure my own mother would have echoed.

Jennie and Maisie have to get back to London and Colleen cadges a lift back to the B&B for herself and Royston. I'm sure they just want to check if there is enough tea and coffee in their room.

"We'll be back to see you in the morning, pet."

"Any time after ten," I say. Knowing them, they'll be round at eight.

"Looks like things are winding down," Noel says, "Shall I go and get a bin bag? We need to clear up all this rubbish."

"In a minute," I say. I'm enjoying the feeling of his arm around me and the pleasant warmth of alcohol in my stomach.

I catch his eye and we are about to kiss when Kurt blunders over.

"Can I borrow Noel for a moment?" he asks. "I've had an awesome idea for a song."

He's got a nerve, interrupting like this but I let Noel go. I should probably go and check on Orchid, anyway.

I walk into the kitchen and try not to mind how much mess there is. I should have accepted Colleen's offer of help. The counters are strewn with open packages, paper plates and empty bowls. If we had a bigger kitchen it might not look so bad but as it is, everything is stacked sky high as if we haven't done the washing up all week.

Never mind, we've had a nice party.

"Orchid?" I call, stopping at the fridge to get myself another drink. I have no idea what I've done with my glass, so I take another one from the cabinet and pour myself a large glass of Cava. It has been an emotional day but a pretty good one, all told. Despite the debacle in church, Orchid has been a hit with our friends and family. Everybody loves her, especially Colleen.

"Orchid…"

I turn my head, distracted by a whistling noise.

What is that?

I catch a flash of light as the projectile zooms towards me.

Firework! Someone's let off a firework in the house!

I duck back against the wall but then there's another one, flying at a different angle.

It narrowly misses my foot and I leap up onto the washing machine. But it isn't over.

"What the…?"

There's another and then another. They're coming at me from all directions. I cannot move fast enough. One zooms over my head and explodes in a burst of colourful energy. Sparks fly everywhere, patches of colour and whizzing noises, punctuated by loud bangs. One stings my leg like an angry wasp and another grazes my shoulder. Then, out of the corner of my eye, I spot a ball of fire flying towards me. I step back, only to fall into the path of another one which detonates inches from my face.

22

I see streaks of colour, like a camera flash going off, then the world descends into a mass of shapes and swirls. There is a throbbing in my ears as if an insect has flown into my head.

"Mummy!"

"Orchid!! Get away!"

"Mummy! Mummy, your face!"

I reach up to touch it, but the pain is like an electric shock pulsing through my body. There are more flashes of colour and everything seems to happen in slow motion. My breathing feels slow and forced, as if I'm wearing a motorcycle helmet over my head. I can't breathe. It feels so heavy...

I feel Orchid shaking me.

"Mummy! Mummy! You're scaring me!"

I reach out my hands and try to push her away, but she clutches me tightly and won't let me go. I feel the fight going out of me and she keeps holding me, enveloping me in her soft, childish warmth. Her hair has a strawberry scent to it from the shampoo we used earlier. She holds me tight and I feel like if I can just keep holding on to her, I will survive.

"Mummy!"

There it is again, that word that I longed to hear for so many years. I try to respond, but I can't find my voice. Bursts of light dance before my eyes. I don't know if they are real or merely an echo of the earlier explosion. The floor is cold and hard beneath me, wet and sticky with my blood.

"Mummy!"

There is movement. Someone is shaking me from side to side. It is a frightening sensation, being carried off into the night.

"Suzannah? Do you know where you are? You're in an ambulance..."

I try to focus but my vision is blurred. I see two forms in green and work out that they must be paramedics.

"Where's my daughter?"

"Orchid is fine, Suzannah. Your in-laws are taking care of her."

Someone squeezes my hand. I know without being told that it is Noel. There is something unique about the way he touches me. A warmth that no one else possesses.

"You're going to be okay, Suzannah."

The more they all keep telling me that, the less I believe it.

TIME LEAPS FORWARD. I'm not in the ambulance any more. There is a wall of green and a strong smell of bleach and disinfectant. I feel a sharp pinprick in my arm and I drift off again. The pain is a relentless electric current. I'm vaguely aware of Noel's voice, trying to reassure me. Then I hear someone counting backwards and I picture myself, falling headfirst into a bottomless well.

· · ·

"Don't try to sit up."

The voice is strong. I try to open my eyes but it's too bright.

"Will someone pull the blinds?" I murmur. It hurts to speak. My throat is so raw. I feel like I've been walking through the desert, under the heat of the burning sun.

"Suzannah, are you back with us?"

"I…I'm thirsty. Can I have some water?"

My body is so weak that it takes me ages to sit up. There is something sticking out of my arm. Tubes everywhere.

"What is this? Where are my clothes?"

"One thing at a time."

A nurse helps me to take a few sips of water. I'm cold now, so cold.

"What do you remember?" she asks me gently.

I remember with startling clarity. Dozens of brightly coloured explosions. All those missiles hurtling towards me.

"There were fireworks in my kitchen. Who…who did it?"

"They don't know," she says gently. "The police think it might have been teenagers. A joke that went wrong."

"A joke?"

"I know, not funny at all. Now, I need to take your temperature."

I submit to being poked and prodded some more.

"Is Noel still here?"

"He went home to take care of Orchid."

"Oh."

"Visiting hours are later. He'll come back then."

"What…what day is it?"

"Monday. You've been asleep a long time."

I'm sitting up in bed when Noel and Orchid arrive. My vision is still blurred and it hurts to turn my head.

I smell flowers and realise that Orchid is carrying a bouquet.

"They're orchids," she tells me.

"Lovely," I say but all I see is an indistinct blob.

I force myself to smile. "Be a dear and put them in water, will you?"

I need to talk to Noel.

"Has she said anything?" I ask, in a low voice. "About what happened?"

"She was in her room. She came running out when she heard the fireworks going off, but she didn't see anyone inside the house."

"She doesn't think it was the ghost, then?"

"The ghost? You don't think…you don't think Orchid did this?" Noel sounds shocked.

"Of course not."

"I know she was naughty before, smashing the mirrors and that but she would never do this, I know she wouldn't."

"Maybe not intentionally…"

But I can't help wondering. There's no knowing what she has brought into our house. Why was I so willing to believe that the spirit was a benevolent one? The clues were right there in front of me. There was a dead rabbit, for heaven's sake, and still I couldn't believe it meant us any harm but now I'm truly frightened.

"You're very quiet," Noel says, "Are you in a lot of pain?"

"I'm okay." I press my lips together. "How are things at home? Are you managing without me?"

"Mum's helping out."

I can't tell from his voice if that a good thing or not. There are so many cues you miss when you can't see a person properly.

"Daddy took me to Nando's!" Orchid says in my ear. "It was so yummy. Much better than home food."

"That's nice."

Where is she? I can smell her breath on my face and I feel stifled, unable to breathe.

"Has the doctor spoken to you yet?" I ask Noel. "I was so out of it earlier, I couldn't take anything in."

He clears his throat. "It sounds like you've done something to your eye. The left one is okay, but there is damage to the right. The doctor will be coming around shortly. We'll know more then."

I'm aware of Orchid jiggling around at the foot of the bed. She moves so fast. It's disconcerting. I sense Noel leaning over me. He brushes my hand with his and it seems like he's about to kiss me then he changes his mind, perhaps put off by all the bandages. There is a rustling sound as he produces something from a paper bag.

"Oh, I brought you some magazines."

"Nice one," I say, but they're useless to me. I can't read. I can't even watch TV.

"Perhaps a nurse could read them to you?"

"They all seem so busy. I doubt they'd have time. Maybe you could bring in my iPod? Then I could listen to some audiobooks."

"Okay."

We lapse into silence. I sense Orchid fiddling with whatever is on the table beside me. Perhaps she's leafing through the magazines though I doubt they would interest her for long.

"Can I have a grape?" she asks.

"Of course."

I hadn't even known they were there.

"Lila and Jennie brought those in," Noel says. "They popped in earlier but you were out for the count."

"Oh, shame."

"Ah, here's the doctor now."

I make out three distinct blobs. The doctor has brought some students with her. Or nurses maybe, I can't tell.

"Good afternoon. Do you mind if we take a look?"

"Please, go ahead."

I try not to object as she peels back the bandages covering my right eye. She shines a tiny torch in my face and I blink into the light.

"I can't...I can't open my eye. Why can't I open my eye?"

"The news is not good, Suzannah. I'm afraid the damage to your eye was extensive. We will not be able to save it."

23

Words float like peppercorns in the breeze. I'm too shocked to ask any of the millions of questions buzzing around in my head.

"You will need surgery. The damaged tissue needs to be taken out. Once it has healed, you'll be able to have a prosthetic eye."

I can't picture it, my dead eye. Is it in pieces, or will they plop it out and leave it in a petri dish? I don't want to see it. I don't even want to think about it.

"I'm going to be sick."

I am in no condition for the physical exertion of heaving. I gasp for air as a violent spasm erupts from my throat. I can't even be sick properly because I haven't eaten anything and each spasm feels like a knife cutting through my skull. When I am done I lie back, exhausted, praying that that is the last of it.

As my head hits the pillows, my mind returns as it often does to the rabbit. That poor, frightened rabbit, with the eyes that bulged out of its head, useless and glassy.

"How long will it take for her to recover?" Noel asks.

"A couple of months. Then she will be fitted with a prosthetic eye."

A couple of months?

I will have no eye for a couple of months. I pinch the skin on my arm and half expect to wake up from this nightmare but it's real. I really have lost my eye.

"No! There must be something you can do!"

"I'm sorry, Suzannah."

"We want a second opinion," Noel says.

"Of course," the doctor says. "I'd want one too in your place but I'm afraid it won't change anything. The damage is too severe."

Orchid has fallen silent. I wish I could see her face properly. It's hard for me to tell how she is feeling. Is she frightened by what's happened or has it gone over her head?

In many ways, it's easier to concentrate on Orchid and how she's feeling than to focus on the pain. I've never been an emotional person, not like some women I know. I recall, with shame, times I've caught Noel crying and haven't been able to say anything, too embarrassed to offer him any comfort. That was just the way I was raised. We didn't show our emotions. Mum and Dad were good, loving people. They didn't need to sniffle and weep to show me how they felt. It was understood as was their overwhelming love for me.

"Well, I'd better get this one home," Noel says. "You try to get some sleep, okay Suz?"

I nod mutely, too stunned to care if they stay or go but after they leave, I'm surprised to find tears leaking through my bandages. Will I still be able to cry once my eye is removed? Or will all my tears be trapped inside somewhere, unable to get out?

I feel a heaviness in my bladder and realise that I haven't been to the toilet in a while. I shuffle to the edge of the bed and attempt to stand up. Slowly, I rise up onto my feet and take a few tentative steps. It feels strange, trying to walk again. There is nothing wrong with my legs (or arms for that matter) but I feel as though I'm on a boat, bobbing about on the ocean. I reach for the edge of the table and miss. I stagger forward and almost end up on the floor. This is ridiculous. If I can't walk to the toilet, what can I do?

A nurse takes my arm. "It will take a bit of getting used to," she says kindly as she steers me around the bed. I'm glad I can't see the faces of the people we pass in the corridor. It is humiliating to need help in this way when I've always done everything for myself.

The nurse waits while I use the toilet and wash my hands at the sink. I peer at myself in the mirror. From what I can tell, my good eye still looks the same as it ever did, but the other one is hidden beneath layers of bandages. Gingerly, I tug on the dressing and try to get a look at it. All I can see is a black hole.

"I wouldn't touch it if I were you," the nurse says, gently. "It will look better, once you've had the prosthetic eye fitted. Lots of people have them these days."

Do they? I've never met anyone.

THE SURGERY IS SCHEDULED for the following evening. Noel has to stay at home and look after Orchid. I tell myself it doesn't matter. He can come and see me afterwards, once it's done. But as they wheel me down to the operating theatre, my teeth begin to chatter violently, and my whole body is filled with dread. I don't want them to take out my eye. What if they are wrong? What if it can be fixed? Maybe not now but in ten years' time. Technology moves fast, doesn't it? What if we're all making a huge mistake?

"I'm just going to mark an x above your eye," someone

tells me, in a jovial voice. "Wouldn't want to get the wrong one, would we?"

This is my cue to laugh but it isn't funny. They are about to remove my eye.

"It might help if you think about something else," the nurse tells me. "Tell me about that lovely young girl of yours. What is she, nine?"

"Ten," I murmur. "She just had her first birthday."

I don't get the chance to explain what I mean by that. I feel myself floating away, into a different time and place. It still smells like disinfectant but the doctor who stands over me is a different one. Noel whispers her name in my ear.

"Doctor Antoinette Sachs. She's supposed to be the best."

SHE HAS a stern face and lank grey hair. Her eyes are small but intelligent and her expressions range from serious to more serious. The pin board behind her desk is covered with baby pictures, presumably from all the happy couples she has helped. I feel a familiar twang as I look at all those beautiful babies and I long for it to be my turn. Mine and Noel's. Why is it so difficult for me to get pregnant, when other women are getting knocked up all the time? Half of them don't even intend for it to happen.

Whoops, I forgot to take my pill and boom, here's a baby!

"Now, we're going to forget everything you've done so far and start over," Dr Sachs says. "I'm going to ask you a lot of questions and put you through some rigorous tests. I may not be able to solve your fertility problem but I will get to the bottom of it, that much I can promise."

I catch Noel's eye and he gives my hand a gentle squeeze. Is he nervous, I wonder, or a little excited, like me? Finally, we're going to get some answers.

I'm used to being examined. We lose a little of our humanity every time we visit one of these places, every time they send Noel away with a paper cup. This appointment takes longer than usual and even after the physical examinations, there are long questionnaires for each of us to complete.

"That's all for today," Dr Sachs tells us. *"We will meet again at the end of next week to discuss the results. My secretary will be in touch to arrange a time."*

I'll have to invent another excuse to be out of the office, but I'm not worried about that. Let the boss think I'd got a second interview. I might even get a pay rise.

Time whizzes forward and I find myself standing outside Dr Sachs's office once more, my briefcase heavy with work to do on the train home.

"Are you ready?" Noel asks.

"Ready as I'll ever be."

I give our names to the receptionist while Noel feeds a coin into the vending machine. A bottle of water rumbles out. Before he can bend down to retrieve it, our names are called.

"I'm going to let you read the report for yourselves," says Dr Sachs, once we sit down. "Take a few minutes to look at it. Then I'll answer your questions."

She hands us each a copy and we read in silence.

I hear Noel swallow. "What about IVF?" he asks in a small voice. "Couldn't we at least try it?"

The doctor lets out a long sigh.

"No, there's no point. Let me state this clearly for you, Mr Decker. You have no sperm. Putting your wife through a painful and invasive IVF programme will not make up for that."

I look at Noel and see his chin quiver.

"Come on," I say, getting to my feet. "I think we've heard enough."

I THINK for a moment that I've fallen into a black and white cartoon. I blink a few times, trying to focus, but the image doesn't get any clearer.

"Hello Suzannah. That's it, take your time. Don't worry, the surgery went well."

It takes me a few minutes to understand what they are talking about. My eye. They've taken out my eye.

I FEEL ridiculous being pushed out of the hospital in a wheel-chair but that's the only way I'm allowed to leave.

"They're afraid of getting sued if you slip on the way out," Noel murmurs in my ear. I don't like the feeling of him pushing me along. It feels too fast, the way the corridors and people rush by. I wish that he'd slow down, so I'd have a chance to focus. I'm still a bit wobbly but I'd rather walk all the same. There's nothing wrong with my legs.

Noel helps me into the car and Orchid jumps up and down with excitement in the back.

"Hooray! Mummy's coming home!"

Noel is a terrible driver, he's the reason we have an auto-matic car. I try not to grimace as he starts the engine and shoots out of the parking space. I look out the window. The view is still blurry but Orchid narrates the journey, calling out the things she sees:

"An ambulance. Another ambulance. A lorry. Lots of cars. Hey, there's Nando's! When can we go to Nando's again, Daddy?"

"Not today, poppet."

"I want to go to Nando's!"

"We can go on Sunday," I say, to shut her up.

I have been in hospital less than a week but it feels much longer. I have missed everything, from the feeling of fresh air on my face to the sound of the birds chirping in the woods. The hospital was so sterile, not like real life at all.

As I step out of the car, I feel the urge to hug the dear old willow trees and kiss the familiar ground. Even with poor eyesight, I can make out the ripples in the stream. Tiger comes rushing up to me and rubs himself against my legs. Normally, I would bend down and stroke him, but I don't want to risk losing my balance. Noel leads me towards the house and I sit down on the sofa, while he brings me a cup of tea. Proper tea, made in a teapot.

"See, I'm good for something," he says.

Orchid chatters non-stop. She wants me to watch a film with her so we all settle down with some of Noel's homemade popcorn. I try to look at the TV but black blotches dance in front of my eyes and the screen is just rivers of colour, like lines on a graph.

"Your vision will settle down," the doctor told me before I left the hospital. But when? I don't want to live like this.

"Are you okay?" Noel asks.

"I'm fine. This is lovely."

"Is there anything in particular you would like to do today?"

I think about it for a moment. "I want to go to church."

"Are you sure? It'll be dark and gloomy in there."

"All the same, I need to go. Can you take me?"

I FIND Howard sitting on the bench outside the graveyard. He sits quietly, facing the hills that rise above the village. My vision is blurry but I know those hills so well that I can picture them, luscious and green.

"I'll take Orchid to the shop to buy some sweets, shall I?" Noel asks, as we approach.

This is met with an enthusiastic "Yes!" from Orchid.

"Fine," I say, giving them the go ahead. "I just need a few minutes."

I walk slowly towards Howard and sit down beside him. He doesn't ask me how I am, just continues eating his roll and waits until I'm ready to speak.

"Do you think God is testing me?" I ask.

"The God I know is loving and kind. He doesn't test people, he accepts them just as they are."

"Then why is this happening to me? After all these years, we finally have a child. But instead of being able to enjoy her, I feel like we are being punished. Were we not grateful enough? Have we not done enough to take care of her?"

Howard swallows the last of his roll.

"I wish I knew all the answers," he says. "I'm still struggling to understand what's happening here. Why Orchid reacted the way she did to the holy water and how you came to be so badly injured."

"And?"

"I feel we must renew our efforts to reacquaint Orchid with the Lord. The child must be baptised. Because until she is, I don't think either of us will be able to rest safely in our beds."

24

"Darling! How are you? Are you getting any sleep?" Lila hugs me gently, then sits down on the seat beside me.

I rub the space around my eyes. "I wish I could bloody sleep but it hurts every time I move."

She glances around. "Where's Orchid? You haven't let her go off into the woods by herself again?"

I don't like the judgement in her tone. Am I too lax in my parenting? I didn't think so but once a social worker, always a social worker, I suppose.

"Orchid is at school."

"Oh," she says, and pulls out her phone to check something. "Why can't I get a signal?"

"Must be the weather. It only takes one tree to go down and we lose coverage."

"I don't know how you can stand it."

"I don't know how you can stand living in London. Don't the crowds drive you crazy?"

Lila smiles. "All the best people are at least a little crazy."

. . .

DILLY'S MUM Emma has kindly offered to ferry Orchid to and from school for as long as I need. It's just as well because although the doctors have assured me I will be able to drive again, there is no way I can right now. I still have pain on the right side of my face and my eyesight is blurred and unreliable. I ought to be able to see properly in time but for now, my missing eye is confusing the good one.

"It's so dark in here, do you want me to open the curtains?" Lila asks.

"No, please leave them. The light hurts my eye."

"It's a good job you're not working," she says, brightly.

"Hmm," I say but I had been thinking of going back now that Orchid has settled into school. I wouldn't be able to do the hours I did before but even part-time work would be good, to keep my brain ticking over and money coming in.

"It's great to see you and all but shouldn't you be at work yourself?" I ask.

"Work, smirk. I was worried about you so here I am. Now, tell me what I can do for you. What do you need?"

"You got the number for a good exorcist?"

I'm only half joking.

"Come again?"

"Howard is coming over to baptise Orchid after school," I tell her. "I've asked him to bless the house too."

There is a moment's silence.

"Will Noel be here?"

"No, he'll be at work."

It isn't that I want to go behind Noel's back but as an unbeliever, his presence may be unhelpful. The more I think about the baptism, the more nervous I become. What if this thing, this spirit doesn't want us to baptise Orchid? I don't know what we are dealing with here and I'm not sure Howard does, either. I feel like we're completely out of our depth.

"Would you like me to stay?" Lila asks.

"Would you?"

I feel like there's safety in numbers, more of us to stand up to evil, should it appear.

HOWARD ARRIVES AT HALF past two. I show him into the living room and introduce him to Lila.

"Yes, we met the last time."

"Oh yes, I forgot."

He lays the holy book out on the table then produces a number of candles and places them at different points around the room. The atmosphere is calm and subdued, like we are about to begin a meditation.

"What if it doesn't work?" I ask, as the three of us wait for Orchid.

Howard places a hand on my shoulder.

"Suzannah, we will cross that bridge when we come to it."

EMMA DROPS Orchid off at a quarter past three. Orchid skips into the living room and then stops, as she sees all the candles, flickering in the breeze.

"Cool," she says, looking around. "Mummy, can I have some crisps?"

"In a minute."

She dumps her backpack on the table and tips out various bits of rubbish, rummaging around until she finds Mrs Seal.

"Orchid, Howard is here to pray with us," I say, softly. "And you remember Lila?"

"Your fairy godmother," Lila supplies.

"She's not a fairy," Orchid objects.

"No, that was just a little joke."

I pat the chair next to me but she has too much energy to sit still. After a few minutes, she settles on the floor by my feet and Howard looks at me and nods.

"Right, I think we can begin."

. . .

ORCHID'S EYES never leave the flickering candles and Howard stands in front of her and prays.

"Do you wish to be baptised?" he asks.

"Yes please."

"Do you turn away from sin?"

"What does that mean?"

"Do you reject evil?"

"Totally! I reject it all the time."

I watch as he produces a bottle of holy water and drips a little onto her head.

"Hey, that tickles!" she protests but there is no screaming or running from the room.

"Lord, I ask that you love and protect us all," Howard says, his deep voice echoing around the room, filling every corner.

I glance nervously about, and catch Lila doing the same but nothing happens. It is over. Orchid is finally baptised.

"WILL I have to wear it all the time?" I ask, as the ocularist takes an impression of my eye socket.

Orchid sits in a plastic chair beside Noel, fidgeting with Mrs Seal.

"Yes," says the ocularist. "It's fine to keep it in. It doesn't matter if you get it wet. You can even go swimming with it if you want."

"Will it ever feel normal?"

"It will move in sync with your other eye so it won't be obvious that it's not real."

"But people will still know, won't they? How could they not know that one of my eyes is fake?"

His moustache twitches slightly. "It will give you a

balanced appearance so no, people won't necessarily know and you should find that it increases the comfort in the eye socket of the missing eye."

The missing eye.

He sounds so matter of factual as if he has just said 'missing shoe' or 'missing key.'

I RECEIVE a phone call from Effie later that afternoon, asking if there is anything she can do to help. Of course, there is nothing.

"As if she'd be of any help," I say to Noel, once I've hung up. "I bet she'd love to come over and point out everything I'm doing wrong. I can just picture it. 'Suzannah, you do realise you just walked into that doorframe, don't you? You do realise you've just dropped your eyeball in the soup?'"

"You're a terrible woman, Suzannah," Noel says with a laugh.

My next appointment is to meet with the surgeon for the pre-op check. She is brief and brisk.

"During the operation, I'll cover your implant with eye tissue. Then I'll connect your eye muscles to allow for natural eye movement. A word of warning, Suzannah - you do need to be aware that your vision will not be as complete as before. That will take some getting used to but don't worry, I have done hundreds of these operations. You're in very safe hands."

She goes on to talk about mortality rates – her stats are impressive.

"So, it's low risk?" Noel says.

"Surgery always carries a risk," she's quick to point out. "But yes, it's relatively low."

"What are the dangers?" I ask.

"It is possible that you will get a rare inflammation called sympathetic ophthalmitis, which could harm your healthy eye.

It is usually treatable but there is always the possibility that it could lead to vision loss in your healthy eye."

"I CAN'T LOSE my other eye," I say to Noel on the way back home.

His hand brushes my knee. "You're not going to lose your other eye. You'll be fine."

"What if I get an infection?"

"Then you'll get some antibiotics. It'll be fine, Suzannah. Stop imagining the worst case scenario."

"I'm just being realistic, that's all."

We return home and I take to my bed, claiming to have a headache. I do have a lot of headaches but it's my heart that's the real problem. I feel wretched and miserable and I can't help longing for an easier life – the life I had before we adopted Orchid.

THE DAY of my surgery arrives and I have my eyelids stitched together, over the eye implant. My eye feels painful and swollen and I'm terrified that I will get an infection. Afterwards, my vision is disturbed. Once again I feel like my good eye is fighting with the bad one. There is no winner, only nausea and an intermittent headache and all I can do is lie about, waiting for my eye to adjust. I knew the prosthetic eye would not give me back my sight and yet on some level, I expected it to and I'm endlessly disappointed when it doesn't. The prosthetic eye feels strange, as if my eye is wedged too tightly in its socket. It will be a while until I start to take it for granted.

Noel is my rock throughout all of this. He comes home straight from work every day. He doesn't stay for drinks or meet Kurt for gigs, like he used to. He is at home as much as he possibly can be, helping me and Orchid. But one night, about three months after the accident, I get a call from him to say the trains are screwed up.

"I might as well go to the office drinks," he says, sounding hopeful.

I bite my lip. "How late will you be?"

"I don't know – not too late."

I hear him breathing down the line.

"Go on, then. I can manage."

I exhale slowly as I set down the phone. There was a time when I wouldn't have minded if Noel stayed out late. When I would curl up quite happily with a book and not even notice the time, but now if feels like a real imposition. How small my world has become.

I fry Lincolnshire sausages for supper and serve them with fluffy mashed potatoes and gravy. The perfect hot comfort food for a winter's night. Orchid is less inclined to play outside after school now that it gets dark so early so we stay in together, the TV on as she works on one of her numerous art projects. I can't get over how chatty she has become. She loves putting on different voices, imitating her teachers at school. Imitating Noel and me. I'm sure she wouldn't be like this if she were really my child. This mad cap sense of humour doesn't run in the Decker line.

I'M NOT able to read her a bedtime story so I ask her to read to me instead.

"Do you want me to read you one of your books, Mummy?" she asks, picking up one my long historical sagas.

"No," I say, with amusement. "Let's have one of your books."

Her reading has improved immensely, so I suppose something good has come of my injury. Afterwards, I listen while she says her prayers, an earnest expression on her face.

"Do you still see the other Suzannah?" I ask, as I tuck her in.

"No, Mummy. I think she's gone now."

"Good," I say. "That's good."

"Sometimes I miss her, Mummy."

"Do you?"

"Yeah. She used to cuddle me and tuck me in."

It occurs to me she might be talking about her own mother or maybe her foster mother, Emily. She hardly mentions her at all any more, it's scary how the human mind works. If only you could choose which things you forget and which you remember.

"Goodnight, Mummy."

"Goodnight, poppet."

I put on her night light and close the door. I had planned on staying up and listening to an audiobook but I'm too tired now. I walk around the house, checking that everything is as it should be. No taps left on, no doors unlocked. I am even more paranoid about such things now because I feel so vulnerable but the house feels peaceful and still as I drift towards my bedroom and shut the door behind me.

I find my way over to the bed and pull back the covers. I'm about to climb in, when I see something lying on Noel's side. I curse my eyes as I struggle to bring the object into focus. I pick it up. It feels soft yet solid in my hands and I get the sense that it's something I've held many times. I allow myself a small half smile as I switch on the lamp.

Has Orchid left my doll here so I'll have someone to sleep with?

The object swims into focus. Yes, it is indeed Suzy, her fuzzy hair fanned around her face. Her smile is as it always was, knowing, mischievous, her nose no more than a little stub. Her left eyes twinkles as if it holds all my secrets but her right eye…her right eye is just a hollow.

25

I let out a loud gasp. I feel as if all the air has been knocked out of me. Hands shaking, I grip the doll by the hair and carry it down the passageway to the kitchen. I hover over the bin for a moment but I can't force myself to let go. I have loved this doll all my life. She deserves better than to be cast out with the rubbish.

I pace from one end of the kitchen to the other. In the end, I stick her in the cleaning cupboard. Bitter tears wet my cheek. I have so many wonderful memories of that doll and now they are all ruined.

Could Orchid have done this?

Maybe she thought she was doing a nice thing, making a doll that looks like me. I check in on her but she is asleep already, her chest pumping gently. Mrs Seal lies on the pillow beside her and I spot Tiger, curled up on her chair. He is a sneaky one, that cat. I nearly mistook him for a cushion.

I leave the room, then on impulse, I open the door again. Everything is exactly the same, except Tiger is now at the foot of the bed. His bright green eyes look a little otherworldly in the dim light and I retreat silently back to bed.

The house has grown cold and the covers feel like sheets

of ice when I pull them up over my shoulders. I lie awake for hours, waiting for Noel to come home. I know he said he'd be late, but I didn't think he'd be this late. Every noise seems magnified as I lie there in the gloom. I hear an animal howling outside then the Grandfather clock plays Ave Maria. I stiffen at the sound. How is that possible? I thought I had turned it off. The music continues, then chimes ring throughout the house, striking midnight. The witching hour, Mum used to say.

I hear the jingle of the keys when Noel comes in. He stumbles as he makes his way through the living room in the darkness. I don't know why he doesn't turn the lights on, but perhaps he thinks he'll wake Orchid. He enters the bedroom quietly. His belt jangles as he removes his chinos and he stumbles again as he wriggles out of them. I pull back the duvet, to show him that I'm still awake. His breath is sour with beer.

"Had a good night?"

"I thought you'd be asleep."

"Yes, so did I."

"I wasn't that late."

"Didn't say you were."

His body feels warm as he slides into bed and I let him wrap his arms around me. I want to tell him about my evening, about Orchid and the doll, but this isn't a conversation I want to have with him when he's had a skinful.

After that fateful visit to Dr Sachs, Noel's ego was shattered. Even trying for a baby was off the cards now. He could hardly look at me. I tried to pretend it didn't matter but I was devastated. I couldn't believe my baby dreams were over.

My world became flat. I didn't enjoy anything anymore. Ice cream tasted glutinous. Books and films bored me. Music gave me a headache. I couldn't get interested in anything.

"It's ridiculous," I sobbed down the phone to Lila. "The bathroom cabinets are still stuffed full of pregnancy tests. So many of them. I can't believe none of them is going to give me those amazing two lines."

"Why don't you throw them out?" was all Lila said, but I don't think she understood.

Jennie called but I didn't feel like speaking to her. She had her children – all four of them. It seemed so unfair when I couldn't even have one.

I continued to take the tests, even though my situation was hopeless. I'd sit on the toilet, staring at the plastic wand, waiting for the result. I threw all my useless tests in the bin but later, I'd find myself going through them again, examining each one, hoping it had changed. One time, I found an extra grey line and my excitement went through the roof. I held it up to the light. Yes, definitely an extra line. It was very faint but it was there all right. I walked from room to room, holding it up to different lights.

"Look!" I waved the stick in front of Noel. "What do you think this means?"

"It's an evaporation line," he said, with a glance. "You get those on old tests."

"But what if it's not? Should I take another one?"

"Take one if you want but it'll come back as negative as all the rest." I didn't like his tone.

"Why can't you allow me one teeny bit of hope?"

"Because it's false hope, Suzannah. Now stop waving that dirty piss stick at me."

I took another test anyway. This time, the result was clear. No second line. Resentfully, I threw on my clothes and went to work. Noel was much nicer that evening. He brought home some expensive strawberry ice cream as a peace offering. We ate it from the tub, the entire thing, huddled up on the sofa in front of a Scandinavian crime boxset.

Once the programme was over, Noel took the remote and switched it off. Then he kissed me, first on the lips, then the neck, then…

I wanted to be with him, I did but then I thought of all those spoiled pregnancy tests and my body froze. I loved Noel but if I stayed with him,

I was never going to have a baby. I honestly didn't know if I could live with that.

"Why don't you let me near you?" he asked in a hurt voice. "Why are you always shutting me out?"

"I'm sorry. I don't mean to."

But that was the thing with infertility, it pitted us against each other. From the moment the doctor lay the blame at Noel's door, I knew it would to be a long march back. There was no undoing those terrible, devastating words, no easy remedy for the loss of his manhood, his sense of self. I silently blamed him and hated myself for doing so. It was all so exhausting. I didn't want it to be like this. I wanted my husband back. I wanted to repair what was left of our marriage and if I couldn't entirely repair it, at least cover the holes in the roof so the rain wouldn't leak in.

26

I ring Howard in the morning. I tell him about the doll and ask for his advice.

"Did you ask Orchid about it?"

"Yes. I asked her at breakfast, but she claims not to know anything and I think I believe her."

"Tell me Suzannah, has Orchid ever seen this...spirit she speaks of or is it more of a feeling?"

"I don't know."

"Well you must ask her," he says. "Let me know what she says."

I wait around all day for Orchid to get back from school. I try to do a little housework, but I'm clumsier than I used to be. I miss objects hidden in my peripheral vision and the more I stumble, the less sure of myself I become. I can't even walk from the living room to the kitchen without tripping over something. Nothing is where I think it is. I can't watch TV or look at my phone, either. Even the simplest pleasures, like sitting by the window and looking out at the wildlife, have become diminished.

When Lila rings, it takes me so long to locate my phone

that she has already hung up. She leaves a voicemail but I don't bother to listen to it. I ring her right back.

"Jennie was saying we should have a big night out," she says without prelude. "We haven't had one in ages and now that you've got your new eye…"

I laugh nervously. She thinks we can pick up where we left off, going out to shows and pubs, and the like but even the journey down to London is a minefield. I would have to catch the train on my own. What if I missed my station because I couldn't read the signs? What if I lost my footing and fell down the gap? There are so many hazards that you don't even think about when you can see.

"What about that other business?" she asks. "Do you think the ghost has gone now?"

"Not quite," I admit. I tell her about Suzy.

"Oh my god, that's so freaky, Suzannah! Honestly, I'm scared for you. Why don't you rent the house out and move somewhere else? Away from that…that whatever it is?"

"Given what we know about Orchid, I have a feeling it would follow us."

"So the problem is really… Orchid, then?"

"Don't say that. She's just a child. It's not her fault."

"Of course, darling. I would never…"

"Listen, I think that's her now. I heard a car pull up."

"Okay, I'd better let you go. I'll give you a call in the week, all right?"

"Okay. Bye."

I set down the phone and feel my way to the door. Lila should never have said that about Orchid, but she was right, wasn't she? The problem is Orchid. She has brought all this upon us, whether she intended to or not.

Orchid walks in noisily and slams the door behind her.

"What's wrong?"

"The twins are having a birthday party and I'm not invited."

"Are you sure you're not?"

"Yes. Priscilla came up to me to tell me. Catriona is going and even Ellie Mae is invited and nobody likes her."

"What about Dilly?"

"She's invited but she says she's not going to go because the twins are being so mean."

"That's nice of her."

"I think it was her mum's idea."

I sigh. It all seems so complicated. They're only ten, for heaven's sake. Why can't they all get along?

Orchid grabs a bag of crisps without asking and stomps off to her room. I don't blame her for being pissed off. I would be too.

I DON'T ASK Orchid about the ghost that night but it comes up the next morning, as she is sitting down for breakfast.

"She came back," Orchid says.

I freeze.

"What do you mean?"

"The other Suzannah. She was here again. She told me to give you a message."

I stare at her, trying to work out if she's for real.

"What message?"

"She said it would soon be time for you to join her."

I lean heavily against the doorframe.

"Mummy? It's okay, Mummy."

She gives me her hand but I move away from her and flop down into a chair.

"Can you tell me what she looks like, the ghost?"

"I can't remember."

"Is she smaller than you?"

"I don't know."

"But blonde?"

"Yes." Orchid picks up the cereal box from the table and takes a handful, cramming it into her mouth.

"And is she…is she moving, when you see her?"

"Of course."

"How does she get in? Through the window?"

"She doesn't need a window or a door. She can walk through the wall."

"You've seen her do that?"

"I tried to do it too, but I don't fit through the wall. I'm too fleshy."

"And she…isn't?"

"No, she's more like the stuff that comes out of the kettle."

"Vapour?"

"Something like that."

"Thanks for bringing her home," I say to Emma, as Orchid bounds into the house later that day.

"It's no trouble. To be honest, I think it's doing Dilly good, spending time with Orchid. She's such a loner, it worries me a bit."

I think of Dilly's dreamy eyes and I nod. I would worry too. That girl is off in a world of her own.

"I heard Dilly isn't going to the twins' party?"

Emma cast her eyes downwards. "No, I didn't think it was fair to Orchid. They've invited all the other girls in their class."

"Oh! Well, thank you. Perhaps Dilly and Orchid could do something instead?"

"Can I have some crisps?" Orchid says, flinging her backpack down on the sofa.

"In a minute," I say, not keen to feed her junk in front of the other mum.

"Perhaps Orchid would like to come for tea one afternoon?" Emma suggests. "She and Dilly could have a little play date."

"That sounds lovely."

"Friday all right?"

"Er, yes, I don't see why not."

I glance at Orchid, aware that I should be asking her but Orchid could use a friend. It should do them both good.

"Can I go down to the stream?" Orchid asks once Emma has left.

"I suppose so," I say. "Just for a little while. I'd better come with you, though."

I'm sure she would be fine on her own, but I don't like the thought of it. It's not like I can go looking for her if she fails to return home.

I set up a camping chair on the bank so I can sit and watch her without getting muddy. It is a bit cold to be sitting outside but I have my flask of coffee. The wintry weather does not stop Orchid from splashing about, endlessly fascinated by the micro life within the stream. I insist she keeps her wellies on. I don't want her paddling barefoot in the cold.

I sip my coffee and listen to the birds. I don't see Robert and Catriona until they are practically upon us.

"Hello Orchid's Mum!" Catriona calls out, as if we're old friends.

"Are you a cyclops now?" Robert asks.

I laugh but there is something in what he says. I do feel like my good eye has moved to the centre of my head, like one of those head lamps miners wear.

ROBERT AND CATRIONA don't venture into the stream but they hang around for a bit. Robert wants to climb one of the taller trees. Catriona insists he'll get stuck but he does it anyway. Lo and behold, he starts yelling for her to come and get him down which, to give her her due, she does.

"Have you seen Arnold?" Catriona asks, as they prepare to go back home.

"Not today."

He might well have been round but I could have missed him with my poor eyesight.

"What about you?" she asks Orchid. "Have you seen him?"

Orchid does not say anything. I can't make out her facial expression but Catriona falls oddly silent.

"Come on, let's go," she says to her little brother.

"But I want to play on the swing."

"The swing's broken," Orchid says.

It's hard to make out but I think she might be smiling.

"I think we should head back now too," I say.

The temperature has dipped and I feel a violent chill down my back.

"Don't you want to look for Tiger?" Orchid asks.

"No," I say, thinking of the bloodied rabbit. "No, I do not."

WE RETURN to the warmth of the cottage.

"I need you to help me turn the oven on," I say to Orchid. "I can't make out the dial."

"Okay."

Orchid does as I ask and then disappears to her bedroom. I hear the crinkle of a crisp packet as she shuts the door. I stand in the kitchen, waiting for the water to boil. I'm making a simple meal of cheesy pasta and garlic bread. The garlic bread is already defrosting on the work top. I'll just need to bung it in the oven at the last minute. It's all so simple and yet I feel overwhelmed, certain that I'll ruin it somehow.

My phone sits atop the microwave and I listen to an audiobook, a historical saga that takes place during the Crimean War. It is well written but some of the details are rather graphic. I was never been one to balk at a little blood and gore but my tolerance has got weaker lately. I'm not sure I can stand to hear about the struggles of a soldier with gangrene or the grieving widow giving birth without assistance.

I hover over the pause button. If I fast forward this bit, will the rest be equally unpalatable? I catch a reflection in the window. There is something behind me. Not Orchid, but another little girl, someone small and blonde. The hairs on the back of my neck stand on end as she glides right past me. She doesn't feel solid as she brushes past the flesh on the back of my legs. Her body appears totally translucent. I don't think she even knows that I'm there.

27

I spin around but I can't see her any more. I wave my hands in front of me but there is nothing there. Whatever it was, whatever she was, has gone. I belt down the passageway, as quick as my poor balance will allow. I pause in Orchid's doorway. She is lying on her bed, flipping through a magazine. I open my mouth to say something but then I hear Noel at the door.

I throw myself into his arms.

"Now that's what I call a welcome!"

His brain has clearly gone in a different direction but romance is the last thing on my mind. I pull back.

"Noel, I saw it. I saw the ghost!"

For a moment, he doesn't say anything. His brow furrows. "Are you sure that's what you saw?"

"You don't believe me!"

"I believe you thought you saw a ghost but think about this rationally! You've not long had eye surgery. The doctor said some people hallucinate. Your eyes are playing tricks on you, that's all."

I stare at him, anger burning deep within me. "I know what I saw."

I seethe as he goes into the bedroom to change out of his work clothes. He closes the door quietly behind him and I fight the urge to go after him and slam it loudly, to let him know how angry I am. I'm so angry that I almost forget to be afraid.

How dare he not believe me? How dare he!

I spin round and realise that Orchid is right behind me.

"Mummy!"

"Yes?" I try to keep the annoyance out of my voice. "What is it?"

"Did you see her, Mummy? Did you see the other Suzannah?"

I let out a long sigh.

"Yes, poppet. I saw her."

I PICK up my phone and call Howard. He goes very quiet as I tell him in detail about what I saw. I expect him to offer to come round and pray with us but he falters and stumbles over his words.

"I'm afraid, this is beyond my understanding and indeed, my remit."

"Are you saying you can't help me?"

"I wish I could."

"Wait! What should I do if I see her again?"

"It's not a her... It's an it. You must remember that, Suzannah. There is nothing to be gained from this apparition, do you understand? Do not, on any account, attempt to befriend the spirit. That's just inviting it in." I hear the tremor in his voice. "Don't approach it and don't speak to it. Definitely don't touch it and don't let Orchid touch it either."

"So, what should I do?"

He draws a long breath. "If I were you, I would pray."

· · ·

I CLOSE my eyes and try to form a picture of the ghost in my mind. She had looked like a child, a small, innocent child. What if Howard is wrong? What if my sister is somehow trapped in our house? What if she needs my help?

I wait for Noel to emerge from the bedroom but he goes into Orchid's room and I hear the two of them talking and laughing together as if nothing has happened.

I serve supper, heaping pasta and garlic bread onto each of our plates.

"Do you think we've got enough carbs?" Noel says, as he sits down.

"It's not easy, trying to cook with one eye."

He puts his hands up,

"Calm down! Just making a joke."

I look him in the eye.

"I am calm."

I HOPE Orchid doesn't notice the hostility between us as we finish our meal. Afterwards, Noel takes her for her bath while I linger in the kitchen rinsing the dishes. I don't listen to my audiobook this time. If the ghost appears again, I will be ready with my camera. I wish she would appear. If Noel could see her, he would have to admit he is wrong. There are some things in life that can't be explained but knowing Noel, he would say it was a trick of the light. It's so infuriating. Just for once, can't he expand his teeny, tiny mind?

Once Orchid is in bed, I try to talk to Noel again.

"Can we just talk about what I saw?"

"I know what you think you saw."

"But this thing was real. I felt it brush against me, Noel. How do you explain that?"

"It was probably the cat."

I cross my arms in front of my chest. "It definitely wasn't the cat!"

He won't listen. His mind is so closed to even the slightest possibility that something paranormal is going on and the more I try to talk to him, the more intransient he becomes.

"I spoke to Howard and he said that if it shows up again, we should pray."

Noel laughs. He actually laughs.

"What is so funny about that?"

"I'm not sure what's crazier," he says. "The fact that you think you've seen a ghost or the fact that you think you can pray it away. Did Ghostbusters teach you nothing?"

He's mocking me!

"Noel, I really did see something. I'm not imagining it. Why can't you just pull your head out of your arse and look around you? There has been so much weird stuff since Orchid came to live with us."

His expression changes from amusement to anger.

"Don't you drag Orchid in this. Don't you dare!"

I watch in astonishment as he grabs his coat. His jaw is set.

"I'm sorry but I can't hang around listening to this nonsense."

"Where are you going?"

He pauses in the doorway and I get the impression that he doesn't know himself.

"To the pub," he finally says. "Don't wait up."

A YEAR before Orchid came to live with us, I was out late at a work do. I worked in the city as a project manager for a top marketing company. I was good at my job but the networking was a killer. Socialising with the senior management team was exhausting, especially when they kept topping up my glass. I enjoyed a drink as much as the next person but I had to be careful not to get so drunk that I spoke my mind. It would never do to tell the boss what I really thought of him. I was really tired by the time I left, so I stood all the way home on the train to ensure I didn't miss my stop. Then there was the long walk up the hill, back to the house.

Mum would have been horrified at the idea of me walking up that hill on my own, in the middle of the night but I never felt particularly unsafe in Little Mercy. I rarely bumped into anyone late at night aside from the occasional fox or deer.

I had tiptoed into the house and made myself a roast beef sandwich; the canapés I'd consumed earlier had done little to satisfy my appetite. I'd spent the evening in a pub garden, breathing in other people's cigarette smoke. It was in my hair and clothes, so I decided to take a shower. I rarely used the shower but that night I couldn't be bothered to wait for the bath to fill. I went into the bathroom and shed my clothes. When I pulled back the shower curtain, I found an empty wine bottle lying on its side.

When exactly, had Noel started drinking in the shower? Or did he just hide the bottles in there? Was this a one off or had it been going on for a while?

28

Noel closes the door carefully behind him and I feel an immediate pang. I can't go after him, not with Orchid already in bed. I can hardly leave her alone in the house, in the dark. Especially when the spirit or whatever it was, might return.

I decide to run myself a bath. Except, I misjudge the amount of bubble bath I need and end up with way too many bubbles. The water is warm and soothing though and I lie back and shave my legs, feeling the curve of each calf with the razor. I used to read in the bath but there is something to be said for doing nothing, allowing all the hurt and anger to seep away.

I can't say how long I've been lying there when I hear the door. I wrap the towel around me and step out of the tub. I'm glad that Noel is back but not sure what to say. Should I be the one to apologise or should I wait and see if he caves first? He is in the wrong, after all.

He is not in the living room or the kitchen, so I walk into the bedroom. Noel is not there, either. The door handle turns and I look up sharply.

Ghosts can't turn door handles.

The door opens ever so slowly. I grab the bible from the drawer beside my bed and clutch it to my heart as I recite the Lord's prayer:

Forgive us our trespasses,
As we forgive those who trespass against us,
And lead us not into temptation,
But deliver us from evil…

The door flies open and the book slips from my hand.

"Mummy?"

It's not the ghost at all but a sleepy looking Orchid. She clutches Mrs Seal by the flipper.

"I heard the door and I was worried. I don't want Daddy to go away. I want him to stay here with us."

"He just needed an evening to himself," I say gently, waiting for my heartbeat to return to normal.

"I want to stay up and wait for him."

"Daddy might be a while. I think we should get to bed."

I shunt Orchid back to her bedroom and check that her window is shut and locked.

"Mummy, can't you read me a story?" she asks, as I start to back away.

"I'm sorry, it's late and my eyes aren't up to it."

"You can tell me a story," she persists. "You don't have to read."

"I'm tired," I tell her, adjusting the duvet so it's not hanging off her bed. "Go to sleep, poppet, I'll see you in the morning."

"Mummy! I haven't said my prayers."

"All right, go on then."

I wait impatiently, as she rattles through them, barely paying attention to her words. She is still not content for me to leave her but I do anyway, promising to check on her in ten minutes.

I put on a jumper and jogging bottoms then I flop down on the sofa in front of the TV. I check the time on my phone. He can't still be at the pub. There are only two in the village, and they both close at eleven. I grit my teeth and text him.

Where are you? Orchid is worried.

Orchid and I are worried, I should have written but it's too late now, I've sent it.

The rain, which had been just a gentle trickle, is now lashing it down. I move to the french windows and look out at the shadows. The darkness has a depth to it. Wind whispers in the weeping willows and I hear rustling in the bushes outside and then the faintest, lightest footsteps, leading up the front door. I wait for the rattle of the doorknob or the turning of the key. Instead, there is a scratching sound, more like a clawing at the door.

Our father, who art in heaven...

The scratching continues and I can't make out what it is. I open the door a little, keeping it on the latch. I feel a rush of warmth as something surges inside, almost knocking me to my feet. Then there is a yowl and I realise it is only Tiger. I shut the door behind him but a puddle of rain has already seeped into the house.

Tiger is cold and shivering and I hold him to my chest to warm him. His purr is loud and strong, and he doesn't even attempt to nibble my hand as I stroke his sopping wet fur. I settle back down on the sofa with him curled up on my lap. I feel safer with him around. Animals can sense danger, can't they? They are more attuned to spirits. I don't remember where I heard this but I feel in my heart that it is true.

There is a crash of thunder and Tiger leaps under the table, his hair standing on end. I watch as the entire wood lights up and then grows dark again. The next crash is so ear splitting, it makes me jump.

The grandfather clock plays Ave Maria then strikes twelve times for midnight. Noel should definitely be back now unless he went back into London. Perhaps he's dossed down at Kurt's for the night. I try ringing him but the phone goes through to answer phone. Maybe his phone is out of battery. Maybe he's still walking home from the pub. Parts of the village have no phone coverage at all.

I ring Kurt and leave him a voicemail, asking him to call me. Then I ring Noel again, in case he's fallen asleep on the train home and then a third time in case he's ignoring me.

"I just want to know you're safe," I tell his voicemail, but he doesn't ring me back.

I CHECK my phone incessantly as I get Orchid ready for school in the morning. Noel normally leaves for work before she gets up, so she doesn't ask where he is.

"Are you all right?" Emma asks, when she comes around to collect Orchid. She has her umbrella up, even for the short walk from her car to the house. I hadn't noticed how much it had rained overnight. The stream has risen several inches and the ground is sodden.

"I'm fine," I tell her. I don't want to say anything more. Not in front of Orchid. Noel will call soon. He has to.

When the phone finally rings, I leap on it but it's only Kurt.

"I'm sorry Suzannah but I haven't seen him. I can ring round and ask his other mates if you like?"

"Please."

I hang up and call Noel's office but he hasn't turned up for work either. There's nothing for it. I have to call the police.

TWO OFFICERS ARRIVE from Greater Mercy. They come in and sit upright on the sofa while they take down all the particulars.

I don't tell them about all the paranormal goings on because if Noel's anything to go by, I don't think they will believe me. I simply say that Noel never came home.

"Has he ever done anything like this before?" asks the female officer, Rebecca something.

"No. Neither of us has ever spent the night away without checking in with the other. Not even when we've quarrelled."

"And had you – quarrelled?"

"Yes but this still isn't like him and he never misses work."

She glances at her colleague, who is frantically scribbling on his pad.

"Have you been out looking for him?" he asks.

"Like I said on the phone, my eyesight isn't very good. It would be hard for me to go out there on my own."

"Right, well I think our next step is to take a look around. I've already rung the landlord at the Plough and he didn't see him last night. We are waiting to hear from Belle at the Cricketers."

"Thank you for taking this seriously," I say.

"Of course. We'll be in touch and if you hear anything in the meantime, please give us a call."

She leaves me her number and I watch as the two of them set off into the woods. They're not dressed for it, in their smart trousers and shiny shoes. I should have lent them some wellies.

My body crawls with nerves. There is nothing I can do to ease the wait so I go into my bedroom and lie down. I shut my eyes but I'm bombarded with visions of what might have happened to Noel. There is no reasonable explanation now. He wouldn't have left me, not like this. And he certainly wouldn't have left Orchid.

I lie there, not fully asleep but not entirely awake, either. It's only a matter of time before the doorbell rings and I'm faced with the same two officers. Their faces are both pale and serious, like they have seen something they will never be able to forget.

Rebecca takes a deep breath, as though preparing herself to speak. I catch a look between her and her colleague.

"Perhaps it's better if we come in?"

I lead them into the house. They take off their shoes and tuck them neatly out of the way. It strikes me as odd. I don't remember them doing that the last time. We walk through to the living room where Rebecca and I sit down on the sofa but he remains standing by the fireplace, eyes lingering on the photographs of my family: mum in her satin dress, dad in his overalls and my wedding photo, with me dressed up to the nines and Noel with unkempt hair and a shaving rash.

They share a look, him and Rebecca and finally, she speaks.

"I'm sorry Mrs Decker..."

"Tell me. Tell me everything."

"Your husband was seen at the train station last night. The train arrived but he didn't get on. A couple of people saw him walking back down the hill towards your house. This was at around nine thirty."

An ambulance siren wails in the distance.

He's broken his ankle or twisted his hip.

"Is that..."

Rebecca sits close and I clutch her hands as I brace myself for what's to come.

"A fallen tree had blocked his way, forcing him to cross the stream at the deepest point. There was a lot of rain last night, as you know and the stones were slippery and wet. It looks like he may have tripped and hit his head. We found him lying face down in the water."

"Is he?"

Slowly, she nods her head.

"I'm so sorry, Suzannah. Your husband is dead."

29

I am paralysed. Frozen in place like a statue. I try to focus on the words but I can't make any sense of them. She studies my face like she's expecting a response but I don't have one. I attempt to move my body but only succeed in raising my arms a little. My mind is lost in the mist.

Someone hands me a cup of tea. My hands shake too much to drink it. I am so cold, even as I feel the warmth of a blanket being placed around my shoulders. My teeth chatter and my jaw moves up and down and I am utterly, utterly lost.

After a while, I sleep. Or maybe I just sit there in a daze. I really can't tell but there comes a point when the initial numbness lifts and the enormity of what has happened begins to sink in. I think I understand it but I can't be sure. My brain is floating in a thick soup.

Noel is not coming back. We will never be able to make up from our argument. I will never be able to tell him I'm sorry. He will never get the chance to admit he was wrong. When I think of him, of everything he means to me, I feel like I am trapped in a vice. Something is squeezing me, crushing my organs so that they squish into one another. The pain is exquisite and yet never quite enough.

The worst part, the very worst, is telling Orchid. Rebecca stays with me until Emma drops her off from school, while her colleague returns to the station. Emma seems to know that something is up when she brings Orchid to the door. Perhaps she has seen the ambulance or the police cars coming to and from Greater Mercy. Perhaps the news has already travelled around the village.

"Oh, Suzannah!" she says and I let her hug me.

Orchid walks in behind her, looking curious but unknowing.

"Mummy, can I have some crisps?"

"Yes."

She squints at me.

"Mummy, are you okay?"

I wait for Emma to leave, before I sit her down.

"Orchid, poppet…"

I try to swallow but I can't quite remember how. The words are already formed in my head, but I can't seem to get them off my tongue.

"Orchid, you know how Daddy went out last night?"

She is rifling through her backpack now, pulling out Mrs Seal. She tosses the toy into the air and catches it again.

"Orchid…"

She looks at me abruptly. "Mummy, when's Daddy coming home?"

I open my mouth to tell her but all that comes out is a squeak.

Rebecca gets down, level with Orchid and looks at her.

"Orchid, I need you to be a very brave girl, okay?"

Orchid looks at her and nods.

"I'm afraid your Daddy is gone. He passed away in the night. That's why he hasn't come home."

For a moment, all is silent. Then I hear the trickle of water and I realise Orchid has wet herself. I rush to comfort her but she runs off to her room, dropping her beloved seal on the floor.

NOEL'S FUNERAL is set for the following Friday. With Colleen's help, I plan a simple affair, just his close friends and family and even that feels too much. Colleen and Royston have booked in at the same B&B as last time, having decided that they 'quite liked it after all'. I tell them to come to the house at eleven and of course they are there at ten but I don't mind. The house is too empty and anyway, Noel was their son. This day is as much theirs, as it is ours.

I don't have a black dress, so Lila brings me a couple to choose from.

"Found them in the back of my wardrobe," she says.

Somehow, I can't imagine Lila in black. Even now, she's in a navy blue dress with an elaborate fishtail. I look at the two dresses she's bought me. They are both a perfect fit, so I suspect that she has gone out and bought them especially for me.

"Can I wear my orange dress?" Orchid asks.

I glance up and see that she's wearing the knitted jumper dress Noel bought her. I don't argue, though Colleen raises her eyebrows.

"Don't you think your velvet dress would be more appropriate?" she asks.

My anger bubbles to the surface.

"I think the orange looks very nice," Lila says, before I lose it.

Colleen lets out a sigh but says nothing more, which is just as well because I am not going to make Orchid change.

Royston picks up Noel's guitar from the wall and hugs it as if he were hugging Noel. He is a man of few words, but I can see that he is broken. Colleen focuses her energy on Orchid, fighting with her frizzy hair.

"She's got lice," she tells me in a low voice. "We'll have to pick up some nit shampoo after the funeral."

I nod in agreement, but I can't even begin to think about it.

"I'll nip out and get some now," Lila says. "We've got ages yet."

THE MINUTES TICK by and Lila returns from the village shop, clutching the nit shampoo. Lila, who refused to buy toilet roll when we lived together because she didn't want anyone associating her with toilets.

"Thanks," I say, setting it down on the counter.

"Here, I got you these," Lila says, presenting Orchid with a cuddly llama and unicorn.

It's strange to see the lack of excitement with which Orchid accepts these gifts. My daughter, who adores presents. The sunshine has gone from her smile and I'm terrified we will never get it back.

WHEN IT IS time to drive to the church, Orchid runs off to her room and refuses to come out.

"Orchid, poppet! It's time to go now. We have to say goodbye to Daddy."

"No! No, you can't make me!"

Orchid blocks the door and so I can't get in.

Colleen tries talking to her but it doesn't make any difference.

"Come on," Royston says. "You don't want to be late for the funeral."

Slowly, Orchid opens the door.

"That's not how I want to remember him. All shut up in a wooden box."

I agree with her on some level.

"You go," Lila says to me. "I'll stay here with Orchid."

"Are you sure?"

"Of course. We'll be fine."

Lila pours us all a Cognac and we drink a silent toast before we leave for the church. I have never known Colleen drink anything stronger than Perry but today is different, I suppose.

Lila offers round the Cognac again but Noel's parents shake their heads.

"Yes please," I say and she pours me a generous measure.

Colleen glances at me but I don't care. I have to get through this day somehow.

"Are you sure you don't want to come?" I ask Orchid, as I prepare to leave for the church.

She shakes her head and makes Mrs Seal wave a flipper.

"All right then. Be good for Lila."

The rest of us pile into Jennie's car.

Howard is waiting outside the church, dressed in his formal robes.

"I'm so sorry for your loss," he greets us and I instantly burst into tears.

I'M drunk before the service even starts and I struggle to listen as Howard talks about Noel and tells an anecdote from his childhood that he must have got from Colleen.

"And now I'd like to invite Suzannah to come up to the front and share some of her memories," he says, giving me an encouraging smile.

I stagger to the front. I'm keenly aware of Royston and Colleen in the front row. I can't even look at them without feeling like there is a huge python wrapped around me, squeezing me from my stomach to my neck. They have lost their child. The pain must be unimaginable.

"Noel was a good man," I say, glancing down at the notes I have prepared. "A man of principle. He lived and breathed his charity work and was constantly looking for ways to improve the world for us all." I look at Colleen. "He was one of that rare breed of men who call their mum every week without asking. He was a good dad and a good..."

The words stick in my throat. I can't bring myself to say it.

"He was a...terrible husband. The worst."

A nervous laughter breaks out.

"He was kind and caring, a cracking cook. Always patient and attentive. But he wasn't always... he wasn't always faithful."

30

I never confronted Noel about the bottle of wine in the shower. I thought for a while that he might be secretly struggling with alcoholism but when I found the bra under our bed, I knew there was another explanation. It wasn't my size or style. It was much more extravagant than anything I would buy. It was the sort of garment a woman might wear if she was trying to impress a man, perhaps at the beginning of their relationship or during an affair.

The idea of Noel the alcoholic had never rung true. Of the two of us, I drank more than he did when we were together at least. This, unfortunately, made much more sense.

I grabbed the bra and I walked with it into the woods. My anger burned like a forest fire as I trailed the silky smooth material through the mud. The bra went from pink to brown, as I trampled though the puddles and when I reached the canyon, I let it go. I watched as it fluttered like butterfly in the wind. It came to settle on the handlebars of the old broken motorbike. Such a pretty bra. Such a shame.

A couple of weeks after I disposed of the bra, I found a lipstick in the bathroom cabinet. I had thought it had been an accident, the wine bottle and the bra. But I now realised she was doing it on purpose, this woman

Noel was seeing. She was leaving me deliberate clues to alert me to her existence. She thought she'd push me over the edge and force me to throw him out.

I was aware of the patterns now, the way Noel was always late back on a Friday night, after going for drinks with colleagues at the office. Even though I knew that the trains didn't run that late and he'd have to get a taxi. She must be paying for it, this affair of theirs, because I was in charge of our finances. I'd soon know if he was hiving off money for fancy hotels and meals out.

"WHY DIDN'T you say anything, babes?" Jennie asks, as we huddle in a corner at The Plough.

She has that gleam in her eye, although she is trying hard to hide it. She has always loved a bit of gossip, as long as it's not about her. She learnt a harsh lesson when she fell pregnant at university but that basic longing is still there. The need to know a secret no one else knows.

"If I told you, that would have been like admitting it to myself," I say. "And I didn't want to. I just wanted to keep my life together."

"You didn't adopt Orchid just to keep Noel, did you?"

"No!"

I'm glad that Orchid was not around to hear those hurtful words but that is the danger of gossip. It hurts anyone who gets in its path. It does not discriminate between good and evil, child and adult. It just blazes a trail and burns everyone who stands in its path.

"You don't think it was a Brokeback Mountain sort of situation?" Jennie says. "I mean, I loved Noel but I always sort of wondered."

"He wasn't gay," I say firmly. "I was married to him for fifteen years. I would have known."

"Would you though?"

"No, it was definitely a woman."

"Just doesn't seem like Noel," Jennie says. "Not the Noel I knew, anyhow."

I shrug. "Tell me about it. I mean, I loved him to bits, but who else would want him?"

THE FRIDAY NIGHTS OUT became a thing of the past, once we were given the go ahead to adopt Orchid. Noel dropped his fancy lady so that we could become a family. I couldn't help wondering if the whole thing had happened because of the way Noel felt after that tactless doctor told him he was infertile. I knew he felt emasculated but he wouldn't talk about it, not to me at least. But when he became a father, he came back to me, to us. Whatever it was that had been going on was not as important as the life we shared together.

We were a good fit, Noel and me. We weren't head over heels any more but I had still loved him deeply and I was sure he had loved me. One of the reasons I never confronted him was that Noel was such a good person, he couldn't possibly be having an affair. He was the kind of person who was always putting himself out for others. He shovelled the snow off our elderly friend's driveway. He was the first phone call that time Kurt was arrested for being drunk and disorderly. He was the kind of man who let other people go first in the queue if they only had a few items. He was kind and loving, but even good men have their faults.

THE REST of our family and friends have arrived now, sitting at the tables I reserved for the wake.

"In-laws at twelve o'clock," Jennie warns me, as Colleen and Royston walk in.

"Let's just stay here for now," I say. I don't feel ready to face them.

I down my drink, enjoying how the abrasive liquid burns

the back of my throat. I've never been one for neat spirits but right now I'm seeking oblivion.

"Don't worry, babes. Lila and I will put Orchid to bed," Jennie says.

I hadn't even thought. Selfish as it sounds, my own loss is so overwhelming that I have temporarily forgotten I have a daughter. I know that sounds terrible but I just need a few more hours, then I'll be ready to be a mum again.

Orchid. I picture her sweet little face. I haven't seen her laugh once since Noel died. She has spent all her time in her room, creating artworks I don't understand. Canvasses filled with dark, shadowy trees and in each one I spot eyes peering out at me. Sometimes a tuft of blonde hair, sometimes a ghostly hand. The girl in the woods.

It seems so unfair. I lost my parents and the sister I never met and now I've lost Noel as well. It's as if everyone I've ever cared about gets taken away from me. It's hard not to take it personally.

"Sod it," I say, banging my drink down on the counter. "Sod Noel and sod God."

"I think maybe you've had enough."

It's Howard.

I look at him and laugh. A long, bitter laugh.

"I bet you deal with a lot of drunk widows."

I can hear the slur in my speech but I can't stop it.

"That I have," he says, with a slight twinkle in his eye. "And widowers too."

I turn to see that Lila has arrived with Orchid. People are trying not to stare as Orchid sits down at the counter and Lila orders her a Coke. Colleen is there in an instant, hugging her and asking if Mrs Seal would like a sandwich. Colleen is a better mum than I am.

The wake goes on longer than it should. Kurt plays a heartrending version of one of Noel's songs. Then Colleen asks him to sing Ave Maria. Ave bloody Maria, of all things.

"Was the food...all right?" the barmaid asks, as she begins to clear away what is left of the buffet.

"There were vegetables in the sandwiches," Colleen complains. "And in the quiche."

"It was just a bit of cucumber and tomato and a sprig of lettuce."

"Disgusting," Colleen says.

Not quite the perfect mum, then. I had forgotten how Noel was raised to fear vegetables but it's good to hear Colleen moan.

Kurt wanders over and stops directly in front of me. He looks like he has something to say but all that comes out is:

"How are you, Suzannah?"

"I'm fine. You?

"Fine thanks, you?"

Still the king of conversation then.

Behind us, Royston starts singing The Lord of The Dance so Kurt grabs his guitar to accompany him.

"Who brings a bloody guitar to a funeral?" Jennie mutters.

I roll my eyes but Noel would have loved it, I know he would.

I have never heard Royston sing before. It's very moving. At least it is the first time, but then he won't stop. He launches into one of Elvis's hits, his voice growing raspier by the minute. Then Colleen grabs the salt shaker that he's been using as a mic and launches into Never can say Goodbye. She's no Gloria Gaynor and Kurt struggles to keep up.

I thought, if I could make it through the funeral then I would start to come to terms with losing Noel but if anything, it gets harder. There have been no more paranormal happenings in the house since Noel passed or perhaps Orchid and I are too distraught to notice them. A small part of me wants the spirit to return so that I can ask if Noel is all right. Despite what Howard says, I still hold out hope that it might be a good spirit and that one day, I will be able to communicate with my parents and Noel as well if only to find out if they all made it to heaven.

Noel was a good man, I'm almost certain that he will be in heaven but there is this little voice inside of me that pipes up every time I go to sleep.

"He was a cheater and cheaters don't go to heaven. Nor do atheists."

Surely God wouldn't hold those things against him? He'll look at his whole record, won't he? Not just the recent past.

31

I don't remember going to bed but I wake up in daylight, dressed in an ugly old T-shirt of Noel's. I have a sick feeling that Colleen must have helped me change since Jennie and Lila have better taste.

I sit bolt upright, certain that this is the morning that I will find Noel beside me. But of course he's not, although the cover is pulled back a little on his side as if he has merely slipped out of bed and gone for a shower. The house is silent, apart from the drip, drip, drip of the bathroom tap. I go in and turn it off as hard as I can. The tap stops dripping but the sound is replaced by the ticking of the Grandfather clock. Why must they make clocks so loud? The noise jars my aching head and I stagger down the passageway into the kitchen where I fall upon the medicine cabinet. I take twice as many painkillers as I'm meant to but what have I got to lose? I pour myself a cup of tea. I know that Orchid must be in her room but I don't go and check. Instead, I drink a second cup and gaze out at the woods, unable to enjoy the view I've always loved.

I finish my tea and glance up at the clock. Orchid is still in her room and I'm annoyed now. What is she doing in there? I thump down the passageway and yank open her door. I feel a pinch in my chest as I study her face. She seems to have grown smaller and thinner in the last few weeks, her eyes have sunken inwards and her arms are wrapped around her body, suggesting a need to be held.

"What are you…"

She rises quickly and comes to the door not because she wants to see me but because she doesn't want me in her room.

I look past her and try not to gape. The greyness of the walls is barely visible now. She has joined several sheets of paper together to create one giant painting. A mural of the woods, including the stream and all the trees. I pick out a deer and a rabbit and little squirrels hiding in the undergrowth. In the middle I spot the face, her eyes bright and penetrating, her head covered in fluffy blonde hair.

"It's beautiful," I tell her, even as the hairs on my arms stand on end.

There is no doubt she is gifted but it's not a gift I would have chosen. There is a strange smell in her room. It seems a little earthy, like she's been out in the woods already.

"I'm hungry," she says, without meeting my eyes.

"I'll make you something. What would you like?"

"Whatever you're having. As long as it doesn't contain meat."

"Oh, you're a vegetarian now are you?"

"Always have been, Suzannah."

Since when?

"Please…" I force myself to lay an arm on her shoulder. "Please call me Mummy."

THE PHONE RINGS DURING BREAKFAST. It's Howard, calling to ask how I am.

"Can you come round later?" I ask.

"I'd love to, only I have a lot of boring church business to conduct this week."

"Right."

It feels odd to hear a clergyman lie.

I glance at Orchid, who is chasing her boiled egg around the plate.

Just the two of us again.

"Can we light some candles?"

"I suppose so. Let's put them on the window sill, above the sink, shall we? We don't want Tiger to knock them over."

I don't even pretend to send the cat home any more. He is currently curled up in the armchair and his presence is the most comforting thing in the house. Only an animal can sit with you while you drip with angry tears and not annoy you by constantly asking if you are all right.

"How many do you want?" I ask, as I get out the candles. I keep them in a box with our torches and other emergency supplies. Noel used to have it all down in the cellar but I prefer to keep it all under the kitchen sink these days, just in case.

Orchid picks out two candles: one long, thin one and another sturdier one, white with gold swirls.

"Daddy liked that one," I say.

"That can be for him then," she says, holding it out for me to light.

"Why don't we just light the one candle?" I say.

"No, Mummy. It has to be two or the other Suzannah will cry."

I swallow hard, wishing she would stop. I don't want to think about the other Suzannah right now, when my heart aches for Noel. I feel like I have a heavy rock in my chest and there isn't room for anything else. When will it go away, I wonder. But I know this is foolish thinking. I'm still grieving for my parents all these years later and I always will.

GRADUALLY, my eyes improve enough that I'm allowed to drive again. It makes me nervous, the idea of driving with limited vision. What if I forget to check my blind spot? There is a lot more of it than before. I go out with a driving instructor a few times and he suggests that I start making small, familiar journeys, like a drive into Little Mercy to browse the shops. As my confidence increases, I make the trip into Greater Mercy and when that goes well, I drive to Winchester, twenty miles away, to have a look at the antiques. I'm thinking of selling the Grandfather clock, since it no longer brings me any joy. I find it creepy, the way it goes off without warning and it doesn't matter how many times I try to turn it off, it still goes off the next night, like it has a life of its own.

Winchester is busy today, lots of people out shopping and meeting up with friends. As I walk down Tanner Street, I spot someone ahead of me. I know that woman but I can't quite place her. She turns to look in a shop window and I see her more clearly. She looks smarter than I remember and she's wearing make up but I definitely know that face. It's Emily, Orchid's foster mother. Emily turns and looks at me too. No wonder I didn't recognise her, she doesn't have a gaggle of children with her.

She walks towards me, stopping just outside the butcher's window.

"I'm so sorry to hear about your husband."

"I must admit, I'm surprised you even heard."

It's not like we run in the same circles.

Emily presses her lips together. "The social worker told me, when I asked her about Orchid. How is she coping?"

"She's devastated," I admit. "We all are."

Both. I should have said both. We are not an all any more, just a both. Orchid is my whole family now.

"It's such a terrible shame," Emily says. "She was so excited about getting the family she'd always dreamed of. So often, the older kids don't get placed with a forever family and they feel so rejected. You see them getting into trouble at school. Getting into fights and turning to petty crime, all because they have so much anger inside them and they don't know what to do with it."

I bite my lip. If I could just have an ounce of her compassion, I would find it so much easier to deal with Orchid.

"Orchid is coping, in her own way," I say.

I feel the need to reassure her. To put her mind at rest.

"We're getting through it together, the two of us. She's been quieter since it happened, but I think she's grown up a bit too. Stopped looking for trouble. No more ungodly happenings, you know?"

She gives me the oddest look. "Whatever do you mean by that?"

I glance around. "You know, the weird behaviour. The broken glass."

Emily blanches. "There is nothing wrong with Orchid that a bit of love can't solve."

I stare at her for a moment. "What about the child she pushed off the swing?"

"I'm sorry, what? Orchid was never been anything but kind to the younger children. She loved them so much. She was sometimes a little over kind, changing their nappies when they didn't need changing, bringing them too many blankets, that sort of thing."

"What about the other stuff? The imaginary friends, the flooding?"

Emily shakes her head. "Orchid never had any imaginary friends when she lived with us and what's this about flooding?"

"She turned on all the taps in the house. Didn't she do that at your house too?"

"Never."

I back away. "I'm sorry," I say. "I must have been given the wrong file."

She shakes her head in dismay. "If Orchid is acting up, it's because she's frightened and confused. You do understand that, Suzannah?"

"Yes, I… but it's more than that. Orchid has been… talking to the ghost of my dead sister."

Emily lets out a noise that might be a snort but she covers it quickly.

"Children have such vivid imaginations," she says, with a shake of her head. "But I'd nip that in the bud, if I were you."

"How do I do that?"

"Just tell her that there are no such things as ghosts. You have to do it, Suzannah, or the poor girl will be clinging to the hope that Noel will come back and that really isn't fair, is it?"

32

I 've been doing it too, I realise. Clinging to the hope that Noel will come back. Is it possible for someone who doesn't believe in ghosts to turn into one? I would love so much to see him again, even if I couldn't touch him. To tell him all the things I never got to say. To yell at him one last time and tell him how much I miss him.

Emily makes an excuse and walks off in the direction of Debenhams and I head back to the car park. Was she telling the truth about Orchid? Does she really not know about her gift or does she choose not to remember?

I DRIVE TOO FAST to the school and sit outside, watching Orchid's classroom until the bell rings. This is the first time I've been here in person since I lost my eye and the other parents studiously avoid my gaze.

The children run out of the class and charge towards their parents. You would think Orchid and Catriona were friends, the way they wave and say goodbye to one another. Perhaps Catriona's mother has told her to be kind but it won't last.

"Mummy!" Orchid cries, her whole face lighting up when she sees me. "Mummy, is it really you?"

I laugh at her disbelief but I feel a bit self-conscious. We walk quickly to the car and I'm glad to escape back to anonymity.

Back home, I hand over a chocolate teacake without even trying to offer Orchid an apple and then I settle down at the computer. I need to see that file again. I had deleted it, as per Lila's request but nothing ever gets truly deleted. It will be there, somewhere in the system. I just have to find it.

I spend half an hour searching through my archives to no avail. I take a break and warm up a tin of tomato soup for supper. I can't be bothered to cook anything more elaborate and Orchid doesn't complain. It is only me who's left with a twinge of guilt.

She hides away in her room after supper, so quiet, I feel the need to check on her. She sits on her bed, scribbling something on her sketch pad. She hums to herself. Ava Maria. I really wish she wouldn't.

"Did you sleep okay last night?" I ask, as I pick up some screwed up balls of paper from the floor and toss them into the bin.

"Much better."

"That's good."

"She wasn't here last night."

"What?"

"It gets so cold when she comes."

I feel a little shiver run down my spine.

"I wish she'd leave," I say.

"But she can't, Mummy."

"Why not?"

"She hasn't got what she wants yet."

I stop and look at her. "And what is that?"

"You, Mummy. She wants to take you with her. You're not going to leave me, are you?"

I cross the room and clutch her to my bosom. My poor, messed up child, who has known so much fear and death in her short life. She doesn't deserve this. She doesn't deserve me. I hold her until I feel her pull away. Is this what love is, this fierce protective instinct that swells inside my heart? I'm beginning to think it is.

Once Orchid is in bed, I return to the computer and try again but it's no use. The email appears to have been wiped from the hard drive. What a shame Noel isn't here. He would have known what to do. I could ask Lila to send it to me again. There must be a record of it on her computer. I pick up the phone.

"Lila? It's me."

"Suzannah! How are you, darling?"

"I'm okay."

"Do let me know if there is anything I can do for you," she says. I hear voices in the background. It sounds like she's in a bar.

This is supposed to be the part where I ask her to resend the file but something stops me.

"What you need is a good night out," Lila says. The way she tells it, you would think drink could cure anything. "You are still on for tomorrow night, aren't you?"

Actually, I had forgotten all about it. Colleen and Royston are coming down for the weekend and Colleen said she would babysit, if I fancied going out. I had thought it sounded like a good idea. My eyesight is a lot better than it was. Not perfect but definitely good enough that I can travel again. I have missed spending time with the girls.

"I'll be there."

"Great, I'll see you then."

LILA WALKS TOWARDS ME, way too close to the platform edge. Her short skirt swishes as she moves, showing off her long, bronzed legs in her trademark pointy boots. She turns heads with every step.

"Darling!" she almost steps on my toes as she clasps me to her. Her breath is a mixture of vodka and mint.

We meet Jennie in a crowded bar, down a dark alley in Soho. I always wonder how Lila finds these places. Whatever part of London we go to, she always knows some little bar, or cocktail place. Must be because she is out every night, while I'm at home, curled up on my sofa.

Several times, I open my mouth to broach the subject of the file but something always stops me. I'm not quite sure what it is, a sixth sense? Hours pass and we drink and dance like we're still at uni. Jennie is on great form, cracking saucy jokes and Lila laughs twice as long and twice as hard as any of us.

"Do you think people will remember me, when I'm dead?" Lila asks.

She often gets a bit morose towards the end of the night.

"How could anyone forget you?" I say. "You're not exactly a wallflower."

That makes Lila smile for a moment but then the melancholy comes back.

"I do worry though. I would hate to be forgotten."

"It's not like you'd be around to care," says Jennie, ever practical. "I for one don't give a stuff what happens to me when I'm nothing more than a pile of dust."

"You will live on through your children," Lila says. "They're your legacy."

"All bloody four of them," Jennie groans. "To be honest, I'll be glad of the rest."

Lila waves her arm and a black cab lurches to a halt right in front of her.

"Wow, you'll have to teach me how to do that," I say, as we all pile in. "Waterloo Station, please."

The driver pulls out into the busy traffic but his eyes return to Lila with such frequency that I fear we'll crash.

"I've seen you in the movies, haven't I?" he eventually says.

"Maybe," Lila says mysteriously, though I'm pretty sure she hasn't been in any despite the fact she spent her twenties auditioning for everything going. Had she actually got a part, she would have rung me. In fact, she would have held a massive screening party and we would have been made to watch it over and over until we felt like we'd been in the film too. The driver asks Lila for her number as we pull up at the station and she scribbles it down on a piece of paper.

"I hope you didn't give him your actual number," I say, as we hug goodbye.

"Oh no. I gave him yours."

I laugh and we part ways, Lila taking the Northern Line, while Jennie and I wait for trains back to the sticks.

"I'm starving," Jennie says as soon as she's gone.

"Me too. Let's go and get a pasty, shall we?"

Nights out with Lila rarely involve food. The shop has run out of pasties, so we have to make do with the sandwiches nobody else wanted. I'm so hungry I agree to a cheese and mushroom melt.

"Does Lila seem all right to you?" I ask as I pick out the mushrooms.

"What do you mean?"

"I don't know, she seemed a bit strange."

"Lila's always been strange. Have you only just noticed?"

"I'm serious."

"So am I. Don't you remember when she had an issue with that girl in her class at uni? What was her name? Alma something. She dragged us all over to Alma's place to gate crash her party."

A memory surfaces. Lila hadn't even been straight with us. She'd told us that Alma had said to bring people along but when we got there, it was clear that Lila herself wasn't even invited. Alma didn't want a confrontation so she didn't forcibly kick us out but it wasn't a lot of fun. It was clear that Lila was only there to piss her off. I wanted to leave the moment I found out, but Lila begged me to stay. It was an odd sort of a night.

"What did she have against Alma, anyway?"

Jennie shrugs. "Who knows? Could have been anything."

NEXT MORNING, I wake to an email from Jennie.

'I finally got around to scanning my old pics from our uni days. I thought you might like to see them!'

Jennie always had her camera. She would pass it around on nights out and as a consequence, a lot of the pictures are rather blurry. All the same, it's fun to reminisce, a bit like stepping back in time. Many of the pictures are a little dark because we were always in some pub or bar. My mind boggles at how much I used to go out in those days. I feel exhausted even thinking about it. I have little desire to go back to that way of life but it's nice to see the pictures.

There are several of me and Jennie posing. Even more of Lila pouting. Whenever there is a picture of the three of us, she always manages to be the one in the middle. I smile at one of Kurt with Lila riding his back like a horse. I don't remember that at all. From their eyes, I'd say they were both a little tipsy. Or stoned. I pause at the pictures of Noel with his guitar, the same guitar that still hangs on our wall. I remember how he would sit and strum it, sometimes for hours.

There is a picture of him and Kurt playing at the Student

Union bar. At the time, there was a third member of the group, an engineering student called Brian. His violin playing was a bit scratchy but it made for an interesting combination. Yes, I remember this gig; Brian is wearing a ridiculous hat that he'd bought at the market and Kurt has his foot in plaster because he fell down the stairs at a party. And there is Noel, the same old Noel, except his hair is really long. He is wearing a 'Free Nelson Mandela' T-shirt, even though Nelson Mandela was already free. I remember the T-shirt and I remember the night. It was the first time Noel played "*The Girl Who Stole My Heart.*" You can see from the expression on his face that he is singing his heart out. It is all just as I remember, except for one important detail. It's not me Noel is gazing at. It's Lila.

Did Noel like Lila?

I try to picture the two of them together but I don't remember them having any particular chemistry. I'd always thought Kurt and Lila could have had something but Noel and Lila? They were comfortable around each other, like a pair of old socks. I never caught him sneaking looks at her or anything like that. Had he liked her once? If so, he'd never mentioned it.

Swallowing my pride, I ring Jennie. She sounds groggy.

"Sorry, I thought you were up?"

"No, I've been up. I just went to bed."

"Sorry, I'll let you go in a minute. I need to ask you something. About Noel. And Lila."

"What about them?"

"Do I really have to say it? Do you think they ever…"

"Not that I know of. Why do you ask?"

"It was one of your photos, actually. Noel is really staring at her."

There is a pause.

"Jennie?"

"I can't speak for Noel. You knew him better than I did. The real question is if Lila liked him."

"Surely she would never…"

"Lila gets what Lila wants. If she had wanted him, she would have had him but I always thought she and Kurt seemed more likely."

I set down the phone, grateful for her honesty. Grateful but uncertain. It shouldn't matter now if my husband fancied my best friend. He's gone now, dead and buried. But in a weird way, it matters more than ever.

33

I drop Orchid at school on Monday then I check the train times. I'm going to call in on Lila and this time I'm going to ask her outright. *Did you have an affair with Noel?*

Would she even tell me, I wonder? Perhaps not, but I might be able to tell by looking at her. People give themselves away, don't they? I think of Orchid sneaking crisps from the cupboard. She'll swear point black that she didn't do it but her face will tell me she did. Lila is not a ten-year-old girl but she still might give herself away. She won't be able to look at me or else she'll fiddle with her hair. If she's lying, I'll know.

I arrive in London later than I intended due to train delays. It is about quarter to one by the time I get there and I cross my fingers that Lila hasn't already had her lunch break. I walk through the campus, noting the bareness of the trees. The weather is colder than it was the last time I was here and the students are dressed in warm turtlenecks and brightly coloured jumpers, looking casual yet effortlessly stylish, the way young people do. I think I recognise a couple of students from her class but I can't be sure. They all look the same: fresh faced and Bohemian.

The theatre is in darkness as I descend the steps and I feel a thud of disappointment. I feel silly for not phoning first but I had it in my head that I would march down here and have it out with her. I wanted to be impulsive for once and catch her unaware. If I told her I was coming, then she would be ready for me. Might even suspect that I'd come with an agenda.

I look around but I can't remember where her office was and there doesn't seem to be anyone around. Is Lila at lunch? She might even have the day off. I don't know her schedule. I follow a signpost that leads me to reception. It is a busy, modern looking one with at least four different members of staff manning the desk and answering the phones. Behind the desk in a gallery are printed pictures of all the members of staff, from A to Z. It fills the entire wall.

I wait behind a man who is at least six feet tall but has the voice of a squeaky young boy. He appears to have fallen behind on his fee payments and I feel sorry for him as the administrator tells him that if he does not pay his bill, he'll have to find alternative accommodation. I am beginning to think we'll both be here all day when another receptionist beckons me.

"I think you're next?"

"Thanks," I say, side stepping the troubled student. "I'm here to see Lila Swann in the drama department. Is she in today?"

The receptionist consults her computer.

"Not in," she says.

"Oh dear!" I turn to leave.

"She's not on the system."

Not on the...

"You might have her down as Delilah Swann? Dr Delilah Swann?"

The woman taps away. "No."

My eye goes to the gallery behind her but I can't find her picture.

The receptionist who is helping the student glances at us. "I remember Delilah! She was a great laugh!"

"She's not here anymore then?"

The woman shakes her head. "Oh no, she was only filling in for a couple of weeks while Norelle was off sick."

My stomach drops. Lila let me believe that she worked here. As if the position was permanent. I cast my mind back. What had she said exactly? Yes, there were definite references to her job. She talked about her students. She told me about shows she was putting on. Fundraisers she was doing with the class and yet she had only worked here for a couple of weeks. Is she living in a fantasy land?

I walk back to the tube in a daze. I don't know what to do now. I am stunned and scared and brimming with anger. I take the phone out of my handbag and dial her number.

"Hi Lila!"

"Suzannah! Are you okay?"

"Yes! Listen, I've got a hospital appointment at Moorfields later. Can I pop in and see you on the way back?"

"Of course. Why don't we meet at Oxford Circus? I know a really great place."

"Actually, I was wondering if we could go back to your flat since it's close to the hospital."

There's a pause.

"My flat?"

"It's just a few minutes from Moorfields, isn't it?"

"Yes but I'll be at work till three."

I'll have to ring Emma and ask if she can have Orchid after school.

"That's about when I'll be finished."

"Oh…"

I can hear the cogs turning and I realise that, for whatever reason, she doesn't want me to come to her place.

"To be honest, it might be best to meet somewhere else. I'm having a bit of drama with one of my flatmates. I'll tell you all about it later."

"Do you want to meet at the college then?"

Another pause.

"Could do. How about the coffee shop next to the car park?"

"Okay, call me when you're there."

I WONDER what she's going to be doing until three if she isn't working at the uni. Could she have lost her job and she doesn't want to admit it? But no, the receptionist distinctly said that she was just a sub. Lila had never held a permanent position at the uni. She merely let me think she had.

The more Lila tries to keep me away, the more determined I am to go to her flat. It occurs to me that I've only been there once, just after she moved in a couple of years ago. Whenever I come to up to London, she always wants to meet me in town. Well, not this time.

I catch the tube to Islington and cross the road, opposite the Angel. The block of flats Lila lives in is on the same road, a pretty maisonette with bay windows. I steel myself as I walk up to the door and press the bell.

After a moment, a young woman comes to the door and eyeballs me with a weary expression.

"Yes?"

"Hi, I'm er...looking for Lila. Lila Swann."

The woman continues to look at me.

"Does she...still live here?"

"Nope."

"Wait, maybe I've got the number wrong. Could she live next door?"

She casts a glance at the next flat.

"Nope."

"Are you..."

The woman lets out a sigh.

"Have you lived here long?" I venture.

"Ain't none of your business."

With that, she walks back into the flat, leaving me staring up at the windows.

This is definitely the place. I've been here with Lila. We did tequila shots in the kitchen. I remember Lila dancing on the table and I remember Jennie falling asleep in the armchair in the corner. There were lots of other people too, no one I knew though. It was Lila's flatmate who threw the party but it was definitely her place. Wasn't it?

A car beeps its horn as I stumble into the road.

Whoops! I'd better be more careful.

"Are you all right?" an old man asks, as I bump into a lamp post.

"Yes, I…"

I drop my handbag, the contents spilling all over the road. I kneel down and gather everything up. The old man hands me a bottle of eye drops that had rolled into the gutter.

"Watch where you're going, okay love?"

I nod and continue on my way to the tube. It's only when I reach the ticket machine that I realise my purse is missing. The crafty old bugger must have swiped it.

I SPEND ages on the phone to the bank, getting them to cancel my cards and then I have to convince the ticket people to let me board the train. I know Lila would lend me some money but I'm not sure I can face her right now. I send her a quick text to let her know my purse has been stolen and I tell her I'll meet her next time. I go through the same palaver when I reach Waterloo and it seems like forever before I'm able to board a train.

Just as the train pulls away from the station, I think I see Lila standing on the platform edge. But it can't be her. We weren't meeting at Waterloo. She wouldn't have known where to find me. I squint at the figure in the tall, zippy boots, her long blonde hair flowing in the wind. She raises her phone to her face and then my phone rings.

It's Lila. My heart jumps into my mouth and I forget to breathe. I don't answer. I can't. A second later, it beeps loudly. She's sent me a text:

Will be in your area on Sunday. Can I come for dinner?

I stare at the message, my mind whirring. What do you want with me, Lila?

I have to reply, or she'll know something's up and if I don't agree to Sunday then she'll just pick another day. You can't get rid of Lila. She's a boomerang.

34

I force myself to cook a proper Sunday roast. Probably the first roast I've made since I lost my eye. I put the gammon in the slow cooker and parboil the potatoes before roasting them in the oven. I'll put the Yorkshire puddings in just before I'm ready to serve. I even chop carrots and cauliflower and boil peas, using the leftover water for the gravy. It's a lot of effort to go to but I need to keep my hands busy, even if I can't switch off my brain.

Lila is arriving by train which means she will have to come down the hill and through the woods. I stand at the window and watch through the net curtains. It's almost time. A tall figure comes into view. I watch as she picks her way through the trees on those high, pointy heels of hers. I see a slight smile on her face and my anger diminishes. What the hell am I thinking? This is Lila, who I know nearly as well as I know myself. I watch as she steps onto the path and I see Tiger slinking towards her like a leopard in the jungle. He sidles up to her and rubs himself against her legs. There is an odd look on her face as she peers down at him. A little half smile that doesn't quite fit her face.

You can tell a lot about a person by the way they treat

animals and Lila is looking at Tiger with an expression of amusement, head tilted, eyes narrowed. I think for a moment she is going to kick him. My stomach twists and I feel sick as I envision her kicking him through the air, but she doesn't do anything of the kind. I exhale as she bends down and stokes him, not caring that her fancy clothes are trailing in the dirt. What was I thinking? Of course Lila wouldn't harm a cat. This is my best friend, the woman I've been closest to for the past twenty years. She may be a fantasist but that doesn't mean she would hurt anyone. I need to get this craziness out of my head.

Tiger permits Lila to stroke him for a bit longer then something catches his attention, and he darts off into the trees. I struggle to compose myself as I answer the door. I still feel reluctant to invite her in.

"Is it cold out?" I ask, as she hugs and kisses me. Her hands are like icicles on my back.

"It's lovely and warm in here," she says, unzipping her fur-lined boots. Only now do I notice how sharp the points on those heels are, like daggers.

She follows me into the kitchen and I automatically switch on the kettle. She tells me about a project she is doing with her students, raising money for kids at a school in Gambia.

"We've already raised three thousand pounds," she says, pulling out a phone to show me the faces of the children she's supposedly helping. They're all gathered around their teacher, their little faces smiling at the camera.

"I want to raise ten thousand by the end of the year," she says. "It won't be easy but my students have lots of ideas. We're going to put on a pantomime at Christmas and we're doing a car wash and a fair."

"Sounds amazing," I say, wondering when she's going to hit me for a donation. I wait but she doesn't say anything. She seems so passionate about what she is doing, but I have a horrible feeling she's making it all up. She doesn't even have any students, does she? So how can she put on a pantomime, unless she's going to play all the parts herself. I nod and smile as she continues to talk but really, I can think about only one thing:

Did you have an affair with my husband?

We drink our tea, lounging on the sofa.

"Lovely cuppa," she says.

"Hmm."

It tastes a little chalky to me and I wonder if the milk is on the turn.

As Lila curls her bare feet beneath her, I notice how pretty her toenails are. They're painted in a rainbow pattern. Each one is flawless and beautiful. It must have taken some meticulous painting.

WE TALK about Noel and I squirm as she brings up funny memories she has of him. The time we held a surprise party for him (her idea, not mine) and he arrived so late half the guests had left. The time we all went to London to see a concert that turned out to be cancelled, and we spent the day in a pub by the river. She seems awfully comfortable talking about my dead husband, dragging his name into whatever topic we happen to be discussing. If she did have an affair with him, she hides it well.

I finish my tea and I jump up to check on the roast.

"Let me help," she says as I pull the potatoes out of the oven.

"You can lay the table."

I don't need to tell her where anything is.

I glance at Orchid's room. The door is shut and she has her music on. She's been printing T-shirts all morning. No doubt her clothes and hands will be covered with ink.

I go to her door and peer in.

"Can you wash your hands for dinner, poppet?"

I don't want to bring her out with Lila here but it will look strange if I don't. Besides, I need someone to act normal because goodness knows I'm making a pig's ear of it. I set the meat down and Lila automatically picks up the knife. It glints in her hand as she expertly slices through the flesh and I fight the urge to snatch it off her. I have to call Orchid a second time before she appears. By then, I have dished up the cauliflower cheese and the Yorkshire puddings. It smells just as it did when my own mother used to cook. What did she make of Lila, I wonder? I can't remember her ever offering an opinion.

I pour the gravy with a shaking hand and concentrate on my food. It is easier to fill my face, than to carry on conversation. I glance at Lila out of my one good eye. It is never this silent when the two of us get together. We rarely go five minutes without a good belly laugh. But that was before Noel died. I have a good reason to be subdued.

Thankfully, Orchid is in the mood for conversation. She chatters on about the mural she is doing at school, painting the brick wall next to her classroom. Lila listens attentively and asks insightful questions. Orchid enjoys the attention. She looks at Lila with full on admiration and is probably wondering if she will ever be as glamorous as her.

"Another glass of wine, Suzannah?" Lila asks.

"Yes, why not?"

I'm careful to drink this one slower. I feel like I need to be on my guard.

After dinner, Lila helps me to clear the table and before I know it, she's rinsing the dishes in the sink.

"That's okay, I've got a dishwasher."

I tell her this every time but for some reason she always rinses each one by hand and leaves them sitting on the draining board.

Drip! Drip! Drip!

She picks up the bottle of wine again and shares the remainder between our two glasses.

"Have you done your homework?" I ask Orchid.

"Yes," she says automatically.

That'll be a no then.

"Bring it to me," I say, and she disappears off to her room.

"I'd better start her bath soon," I tell Lila.

"Yeah and I'd better get going," she says, taking the hint. "Got some marking to do."

"Would you like a lift to the train station?"

"Oh, no. I wouldn't want to put you out."

"It's no trouble. I've got to pop to the shop anyway."

Fifteen minutes later, I sit in the car with Orchid, watching as Lila boards her train back to London. I still have a bad feeling about her. Even though she hasn't done anything. Even though she's been kindness itself. I wish I'd asked her outright but I couldn't get up the courage.

"Why aren't we leaving?" Orchid whines as the train pulls away. "I'm bored."

"I just want to sit here a little longer," I say.

"But I'm bored!"

"I'll put the radio on. You can choose the station."

We sit there until the next train comes in. I need to be sure she hasn't come straight back. I feel a bit silly as I drive back home. Of course Lila isn't dangerous. My mind is leaping to conclusions, that's all.

Back home, I run Orchid a bath then listen while she reads a story and says her prayers. Once I've tucked her in, I go to my own room, ready to dive under the covers. There is something in my bed. It looks like my doll. I switch on the light, so that I can see it more clearly. Yes, it's Suzy, except now she has no eyes at all.

35

I stare at the doll for the longest time. I can't imagine what
it would be like to lose both eyes. It would be unthink-
able. Is the other Suzannah sending me a message? Is it
Orchid, fooling around? Or could it possibly be Lila? It's hard
to imagine how she would have had the opportunity. I saw her
arrive and I saw her leave. She didn't leave my sight once
except for five minutes to use the loo. Even then I saw her go
in and out. There's no way Lila could have done this and yet I
have an unshakable feeling that it's all connected somehow.
There is a gnawing feeling in my gut. A feeling that tells me I
need to go and check on Orchid. Right now.

Orchid's door is open slightly and she lies silently in the
bed, her body facing the wall. She clutches Mrs Seal a little
too tightly as if she's afraid to let her go. I watch her for a few
minutes and she doesn't stir and yet there is something not
quite right. I step inside the room and a sharp wind blows in
my face and ripples through the paintings on the wall. It
shouldn't be this cold. I touch the radiator but it's warm. I
move over to the bed. Orchid murmurs something into her
seal but she doesn't wake.

Quietly as I can, I part the curtains and find the window

hanging open. Someone has been here. Not a ghost, but a person. My hand trembles as I shut the window and secure it. Then I take another look around Orchid's room, checking inside her wardrobe and under her desk to make sure there's nobody hiding in the shadows because I'm not so sure it's a ghost we're dealing with anymore.

I leave her room and stand in the hallway, listening for the sound of movement. With my back against the wall, I move slowly through the house, checking every door and window. I have a horrible sense of foreboding as I reach the cellar door, but I don't dare go down there. Instead, I take a heavy plant pot and drag it in front of the door. If there's anyone down there they can starve to death for all I care. There's no way I'm letting them out.

Should I ring the police? They would have to send someone from Greater Mercy and I know from experience how long that would take. If only I had friends in the village. I think of Emma, but she's on her own. I could hardly ask her to drive out here with Dilly in tow especially if there is someone in the house. I could pack Orchid in the car and drive over to Catriona and Robert's house. They are about the nearest and their dad is built like a tank but there's still bad blood there. What if he doesn't let me in?

I hear a sound outside like boots shuffling through the leaves. I race to the window but it's hard to see. Is somebody out there or is it all in my head? I need my phone but where is it? I search the kitchen and the living room before I finally find it in the bathroom, sitting on the side of the bath. I don't remember leaving it there. I pick it up and stare at it for the longest time before I know who to call.

"GOOD JOB you're such a night owl," I say.

Kurt smiles weakly but his brow is furrowed.

"To be honest, I was worried about you. What you were saying about ghosts and Lila. I don't know what to make of it all. Do you think maybe…you should see a doctor?"

I stare at him open mouthed. "It isn't a doctor I need, it's proof."

He looks unconvinced. I can see it in the slight tilt of his head and the way he keeps brushing his hand through his hair.

"All this stuff about her flat and her work…"

"Have you been to her flat?"

"No," he admits. "I only see her at parties and stuff but this is Lila! We've known her for years. Are you sure you got the right place?"

"I'm not going mad," I insist. "I think there's something going on with her. Think about it, she's always been a bit off the wall."

"That she has but that's just Lila. She's always been a bit funny and daring."

"She's clung to me like a limpet. I don't know why I didn't see it before. She's the one who always rings and asks when we're going to meet up. She's the one who wants to know all about my life. I thought she was just interested but I'm not so sure now. I'm not sure I trust her anymore."

"What do you want me to do first?" he asks.

"Check the cellar, if you wouldn't mind. I'm too scared to go down there."

"Okay."

I lead him down the passageway to the cellar door. He pulls a powerful torch from his bag and shoves the plant pot out of the way. I watch nervously as he pulls the door open.

"I'll stand here," I say. "And make sure it doesn't close."

Kurt shines the torch around. "All looks fine to me. Do you really need me to go down there?"

"If you wouldn't mind."

Slowly, Kurt descends. I feel a shiver up my back as he

reaches the bottom and I keep glancing behind me, terrified that someone's going to push me down the steps.

"It looks clear!" Kurt calls out from below. "I'm just going to take a look behind these crates and make sure."

"Thank you!"

He moves into the darkness and I hear him moving things about.

"Are you all right?" I call, after a bit.

There is no answer.

"Kurt?"

"I'm... argh!"

"What is it?"

Without warning, he comes bolting back up the steps and slams the door shut behind him, panting heavily as he blocks the door.

"What is it?" I ask, impatient for him to get his breath back.

"I don't want to alarm you," he says, wiping the sweat off his forehead, "But you've got mice."

"Ugh."

Horrible as that is, I am relieved as we walk towards the living room. Mice, I can deal with. Better than having someone hiding down there. Kurt takes a step towards the computer. "Maybe I should take a look for this file of yours? I'd like to see some evidence before we start accusing Lila of anything."

"Of course."

I open up Outlook for him and he takes a seat.

"Do you think you'll be able to find the deleted file?" I ask.

He pushes a strand of hair behind his ear. "If it's in there, I'll find it."

I potter around, tidying up Orchid's mess which has, as usual, spread from her room out to the living room. There are art supplies everywhere and freshly painted T-shirts hanging from every door frame. I pick up stuffed toys and place them in the toy box and pack playing cards back into their box.

"Yikes!" Kurt exclaims.

I look up to see Orchid standing in the doorway. She is as still as a statue, her face as pale as moonlight in her long white nightgown.

"Orchid, how long have you been standing there?" I squint at her outfit. "Where did you get that?"

"It was under my bed. I thought you put it there?"

"No! Maybe it was Nanny?"

I picture Colleen. She loves to bring Orchid presents and the nightgown is kind of pretty, in an old-fashioned way.

"What are you doing up?" I ask.

"I want a glass of water."

"Didn't you take your bottle to bed?"

"Yes, but you didn't fill it up for me."

The accusation stings. Of course, Orchid is old enough to fill her own bottle. But it's something Noel always did for her, one of his little indulgences. I should have thought.

"Sorry," I say. I go to the cupboard and take out a glass and fill it from the tap.

"Who's he?" she asks, looking at Kurt with eyes as wide as saucers.

"Don't you remember Daddy's friend, Kurt? He's helping me with something."

"Oh. Is he dead too?"

"No!" I say, darting a glance at Kurt. "Why would you say that?"

"He looks a bit dead," Orchid tilts her head slightly and looks at him critically.

"Well he's not."

Kurt has an uncomfortable expression on his face.

"Sorry,"' I say.

"I'm fine," he says.

"He's fine," I repeat. "Now go to bed."

. . .

ORCHID PADS off to bed and I tuck her in again. I check her window again but it's still locked and the room feels a little warmer now. I walk back out to the living room and catch Kurt mid stretch, his mouth wide open.

"Tired?"

"I'm all right. It's just harder than I expected."

"No luck then?"

"It's downright strange," he says. "There is no trace of it. I ought to be able to find some record, a ghost file if you like, but there's nothing."

"So you think it was Lila?"

His frown deepens. "I'd be surprised if she knew how to do this. I don't recall her being particularly tech savvy. Maybe it was the person she got the file from?"

"But what if no one gave her the file?"

"What are you saying, Suzannah?"

"I think she might have fabricated the whole thing. Got a copy of my file somehow and then added stuff of her own on the end to freak me out. I don't think that file was real, not after what Orchid's foster mother said."

"But Lila really was a social worker…"

"Was she though? Think about it, Kurt. When did she first mention that she was a social worker?"

"I don't know, it was a couple of years back I think."

"Because I don't remember anything about it until I told her I was planning to adopt. And I know we all get wrapped up in our own lives but I could swear she never mentioned it before then and suddenly she had all this knowledge."

"Perhaps she played one in a show," Kurt ventures but I still don't think he believes me.

"She knows her stuff, I'll give her that. She sounds exactly like a real social worker."

"Perhaps she had one herself when she was little."

I stare at him. This explanation sounds better than any I've been able to come with.

"I've never met Lila's parents, have you?"

"No."

"She said she'd left home at sixteen because she didn't want to live by their rules. I'm wondering now whether Lila ever had a normal home at all. Wouldn't that explain why she hangs on to her old friends so much?"

"Maybe we are her family."

"She's totally unhinged. I can't believe it's taken me this long to realise." I stare off into the distance. "But what about the ghost? Things have happened in this house. Things I can't even begin to explain."

Kurt doesn't answer. He is looking at the bookcase. My mother's bookcase, actually. Still filled with all her favourite books. Mum preferred the classics, many of them in the gothic tradition: My Cousin Rachel, Wuthering Heights, Rebecca...

Suddenly, I see it all as he does. There are a lot of books about the supernatural up there, clues that I might at least entertain the idea. And Lila is one of the few people who knows about the ghostly encounter I had when I was a kid.

"But my dead sister, that wasn't fabricated. The grave was real. Howard knew about her, and that newspaper article I found at the library seemed real enough."

"Could Lila have been stalking you when you discussed her with Howard? Perhaps she took the idea and used it to get into your head."

"Maybe...I thought maybe you liked Lila once," I say, cringing as I say the words out loud. I don't mean to be nosey, really, I don't...

"Yes," he says, "I was quite into her at uni and it took me a long time to get her out of my system. There's just some-thing about her. She has a way of putting you under her spell."

I stare at him, amazed we're having this conversation. This

is the most I've ever got out of Kurt in all the years I've known him.

"Honestly Suzannah, we both liked her at first, Noel and me. That's why I never went for it, and he didn't either. Noel was loyal like that. And then, he fell for you and the rest is history."

IT MUST HAVE DRIVEN Lila crazy, that neither one of them seemed to want her. Lila thrives on attention. But she got Noel in the end, didn't she? She waited until he was at his lowest ebb, after the doctor told us he was infertile. I picture her approaching him in a bar, slipping her arms around him, whispering sweet nothings in his ear. Lila knows how to make a man feel special. She's got a gift that way. All the men want to be with her. All the women want to be her. I thought I was lucky, having her as my best friend.

I picture them together, laughing and drinking wine in the shower. Tumbling into bed together. Our bed. It seems preposterous and yet...

"Did you know? About Noel and Lila?"

He won't look directly at me. "Not for sure. But I had wondered. He seemed...distracted for a while, and he kept leaving practice early. It wasn't like him..." He fiddles with a loose thread hanging from his shirt. "When he couldn't give you a baby, I think it really ate him up inside. He told me once, that he didn't feel like a man any more. Of course, I told him that was nonsense but you couldn't reason with him once he got something into his head."

"Tell me about it!"

He returns to the computer.

"I'll order a pizza, shall I?"

"Cool."

"What do you want on it?"

"Whatever," he says without looking up. "Just no mushrooms."

"Mushrooms are not food."

"You're telling me."

I think of the trillion pizzas we must have ordered together in the past. We spent a lot of time together at uni, the five of us. Loafing around on the old sofa at Noel and Kurt's flat. I remember the time Kurt accidently set fire to it and we were all running between the living room and the bathroom with buckets full of water. We should have called the fire brigade, but we were young and reckless and thought we had everything under control. I remember how Lila loved it, the excitement, the drama. I can't believe that same Lila could be the person who has done all this. I can't put them together in my mind. Not my Lila, who I have loved like a sister.

THE PIZZA ARRIVES on the stroke of midnight. The Grandfather clock chimes as I pay the delivery man.

"Everything okay?" he asks, as I glance behind him, into the woods.

"Fine," I say, forcing a smile.

But I can't take any chances. I lock and bolt the door.

I carry the pizza box to the table and lift up the lid. The smell of melted cheese and tomato wafts out. Kurt and I grab a slice each and I'm just about to bite into mine, when I hear a sound.

"Orchid!"

I rush into her room. "What's wrong?"

Her eyes glisten in the darkness and she shakes with spasms of grief that I understand all too well.

"It's all right, poppet." I kneel down beside her bed. "You had a bad dream."

I hold her to my bosom and breathe her in, her salty tears mingled with the good smells of her strawberry shampoo.

"We were in a fog, Mummy. I feel like we are all wandering, lost in the woods. First, I lost Daddy and then I couldn't find you, either. I was all alone and I was so… scared."

"I'm not going anywhere," I promise her. "It will be you and me forever."

I wait with her until she falls asleep. Then I head back to the living room, where Kurt is packing up his stuff, along with Noel's music books which I told him he could have.

I swallow my pride. "Kurt, I have another favour to ask. I want you to stay the night."

36

M y cheeks burn brighter than a Belisha beacon. "I didn't mean…"

Kurt raises his eyebrows. "I know what you meant, Suzannah and it's fine. I'll stay."

My cheeks are warm with embarrassment but I also feel calm.

"Good. That's good. Can I get you anything else? Tea?"

"I'll have something stronger since I'm staying. If you've got anything?"

I think of Noel's beers sitting at the bottom of the fridge. He would probably want Kurt to have them. In fact, if he had made a will, I can imagine what it would say:

'And to Kurt, I leave all my alcoholic beverages… and just possibly, my wife.'

Where did that come from?

I have never had those sorts of thoughts about Kurt but then I have never spent much time alone with him before.

I grab a beer from the fridge and pour it into a glass for him.

"You can't tell, you know," he says, as he takes it. "About your eye."

"Thanks."

It is amazing how quickly I forget about my eye. The fake one has become a part of me, something totally normal. I almost forget that I used to have two. Just as I forget what life was like before I had Orchid. I can't believe we had to wait so long for her to become part of our lives and then the three of us were together for such a short time.

———

Kurt stays up late working on the computer. I get myself ready for bed, then return to find him hunched over the keyboard, his T-shirt riding up to expose his belly. It's not a warm night and the living room is cold without the fire on. I fetch him a blanket and cover him with it.

"Thanks," he murmurs, opening one eye.

"Sorry, I didn't mean to wake you." I take a step backwards.

"Suzannah?"

"Yes?"

"I miss him too, you know. He was my best friend."

I am surprised to see a tear trickle down his face and even more surprised to find myself moving over to him and wiping it away with my finger.

His cheek is extremely smooth in contrast to the stubble that protrudes from his chin.

He reaches up and touches my hair, the way Noel used to and if I close my eyes I could almost believe he is Noel. He has a similar scent. Perhaps he uses the same aftershave.

"I should get back to bed," I say. But I don't. Instead I move closer and he wraps the blanket around the two of us.

"I'm so glad you called," he says. "It means a lot to me that you were able to trust me with all this."

"I didn't know who else to turn to and you were always such a good friend to Noel. To us."

"Well you did the right thing."

His lips press against mine and then he pulls back and looks at me, like he is trying to read my expression.

"I won't let anything happen to you or Orchid. He really loved you both, you know."

I can't reply. There is a strange sensation in my stomach but it isn't hunger. I want him. I want him now and yet it feels wrong. Kurt is Noel's best friend.

He wraps his arms around me. He is more muscular than Noel and I enjoy the weight of his body as he presses against me. I pull his T-shirt over his head and run my hands all over his warm, soft middle. I always loved Noel's chest, by far the best part of any man. My heart does a somersault as he tugs at my pyjamas and before I know it, it's happening. Kurt and me, and I don't fight it any more. It feels so right…

It's daylight when I wake and I realise with a start that I have slept curled up on the sofa.

I scramble to my feet and gather up my clothes which lie in an untidy heap on the floor. Kurt is still sound asleep, so I dress quickly and cover him with a blanket.

There is a scratching sound at the back door. Cautiously, I open it, but there is no sign of Tiger. I close the door again and stare out the window into the woods. The woods are never still. There's a rustle in the bushes and wind in the trees. Absentmindedly, I flick on the kettle to make myself a brew.

"Mummy?"

I realise that I've missed the cup and there is tea all over the floor. I still make mistakes like that sometimes, my left eye never quite compensating for the right. I get a cloth and mop it up, while Orchid chews her way through a bowl of cereal. I watch as she pours more milk into her bowl.

"Do you want some?" she asks, seeing me watching her.

"No, you're all right."

Noel would have. I can just picture him sitting beside her, enthusing at the unicorn on the back of the box. He was a big kid sometimes. It was charming and annoying in equal measure. I used to ask him when he was ever going to grow up but now he won't have to.

I swallow hard. He would be on his way to work now, trekking up the hill to the station, headphones in, head bobbing slightly in time. He'd be listening to some noisy rock band, something alternative with depressing lyrics. Sad tunes made him happy. Perhaps that's why he liked Kurt's stuff so much.

"He's awake," Orchid points out.

I turn and see that Kurt has his eyes open. There is a faint red line across his forehead, where the arm of the sofa has imprinted itself upon him and his hair is tousled and wild.

"Do you want some?" Orchid asks. "It's really yum."

Kurt manages a crooked grin. "Yeah, why not?

He walks stiffly over to the table and plonks himself down. I set out an extra bowl and grab some bread and jam too because I really can't eat that stuff and I don't want to just sit there, watching them both.

We all busy ourselves with our food, Orchid munching her cereal as noisily as she can.

I feel Kurt's ankle rub against mine but I can't look at him. I can't believe last night was real.

"So, how's school going?" Kurt asks Orchid after a few minutes.

I look down at my plate, wishing he wouldn't. I've learnt by now never to ask direct questions about school. Information can only be extracted from ten-year-olds like a delicate operation. I picture myself in an operating theatre plucking facts from the patient's stomach with a pair of pliers. You get a grip on the truth and extract only very carefully. One nudge and you drop the lot and have to start again.

"I want to join the hockey team," Orchid says. "You have to try out first, though."

I stop myself from gasping out loud at this unsolicited information.

"You have to try out?" Kurt says. "That's harsh."

"It's okay," Orchid says, reaching for another handful of cereal. "It helps them decide what position you should play. I want to be goalie."

"Got much competition?"

"Catriona wants to be goalie too and she totally thinks she's going to get it. She's fast but she's not as tall as me and less brave." She pauses dramatically. "I am thunder."

Kurt catches my eye and I try not to laugh.

EMMA COMES to pick up Orchid and I wave her off.

"Thanks, again!" I say. "I'll be ready to do it myself again soon. Just need a bit more practice."

"It's no trouble," she says, waiting patiently as Orchid searches for her left shoe. "You know it does Dilly good to have the company. Orchid's such a bright, chatty girl. She makes us howl with laughter, the things she comes out with. You know what she's like."

I try to think of the last time Orchid and I laughed together but I can't. Not her fault of course but now I wonder. Is she different around other people than she is with me? Do I make her more sombre, more withdrawn? I watch guiltily as she plucks the missing shoe from the back of the cupboard and wedges her heel inside.

"Have a nice day!" I call, as she disappears outside.

I notice Dilly sitting in the back seat, staring out at the woods. Has she spotted something out there I wonder or is she just being her usual dreamy self?

"Well…" Kurt says, now that we are alone again.

"Well…" I say in return.

We exchange an awkward smile. I wish I knew what he was thinking. Was it a mistake last night? A moment of craziness? But no, I still feel an attraction, which is odd because I could swear I never looked at Kurt before, never once considered it in all the years I've known him. If I were better at these things I'd ask him outright if it meant anything but I don't want to put him on the spot. I don't think I could bear the rejection. Better to leave things as they are and wait and see if he calls me.

I clear the table, pretending that the washing up is the most important thing in the world.

"I'd best be off, then," Kurt says.

"Thanks," I say, as if he's done no more than work on the computer.

He stands by the door looking as crumpled as a paper bag.

"Are you going to work like that?" I ask.

"No, I'll have to swing by my house and change."

"Won't you be late?"

He shrugs. "I haven't got any meetings till this afternoon."

I think of Noel's clothes hanging useless in his wardrobe. I open my mouth but I can't make the words leave my lips. Maybe I will give them to him when I'm ready but now is too soon.

AFTER HE LEAVES I put on the TV and watch some trashy daytime soaps, programmes I haven't bothered with since my student days. More unwelcome memories flood back. I remember sprawling on the floor with Jennie and Lila, eating popcorn and talking about everything and nothing.

I can't believe how many of my memories are tarnished now. It's not like I can take a cloth and wipe away everything with Lila in it. We had so much fun together before all this. Did she always have it in for me? Was any of our friendship real?

I take the blanket I gave Kurt and wrap myself up in it. A new sitcom is just starting, and I could do with a bit of a laugh. It's not a particularly good show but I feel myself decompressing just enough to fall asleep.

WHEN I WAKE UP, the TV has switched itself off again. I rub my eyes. The right one feels a little sandy. Perhaps I've got some grit in it. I pop it out and go to the sink to wash it. The water feels ice cold even after I've let it run for a while. I switch the kettle on for some hot water but nothing happens. I flick the lights. Nothing. Too late, I glance outside and see Kurt's Honda which means he never left.

37

I set my prosthetic eye down on the counter. Quietly I edge over to the window. Kurt is not in his car and I can't see him anywhere nearby. What could have happened to him?

Is he in on it?

I picture him and Lila laughing as they conspire against me but no, it doesn't feel right. One of them might be bad but not both, surely? I open the door and stick my head out. Bird song fills the air. I take a few steps and hear the familiar trickle of water from the stream. I've hardly ventured into the woods since Noel died. It hasn't felt right, not yet.

I dart back into the kitchen and look around for my phone but it's not in its cradle. Could I have left it in the bedroom? I go from room to room scanning all the usual places, but it's nowhere to be seen.

I glance outside again. It's like watching a moving jigsaw, all those tiny pieces. A rabbit sits boldly on the path, ears cocked, whiskers twitching.

What can it hear that I can't?

Cautiously, I pull on my coat and boots. I open the door slowly, frightened to step outside. I feel something behind me and whirl around but it's just Tiger. He rubs himself against me, purring loudly. I bend down and stroke him. His fur is cool and smooth and I long to pick him up and snuggle him. But this is not the time.

"Go on in, Tiger. Stay safe inside."

My voice cracks slightly and I wish he was a dog. I would feel so much safer with a big German Shepherd beside me.

I inch over to Kurt's car. I half expect to find him slumped over the wheel but perhaps I'm being melodramatic. I try the door handle and find it locked. What does that mean? Did he walk off into the woods? Perhaps he wanted to see the spot where Noel died.

The weeping willows droop with water as I stray further from the house. They stand over me, like discarded umbrellas, water droplets muddying the path. I push past the leaves, and something glints at me from one of the rhododendron bushes. There is a silver keyring caught in the leaves. I recognise the logo from Noel's band. I tug on it and find it is still attached to Kurt's backpack, the whole thing hidden in the bushes. I pull it out and look inside. It contains Kurt's laptop, the front of which looks battered as if it has been dropped from a height.

I look up but there is no one in the trees above. I flip the laptop open. If I can get it working, I might be able to Skype somebody for help but despite my frantic attempts, the laptop refuses to start. Either it's broken or it's out of battery.

I sense movement in the distance. A rustle in the bushes. The next noise I hear is like the hiss of a snake. I've never encountered any snakes in these woods, aside from that one time my father captured a grass snake and I ogled it like it was the most exotic creature I had ever seen. There it is again. Less of a hiss, more of a gasp. I'm getting closer. A sixth sense propels me onwards. The noise is coming from the rope swing.

I run towards the clearing, my hands trailing the trees to guide me along. I find the large oak tree with the branches that look like arms. The tyre lies discarded on the floor but the rope is in place and dangling from the rope is Kurt.

A cry escapes my throat and I stare at him in horror. His face is as pale as the moon and his eyes are red and glazed. There are claw marks on his neck where he must have tried to pull off the rope, but now his arms hang limply by his sides. His tongue hangs out of his mouth, saliva dripping slowly down his chin. His jaws are clenched, his hands balled into fists. His heart...I pray his heart's still beating.

"Kurt! It's okay, I'm going to get you down."

His body twitches and he grunts like an animal. Does he even know I'm there? I can't be sure.

I tug at the rope and try to widen his airway but the knot holds tight and I can't loosen it by much.

"Help!" I yell, "Help!"

If I yell loud enough, someone might hear me at one of the neighbouring farms. I pull the rope harder and manage to loosen it a fraction more, but not enough that he can breathe easily. His feet are still touching the ground, his weight pulling him down. I pull harder and loosen it by about an inch.

"She won't be happy..." he splutters. "Until she has destroyed us...all..."

"Don't try to talk! I'm going to cut you down."

I run back towards the house. I don't know if he has seconds or minutes but I have to do something. I burst through the kitchen door, every nerve ending inside me electrified as I charge towards the cellar. I pull the pot plant to one side and open the door, staring down into its dark depths. I hear a rustling sound and remember the mice.

I need a light.

I run to the fridge but my torch is missing. I spin around, taking one last look for my phone but there is no sign of that, either. I grab a pair of candles and a lighter instead. These will have to do.

I race back to the cellar and wedge open the door with the

heavy pot plant. Then I light the candles and head down into the darkness. I hear more noises: scratching and rustling.

Mice!

They're just harmless little mice. They're more afraid of me than I am of them. I descend the steps carefully, aware that the clock is ticking. An axe hangs on the wall at the bottom of the stairs. It's just what I need. I can still hear them scuttling around the cellar, nibbling through boxes with their teeth. My hands close around the axe and then I hear something else.

Lila?

I glance up the steps but I cannot see anyone. I hear the sound of sharp, pointy heels clacking across the kitchen floor. I forget to breathe as I propel myself back up the steps with the axe, my thighs burning with pain. The footsteps are getting closer.

I'm sorry, Kurt. I don't think I can make it.

I burst through the door and out into the passageway. I glance left and right. I can't see anyone but I suspect she's still here, lurking in the shadows. I sprint for the kitchen door and then I'm out into the woods, tearing along the path to the spot where Kurt hangs limp and lifeless.

He has stopped gasping for air and his face has turned from pale to blue.

"C'mon!"

Desperately, I hack at the rope with the axe. I can't go any faster, for fear of decapitating him. The rope is hanging by a string now and I slice through it carefully, desperate to cut him free. One last stroke of the axe and the rope gives way. The axe clatters to the ground as Kurt falls through my arms like a tree. There is a rushing sound in my ears, like a dam bursting.

"Kurt! Speak to me!"

I turn him onto his front and press down on his chest, then I tilt back his chin and blow. I took a first aid course when I applied to adopt Orchid but the lessons have become scrambled in my head.

"You found my clue!"

I spin around to see Lila. Her blouse is torn and dirty and there is blood dripping from her left arm.

"Lila! You're hurt!"

"Don't just stand there," she says, grabbing the axe from the ground. "Run!"

She grins broadly and I think for a moment she's joking, but then she takes an exploratory swing that lands way too close to my leg.

"Didn't you hear me, Suzannah? I told you to run!"

This time, the axe comes down right by the heel of my shoe, a millimetre closer and she would have got my foot. There is nothing for it but to run, leaving Kurt lying motionless on the ground.

I bolt through the woods, grasping wildly at the trees that block me at every turn. I glance back over my shoulder but my vision is indistinct, a blur of green and gold. I stumble madly, trying to get my bearings. A creak in the undergrowth tells me all I need to know.

She's coming.

I propel my legs onward, forcing my way through twigs and sodden leaves. A thick branch twangs in my face and a cry escapes my bloodied lips. My hand goes up automatically, rubbing the nothingness where my right eye should be. My heart ticks like an unexploded bomb and I gasp, desperate to catch my breath. And still, I run, pushing myself desperately onwards. I keep on running, right up until the moment I fall through the undergrowth. And then all is still.

38

I blink. The sun shines in my eyes and it takes me a moment to realise where I am. There is a dank smell in the air, a whiff of damp earth and fungi. I glance at the broken computer and then I catch sight of a tyre. I have fallen down into the canyon not more than five hundred yards from my house. I squint up at the sky and see that the light is different now. The sun hangs directly above my head.

How long have I been down here?

I rub my face. My hand automatically goes to my hollow right eye. It feels wrong, like I've lost it all over again. I hear a movement above me and I look up. Lila sits on top of the canyon, her pointy heels swinging above my head and in her hands, she is holding my prosthetic eye.

There is a dull ache that stretches all the way from the back of my head to the length of my nose. I sit up slowly and Lila's face moves in and out of focus. I see the laughter in her eyes. She was always laughing. I used to find it infectious, like when you see someone yawn but now I see it as a sign of a deranged mind.

"We need to get help," I call trying not to wince. "Kurt's in a bad way."

"Kurt's dead."

"You're lying!"

I can't tell from her face if she is or not.

"It's your own fault, you know. You were supposed to save him."

She tosses my eye from one hand to the other like a marble.

"Careful!" I say, realising too late that there's no point because *Lila - the best friend* is a fiction. This person sitting up there is my enemy. Maybe even the devil herself.

I glance around at all the dirt and rubbish. I played down here often as a child. It was easy enough, climbing in but much trickier to get out and I was a lot fitter then.

Please, God.

"How did you figure out it was me?" she asks. "I could tell you knew, when I came for Sunday dinner. The way you wouldn't take your eye off me, not even for a minute."

I suck in a breath. "Of course, I knew. It was obvious. You always were a terrible actress."

I enjoy the look of shock on her face as I aim for her Achille's heel.

"Remember that terrible play of yours?" I force myself to laugh. "It just went on and on, didn't it? I thought it would never end."

"You loved my play!"

Her voice is ripe with indignation.

"Are you kidding? It was terrible! Good gracious, you never even read the reviews, did you? We had to stuff them in the bin before you saw them. They slated you!"

She leans forward. "You're lying! No one even came to review me."

"That's what we told you."

She's takes the bait. Panic rises off her like steam from a prairie. It's there in the slight flair of her nostril and the narrowing of her eyes. It's not even true but it could be. It would only take one mean spirited critic to put something out there. Lila would have been mortified.

"You loved my play."

"No, Lila. No one did."

Her eyes well up and I realise this pill may be too bitter to swallow.

"You let me down."

I shake my head. "I helped you. I was out there, flogging tickets every night."

"You let me down! Don't you remember? The last night of my play, the night you stole Noel."

"I didn't steal him! I didn't even know you liked him."

"You must have known! That's why you sabotaged my play."

"What are you talking about?"

She wipes her damp eyes with her sleeve.

"My play was sensational. Everyone thought so but instead of helping me, you drove them all away."

"I did not!"

I cast my mind back.

NOEL and I had been handing out flyers but it was a hard sell, especially that final show. No one wanted to spend their Friday night at the theatre, watching a one woman show. Not when the pubs and bars were heaving. I remember Noel and I were both cold and fed up and there came a point when I had looked at him and he had looked at me and something magical passed between us. We had been noticing each other for a while. It was always on the cards but that was the moment when we admitted it to each other. When the rain came down, we barely even noticed. While other people ran for shelter, the two of us huddled together in the middle of the street, his lips pressed against mine and I got my first taste of him, salty and delicious. He warmed my heart, as no one had ever done before.

"Let's go back to mine," he'd whispered.

I'd nodded and let him take my hand. Our shirts clung to our backs and our jeans were heavy with rain. The street was empty as we walked away. We couldn't have flogged any more tickets if we'd wanted to and besides, love was the only thing on my mind.

"THE AUDITORIUM WAS ALMOST EMPTY," Lila says. I hear the pain in her voice. "I looked out at the audience but I could barely see anyone. It was just a handful of people, but the show had to go on. Half of them didn't even return after the interval. I was left with an audience of two: a batty old lady and a hobo. Suzannah, the hobo wasn't even awake."

"I'm sorry that happened to you," I tell her. "But it wasn't my fault. What you were doing was so incredibly ambitious. How many people do you know who have put on a show all by themselves? My goodness, you even staged your own special effects."

I had forgotten about Lila's special effects. She had set them all up herself. You wouldn't think you'd need them for a show that is basically about a woman who lies in bed until she dies but there were dream sequences and all sorts of strange digressions, some of them funny, some of them less so.

"That's how you made the ghost appear, isn't it?" I say. "You made it brush right past me, but it wasn't real was it?"

"I used a projected image," she says, "And yes, that was me you felt. Your eyesight was so poor you didn't see me in your blind spot. You were so bloody gullible, so willing to believe anything. You thought you were careful because you locked your doors but then you left your windows open. You only had to do it that one time, Suzannah. I waited until you went out and then I borrowed your spare key and had it copied. After that, I could come and go as I pleased."

I feel in my pocket, wishing I had my phone so I could tape all this. She'd go down for years, the way she's shooting her mouth off.

"It was you who smashed my mirrors, wasn't it? And cut up my quilt?" I ask, almost hopeful.

Lila cackles with laughter. "You claim to love your precious Orchid but you were so quick to judge her. It wasn't even good, that file I forged. I wrote it in about ten minutes flat and you swallowed it hook, line and sinker. You wanted to believe there was something wrong with her. It was easier than admitting you were a bad mum."

I let out a breath, the anger welling up in my chest.

"Who are you to judge me? You've never had any children! You've no idea how hard it can be. What I can't understand is why you had to drag her into this."

"Because she's the reason Noel stayed with you. It wasn't because he loved you, was it? Nobody could love someone as frigid as you."

"If you cared about Noel so much, then why did you kill him?"

She eyes me dangerously. Even the wind stops blowing through the trees for a few seconds, as if all the animals in the woods are waiting for her confession. Her voice goes so quiet, I have to strain to catch it.

"If I couldn't have him, nobody could. Not you and not Orchid."

"Noel was never going to leave me, was he? Even if I had confronted him about the affair. We would have worked it out and once we got Orchid, we were even more solid."

"You're such a pushover," she complains. "What kind of woman lets her man have an affair and doesn't kick him out?"

"Hillary Clinton."

"You honestly want to be like her?"

"It beats being like you. Why did you want him so much anyway? I can't believe you ever really loved him. You just liked the challenge didn't you? You couldn't believe any man could resist you, let alone two. Noel and Kurt did not deserve to die for the sake of your ego."

Lila snarls at me and her face becomes venomous. It amazes me how even the whitest, straightest teeth can look dangerously sharp when a person is agitated. There really is a mad dog look about her. I can't believe I didn't see it before. I expect her to start barking or something. Except I'm not sure she's that kind of insane.

She gives me a superior look, like she knows something I don't.

"When you die, I get Orchid. I'm her godmother, after all."

"It doesn't work that way. Noel's parents would get her. It's in my will."

Her mouth curls downwards and she purses her lips. She can't stand being corrected.

"It's time to finish this, Suzannah. Time for the grand finale."

She picks up the axe and runs her finger along the tip, checking its sharpness. It glints in the sunlight. It looks like it's been polished just for the occasion but that's impossible. She can't have known I would fetch an axe.

She picks it up and feels its weight in her hand. I back towards the canyon wall. If she throws that thing at me, I've got nowhere to hide. I watch as she grasps the shaft with both hands, bringing it up to eye level then pulls it back over her head.

"Lila!"

I scream as the axe somersaults through the air. My brain tells me to move but my legs freeze as if they're stuck in the mud and so I stand there, rooted to the spot, as the axe comes down right by my left ear.

Breathing fast, I pull it out of the earth, wondering if there is any way I can hurl it back at her. No, I'm too far down. Likely as not, it would fall back down on me, like a boomerang.

"Incoming!"

I look up and see that she has two more axes, one in each hand.

"Lila!"

She holds them behind her head and grunts like a tennis player as she flings them both in my direction. This time I move, losing a shoe as I throw myself out of the way. The axes embed themselves in the wall. I think about getting them down but Lila is ready again. This time she's swinging a hammer.

"Stop it!" I scream. "There's no way you can get away with this. The police would know it was you!"

The hammer comes right at me. I duck as it bounces against the wall and hits me below the shin.

"Argh!"

My leg feels like it's on fire. I feel blood trickling down into my shoe, but I don't dare look down in case Lila has more weapons. She has her back turned to me and I can't see what she's doing. Perhaps she has a stockpile up there and she's choosing what to throw next.

I dash across the canyon, my leg screaming as I get down behind the broken motorcycle. I'm not sure how much cover it will afford me. Perhaps I should pile up some other junk on top? I look up at Lila and realise she's talking to someone. With a jolt of hope, I wonder if it's Kurt. I steal a little closer. Yes, there's definitely someone with her. My heart pounds when I see who it is.

"Mummy!"

Please, God!

Orchid stands at the top of the canyon. Her shirt is untucked and her hair puffs out around her, the way it always does after a long day at school.

"Mummy I got an A for my art homework!"

"That's great! Where's Emma?"

"She's helping Daddy's friend."

"Kurt? Is he all right?"

"We found him sleeping on the ground. What are you doing down there?"

"We're… playing hide and seek," I say, quickly. "And it's your turn to hide. Run Orchid, quick!"

I stare at Lila, wondering which of us she'll run after, because she can't get us both. Then I see a look pass over Orchid's face. She looks at the final axe, lying on the ground and I see the light go on behind those intelligent brown eyes.

"Orchid! Get away!"

"You get away!" she yells back.

When did Orchid ever listen to me? I watch in horror as she grabs the axe and holds it high above her head.

"Careful!"

I scramble up the side of the canyon, dragging my bleeding leg behind me. I can't see what's happening but I hear the sounds of the struggle.

"Hold on, Orchid. Mummy's coming!"

I spot a dip in the stone wall and a memory comes back to me. I used to climb up this way, when I was little. I used that bit as a foothold. There should be another one further up. It had felt like a big gap when I was young but now that I'm fully grown, I can reach it easily. I wince as my leg makes contact with the hole.

"Mummy!"

Lila and Orchid are wrestling just above my head. Any minute, Lila is going to get the axe…

"No!"

Orchid's shout hastens my climb and I search desperately for the next handhold. I find a thick branch sticking out of the wall and grab onto it. I'm not sure if it's strong enough to hold me but I will have to try. It feels like the earth is shaking as I pull myself up. I raise my head up above the pit and see Orchid on the ground, still hugging the axe. She kicks her legs as Lila tries to get it.

I raise myself out of the hollow but there is no time to rest.

Orchid is putting up a good fight but she's getting tired. She won't be able to fend Lila off for much longer. I reach out and grab one of Lila's boots, causing her to stumble. A strange noise pierces the air as she falls directly on top of Orchid and the axe.

"Mummy!"

Lila has gone limp. Gently, I roll her off Orchid. Her eyes are still open and her face is the colour of cornflour.

"Are you all right?" I ask Orchid.

"Are you all right?" Orchid asks and I laugh. Then I see the patch of blood on her stomach.

"Is that…"

"I think it's Lila's."

I turn to look at Lila. Her body is splayed out on the forest floor, the axe buried deep in the soft, pink flesh of her breast. She moans in anguish and grasps my hand in hers. For a few seconds, she is my best friend again. The funny, quirky woman I've shared half my life with.

Her breath comes hard and fast and she lets out a series of deep moans. I hear helicopters overhead and pray that Kurt will make it.

"It's going to be okay," I say and in one swift movement, I wrap my hands around the axe and yank it out, flinging it down into the canyon below.

"You've… killed me," Lila gasps, as blood spurts from her chest. I watch in grim fascination as it pours out like a waterfall and pools on the ground beside her. Orchid leans over her and kisses her gently on the cheek.

"You're going to die now," she says. "If you see my Daddy, can you tell him I said 'hello?'"

"She's not going to see him," I say, taking Orchid's hand and pulling her away. "There's no way she's going to heaven."

I don't know how long it takes Lila to die. We don't hang around to watch.

EPILOGUE

Miss Gibb greets me at the classroom door.

"Mrs Decker?"

She stops and stares at my eye.

"Yes?"

"Since you missed parents' evening, I thought you'd want to know that Orchid is doing just fine."

"She is? That's good to know."

"Yes, she's knuckled down these past few weeks and we've seen a big improvement in her work."

"That's great."

"And she's made a good friend…"

"Dilly?"

"I was thinking of Catriona, actually. I've had to separate them in class because they won't stop talking, but they play together most break times. I think Orchid seems a lot more settled."

"Great," I say, a little stunned. "Thank you for letting me know."

. . .

I HEAD BACK to my car. Emma is coming over for a cuppa in a little while and I want to have a quick tidy round before she arrives. It feels a little scary letting someone new into my life, but Noel was right. I need a friend in the village. I still find it hard to trust people but given enough time, people will show you who they really are. If only Lila had revealed herself sooner, maybe I would have been able to do something. I doubt I'd have been able to save her but I might have been able to save Noel.

It still hurts that Noel betrayed me but I choose to remember him the way I knew him, as a kind, loving man. I'm still angry that Lila took him away, not just from me but also from Orchid, who deserves only the best in this world. But Orchid is young and I'm determined to make it up to her, in every way I can.

Colleen has decided that the distance between Hampshire and Birmingham isn't as great as she once thought, and she now makes the journey down regularly. With all her experience, she is a great help in raising Orchid. Not that I'm totally on my own now; we've got Brutus, our beautiful Great Dane. I'm glad Orchid will get to grow up with a dog and it makes me less nervous when she's out in the woods.

Kurt was barely breathing when Emma found him in the woods that day. When she dropped off Orchid and found the house empty, they came looking for me and found him sprawled out on the footpath. It looked like he'd been trying to raise the alarm but hadn't made it more than a few metres. And while Emma was helping him, Orchid ran off looking for me and that's when she found Lila.

KURT HAS MADE a full recovery since then, though I bet he still has nightmares. He's asked me to go to a concert with him, one he and Noel had planned to see together. We text one another often and I like knowing he's just on the end of the phone but I don't know if I'm ready for a serious relationship so soon after losing Noel. I still miss him every day. I miss all the stupid stuff we used to do together: the evenings by the fire and the lunches at the Plough. I miss having him to back me up when Orchid throws a tantrum and I missed having him by my side when she saved a goal in her first hockey match. I know he would be so proud of her and I'm so very angry that he's not here.

I still hold out hope of seeing them all again one day: my sister, my parents and Noel.

Despite what Kurt says about tricks of the light, I'm still satisfied that I have in fact seen a ghost, even if it was only once in my life.

I SWEAR I will be a better mum, Orchid. I'm going to try much harder from now on, I promise. I can't make up for our bad start, but I have my good eye open now and I can finally see.

ALSO BY LORNA DOUNAEVA

MCBRIDE VENDETTA SERIES BOOK ONE

FRY

She acts like she's your new best friend, but is she really a deadly enemy?

When Isabel nearly runs over mysterious Alicia, she is filled with guilt. She helps Alicia get a job at the supermarket where she works and soon, Alicia is acting like her new best friend. Then fires break out all over town and she suspects Alicia knows more than she's letting on, but it's Isabel the police suspect. In order to survive, Isabel must question her own innocence, her sanity and the very fabric of her morality.

Lorna Dounaeva's debut novel is a sizzling psychological thriller that will make you question how well you can ever really know a person.

FRY is a very British fast paced psychological thriller.

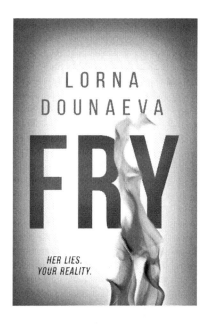

Angel Dust

It's every parent's worst nightmare…

When Isabel's daughter, Lauren is snatched from outside her school, she suspects Jody McBride is behind the kidnapping. Yet the detective in charge of Lauren's case seems more interested in picking apart her statement, and investigating members of her family.

Can Isabel persuade the police to take her seriously, or will she have to take matters into her own hands? In order to save Lauren, she must take a stark look at her own relationships, and consider how well she really knows her daughter.

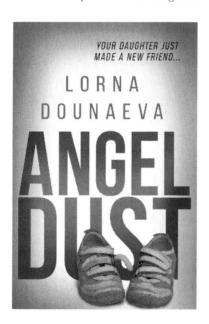

ALSO BY LORNA DOUNAEVA
MCBRIDE VENDETTA SERIES BOOK THREE

Cold Bath Lane

Who will pay the price for her silence?

Nine-year-old Jody is does well in school, despite living in a run-down part of East London.

Then one terrible night, her life changes forever, and Jody is forced to make an impossible choice between telling the truth and keeping her family together.

The police bring her in for questioning, and pressure her to tell them what really happened but is Jody ready to admit it, even to herself? Will the truth win out, or will Jody be sucked into a web of lies in order to protect her family?

This disturbing crime novel is utterly gripping and impossible to put down.

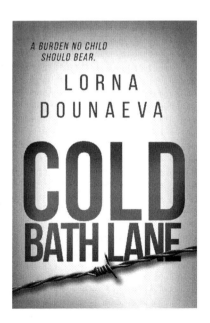

ALSO BY LORNA DOUNAEVA
THE PERFECT GIRL

She was beautiful, popular and successful, the one they all wanted to be. So who, or what, was she running from?

When reclusive writer, Jock falls for vivacious Tea Shop owner, Sapphire, he is amazed that she seems to feel the same way about him. He watches with pride as Sapphire is crowned May Queen at the town's May Day celebrations, but his joy turns to heartbreak when she runs off into the crowd, never to return.

As the days pass, he becomes increasingly desperate. Everyone he speaks to seems to love Sapphire. No one has a bad word to say about her. So why did she run away like that, and what is stopping her from coming back?

The Perfect Girl is a claustrophobic British thriller set on the English/Welsh border.

(The Perfect Girl was previously titled May Queen Killers)

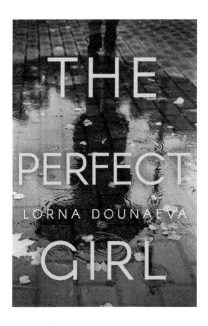

AFTERWORD

You can now join my readers' club to receive updates on new releases and giveaways at www.lornadounaeva.com

You can also contact me at info@LornaDounaeva.com

ABOUT THE AUTHOR

Lorna Dounaeva is a quirky British crime writer who once challenged a Flamenco troupe to a dance-off. She is a politics graduate, who worked for the British Home Office for a number of years, before turning to crime fiction. She loves books and films with strong female characters and her influences include *Single White Female* and *Sleeping with the Enemy*. She lives in Surrey, England with her husband and their three children, who keep her busy wiping food off the ceiling and removing mints from USB sockets.

facebook.com/LornaDounaevaAuthor
twitter.com/LornaDounaeva
instagram.com/lorna_dounaeva

Made in the USA
Middletown, DE
30 April 2024